"Jeremiah Knight has written the beginning of an epic sojourn into the good and evil of science, and more importantly, of man. *Hunger*, the first book of the Hunger Trilogy, is a must read for all!"

—Suspense Magazine

"Just when you think that 21st-century authors have come up with every possible way of destroying the world, along comes Jeremiah Knight."

—New Hampshire Magazine

"A wicked step-child of KING and DEL TORO. Lock your windows and bolt your doors. Jeremiah Knight imagines the post-apocalypse like no one else."

—The Novel Blog

ALSO BY JEREMIAH KNIGHT

The Hunger Series
Hunger
Feast
Famine (2017)

The Berserker Saga
Viking Tomorrow (2016)

JEREMIAH KNIGHT

BREAKNECK MEDIA

FEAST

ONE

"Mmm, wow," Anne said between wet, crunching chews. "Oh, now this...this is good." She took a second bite of the plump, uncooked corn and leaned back against a tree. Juice oozed from the sides of her mouth, as she chomped again and again, moving the food along her lips like a typewriter. She made no effort to wipe her face as she chewed, mouth open, corn sticking to her chin.

When she spoke again, this time to her mother, the twelve year old girl's words were garbled by the food. "I mean, I've had corn before, but this is amazing. And it's not even cooked. You guys didn't just make it grow like crazy, you made it *taste* better, too."

"You left out the part about how that vegetable turns people into monsters," Jakob said, staring at his younger sister. They'd only met a few weeks ago, but they already bickered, teased and fiercely protected each other like lifelong siblings.

"*Zea mays L. var. rugosa Bonaf*," Ella Masse said, rubbing a hand over her shaved head. She spoke the words whimsically, like recited lines from a play in which she was the star. She watched her daughter take another bite, the juices making clean streaks through the dirt that covered the girl's chin, and the rest of her exposed skin. The dirt wasn't out of place. They were all covered in soil. It was camouflage for their white skin and human scents. "Sweet corn. And it's not a vegetable. It has vegetable features, and fruit, but it's actually a grain."

Ella looked at the corn for a moment, as though lost in thought. Then she stood up and walked away. The world around them, lush with her mankind-destroying creations, was a constant reminder of the biggest blunder in the history of the world. Ella's blunder, at least, in part.

"Really big grass," Jakob said, still watching Anne eat. A bowl of food sat in front of him, composed of foraged leaves, mushrooms, weeds and mosses. All of it grew in the wild and had no ExoGenetic traits, which meant it lacked RC-714, the gene that had turned the rest of the world into monsters by unlocking dormant adaptations going back to the beginning of life on Earth. The gene had also unleashed an unspeakable hunger in all who had consumed it. Those who had eaten the crops unleashed by ExoGen, the biogenetic corporation for whom Ella had developed RC-714, became ravenous predators. Their bodies rapidly adapted to new environments, which included being surrounded by other rapidly adapting predators. Those who adapted faster, killed and ate those who hadn't. Over a period of two years, the world's population had eaten itself nearly to extinction, until only apex predators remained. They still hunted each other, and still looked to devour the small pockets of humanity who had not yet consumed ExoGenetic crops. At the moment, that included Jakob.

Anne was torturing him on purpose, he knew. It was part of her job description as a sister, a role she took seriously. He picked up a mushroom in defiance and forced a smile, as he popped it in his mouth. It tasted earthy and sour, but it wouldn't make him sick, make him trip or kill him. Still, it was hard to enjoy while he could smell the sweetness oozing from Anne's corn.

"Oh my God," Alia said, eyes closed, nose raised and sniffing. "It smells like a candy bar."

"Normal sweet corn has twice the sucrose of field corn and ten times more water-soluble polysaccharide." Anne took another bite, juices rolling down her chin.

"Sucrose?" Alia asked. "Polysaca-what?"

"Sucrose is sugar," Anne said between bites. "Polysaccharides are a bunch of other things you won't understand, either, so best to move on."

"I'm not stupid," Alia said, glaring at the younger girl.

"That has yet to be determined." Anne took three more bites and smiled at Alia, the gleam in her eye revealing that she hoped the older girl would take the bait. But Alia had quickly learned to not match wits with Anne. She wasn't just smart, she was also ruthless—a habit picked up while traversing an ExoGen-populated countryside with just her mother. That was, until a few weeks ago, when they had showed up at Peter and Jakob's doorstep with a horde of monsters following in their wake.

"ExoGen corn is a super-sweet strain that has seven times the sucrose," Anne said, staying on topic, oblivious to the brewing teenage tension. She looked away from her food, like she was seeing something not there. "That's why it tastes good. Why *all* the crops taste so good. Why people couldn't stop eating them. Why the Change happened so fast."

"But not to you," Jakob said.

"That's great for her." Alia pushed her bowl of foliage away. "But she could at least try not to rub it in."

Uh boy, Jakob thought, *here we go.*

He sometimes wondered if Alia remembered her twelve-year-old self. It had only been four years ago, after all. He'd been through seventh and eighth grades, and had learned to avoid unnecessary clashes with his female classmates, especially those who were smarter, or bigger, than him. They might not get violent—though that wasn't always true with Anne—but they dragged them out. What could be resolved with a few punches between boys might last months or years with the girls. They weren't fights. They were feuds, and he really hoped that wouldn't happen between Anne and Alia—his sister and his girlfriend. There weren't any daytime talk shows left to help them resolve it.

"First of all," Anne said, "I can only eat this corn because I was *grown*, in a lab, from DNA that Mom..." She pointed at Ella. "...*stole* from Dad." She motioned to the forest surrounding them, where Peter was on guard. "I'm a genetically engineered freak, who, yeah, can eat corn. But I've also got a USB port in the back of my head." She stabbed a finger at Alia. "Do *you* have a USB port in the back of your head? No? Too bad for you. It's sooo fun. If you want, I can drill a hole and shove a—"

"Keep it down." The deep, serious voice made them all flinch, but everyone relaxed when Peter stepped into the small clearing where they were enjoying—or trying to enjoy—their foraged lunch.

"Did you see something?" Alia asked, nervous. Of the five of them, she was still the most shell-shocked. They had become adept at avoiding trouble over the past few weeks, but the events that had brought them together and taken her father's life, had left her in a constant state of nervousness.

"We're clear," Peter said, and then he focused on Anne. "But *you* are being too loud."

Anne said nothing, but took a another bite of corn.

Jakob picked up a still-full bowl of greenery and handed it to his father. In the past few weeks, his father had gone from looking like a tough-looking Dad to a chiseled warrior. Caked in mud, head shaved and carrying weapons that included a high-powered bow and arrows and a suppressed M4 rifle, Peter looked more like Arnold Schwarzenegger in *Predator* now, but a little less bulky and half a foot taller.

Alia said Jakob looked like his father, and to an extent, he agreed. They had the same facial features, dark eyes and shaved brown hair, but that was where the comparison ended. Seventeen-year-old Jakob lacked his father's mass. He wasn't sure if he would ever be as strong as Peter, but he hoped he'd put on some muscle soon, if only to not disappoint Alia before she realized he was scrawny. He wasn't exactly the pinnacle of masculinity yet. But Alia...she was everything Jakob could have asked for. Kind, funny, and beautiful, with her mother's tan Arabian skin, dark eyes and black hair. In this post-apocalyptic nightmare world, she was a flower blooming in the desert. Jakob felt more like a misshapen cactus.

Peter took handfuls of vegetation, shoving them in his mouth and chewing with efficiency. He was done in under a minute, and like Jakob, he was clearly not satiated by the meal. But he wasn't going to complain about it. Never did. Instead, he'd keep them moving, focused on their destination: George's Island, off the coast of Boston, where a laboratory had been set up before civilization had come to a screeching halt. Ella claimed she could rework the human genome so that ExoGenetic food wouldn't transform people into monsters. She couldn't reset the world, but she *could* increase their chances of survival and ensure the human race's continuation.

If they made it that far.

Apex predators hunted day and night.

And ExoGen, whose executives had known what the RC-714 would do to the world, and had prepared for it, were likely still searching for them. Still trying to stop Ella from freeing the human race. They didn't know why. Only that the corporation had a large, well defended facility in what was once San Francisco, and that they had sent their own private army in search of Ella. And in search of Anne, who held the key to mankind's future in her head...or rather, in the USB drive in her head.

Peter tensed. His eyes flicked up. They were surrounded by trees—maple, birch and oak—and they were sitting on a carpet of potato plants. "Finish eating."

No one asked why. They just shoved what was left of their food into their mouths and consumed it quickly. Food was sometimes sparse, and they were loath to waste any of it. Unless danger was charging straight for them, jaws agape, they finished all of their meals.

Jakob had just finished swallowing when he noticed what his father had already picked up on. The canopy above was still thick green with summertime foliage. But that didn't stop the sun from filtering through the myriad cracks in the armor of thick luminous leaves. Nor did it stop him from detecting the enormous shadow flitting past above them.

A bird, he thought, holding his breath.

Birds were among the most dangerous apex predators, mostly because they could spot you from miles away and strike from above, without warning. So he was told. He hadn't actually seen an ExoGen bird yet. He had seen a few species of normal birds, which fed exclusively on non-ExoGen plants, like hummingbirds, but he'd seen none of the man-eating super-birds of prey said to be circling high in the atmosphere.

But now...was the shadow so large because it was low in the sky? Or was it just enormous? Experience told him it was the latter, and that it was close because it was hunting them. But they were concealed in the trees. How long would the ExoGen bird wait before giving up?

Fifty feet away, the canopy exploded downward, as something large pierced through the trees and struck the ground.

About that long, Jakob thought, getting his first look at an ExoGen bird and quickly wishing he hadn't—not just because it was a hideous sight, but because it wasn't alone.

There were two of them.

TWO

Peter nocked an arrow and took aim before the first massive creature struck the ground. One good shot from the powerful bow could drop most anything alive—before the Change and after it. But when the creature reared up after landing, Peter held his fire. The two creatures were focused on each other.

And that was a good thing.

A small voice in Peter's mind shouted at him to run, to sneak away with the others and never look back. But this was the first time he had ever seen two ExoGen creatures locked in combat. And from the looks of them, they were both top predators, whose recent rapid evolutions had taken them in divergent directions. He crouched with the others, peering out from behind a thick oak trunk, watching the two behemoths tear at each other.

Peter guessed that the creature on the bottom, which might have once been a crow, was what he'd detected flying above them. Perhaps it had been zeroing in on their scent, despite their best efforts to mask it. Its ten-foot-long wings were covered in black feathers, but the rest of its dark body was cloaked in what looked like long black hair. A line of long spines jutted from its back, flaring up as the bird-like thing snapped at the second creature's exposed neck. The biting jaws, filled with sharp teeth, fell short, but one bite would be enough. Its long legs, ending at massive, talon-tipped, three-toed feet, kicked and scrambled, but to no avail. It was pinned by its larger adversary.

The second creature, which had no doubt dived down on the giant crow-thing from above, might have once been a falcon, but Peter had a hard time spotting any features resembling a pre-Change bird. This featherless beast, with an elongated beak, twitching, sinewy muscles and taut brown skin, looked prehistoric. More like a pterodactyl, but with long powerful legs for running and a long tail tipped with a tuft of feathers. A blood-red crest rose up behind its yellow eyes, which were focused on its equally hungry prey.

The crow-thing gave up trying to bite the larger creature's neck and opted for a less deadly attack. It twisted its own long neck to the side, clamped its jaws around its enemy's lower leg and sank those long teeth deep into the flesh.

The Exodactyl's eyes just widened, but Peter didn't think it was from the pain. The creature looked excited, like this was the moment it had been waiting for. With startling speed that made Peter flinch, the creature jabbed its long sharp beak downward. The strike began and ended in less than a second. The crow didn't even notice the gaping hole in its neck. But it slowed its biting and thrashing, as blood pulsed from its throat.

When its flailing limbs finally fell still, the victorious creature leaned down close to the bloody hole.

Peter expected it to start tearing the dead bird apart, rending it with beak and talons, but that was not what happened. A long tube-like tongue extended from the beak's tip, sliding into the open wound. It then began to twitch, as a slurping sound filled the air.

It's drinking blood, using its tubular tongue like a straw.

Despite having seen combat violent enough to cause a bout of PTSD, not to mention the past few weeks of ExoGenetic horrors, Peter found himself getting queasy. As a former U.S. Marine Critical Skills Operator—part of the most elite fighting force within the Marine Corps—he had been trained to keep his emotions, and his stomach in check.

But the others...

A gurgling sound followed by a wet smack made him freeze in place. He glanced over his shoulder and saw a glob of partially chewed, now regurgitated corn kernels laying atop a flattened potato plant stalk. Anne. As tough as she wanted to be, or wanted everyone to think she was, she was still a twelve-year-old girl. And yeah, she had seen some shit that would leave most adults damaged for life, but she still processed trauma like a kid. Sometimes, that meant puking at something gross.

Without moving his head, Peter swept his gaze back to the Exodactyl. Its body hadn't shifted position, but the slurping sound had stopped, and its tongue no longer twitched. Peter nearly shouted in surprise when he spotted the baseball-sized yellow eye turned straight toward him.

Man and beast locked eyes and froze.

Would it attack with a fresh kill underfoot?

Did it think of them as prey? As competition?

Was it even thinking at all?

No, Peter decided. *And it's not going to let us leave.*

That was one of the defining attributes of ExoGenetic creatures—ravenous hunger. Unceasing. Despite having a meal underfoot, it would hunt them all down, kill and consume them and then return to the mutated crow. Or some variation of that.

"Everyone get ready to run on my mark," he whispered. He didn't expect to hear confirmation or see any nods. They would follow his lead, knowing full well that to stray from the plan, even an evolving plan, would likely lead to a horrible death for one of them, if not all of them.

"Now," Peter hissed. "Run."

As he heard the others turn and run, he stood up, in clear view, arrow already nocked and drawn back. Their movement freed the large bird-like creature from its predator rigor mortis. It turned to face Peter, leaning toward him. It then opened its beak wide and let out an ear-piercing squawk.

Peter's fingers withdrew from the string. It snapped forward, propelling the arrow at three hundred seventy feet per second, meaning the arrow left his fingers and entered the creature's open maw before it could react to the sound. The Exodactyl's beak snapped shut, and its head twitched back in surprise. Its wide eyes had an almost humorous 'what the fuck' look about them. But the arrow hadn't lodged in the bird's throat. Instead, it pierced the layers of flesh and skin, emerging on the far side and striking a tree, twenty-five feet away. It was the one free shot Peter would get, so while the creature was distracted by the confusing pain, he turned tail and chased after the others.

Ten steps into his run, he began to second guess his flight.

I should have taken a second shot, he thought. *Should have put it down for good.* He'd killed other ExoGenetic monsters before. Why not this one?

There's no way to know if more arrows would have done it, he told himself. *The first arrow only confused it. How many more would it take to kill it? I'm not even sure where its vital organs are. It could have two hearts, for all I know.*

They were all logical arguments. To a point. But none of them was the truth.

The truth was that he was afraid. The moment he saw those sinister eyes and the blood-sucking tongue, the mental switch in his psyche that was normally switched to 'fight' got flicked over to 'flight.' In a world of predators, no matter how well prepared or armed a person was, true humans were still prey, and those instincts couldn't always be overcome.

But there was no sense in second guessing his decision to run. He was committed to it. He knew if he reached the road, just a few hundred feet ahead, he would reach the truck. The kids had nicknamed it *Beastmaster*, on account of its many spikes and metal shields. Peter had argued that *Mad Max* was a more appropriate nickname for the post-apocalyptic death machine, but Anne's ceaseless arguing had won the day. Peter tried to explain the *Beastmaster* movie to them, but they didn't make it past the thongs before bursting into laughter. It had been a lively debate, and a good day.

But not all days were good. Most were defined by fear and violence.

Like today, Peter thought, glancing back, as the Exodactyl let out a shriek.

The massive creature tilted its body forward, its tail rising up as a counterbalance. Then, with eyes locked on Peter, it lunged forward and ran.

The dead crow-thing's jaws, locked in a death grip, still clung to the Exodactyl's leg. But the larger predator didn't slow or try to pry itself free. It just charged forward, dragging the corpse along for the ride, leaving a trail of blood in its wake.

With the chase in progress, there was no reason to be quiet anymore. "How close are you?" he shouted.

"Nearly there!" Ella replied.

Peter couldn't see the others through the maze of trees, both standing and fallen, but he knew they weren't too far ahead. They'd have just a few seconds before he, and then the hellish Big Bird, entered the clearing ahead.

He angled his course, aiming for the road behind the armored, black Dodge Ram, and guesstimated his ETA. "Seven seconds! Behind the truck!"

"I'll be ready," Jakob replied. "Don't stick around."

Peter understood the message and poured on the steam. The forest floor began to shake with each of the Exodactyl's footfalls, but more so when it stepped with its left limb, slamming the still-attached, giant, dead crow into the ground.

Rounding a tall pine to confuse the predator on his heels, Peter looked back and shouted in surprise, as the massive beak snapped shut just inches from his face. It sounded like two wooden planks clapping together, the noise loud enough to hurt his ears.

As the Exodactyl rounded the tree behind him, momentum carried the crow out in a wide arc. Its limp body wrapped around the trunk of a sturdy maple, bones cracking. The snagged corpse pulled the larger creature's limb back, keeping it from lunging one more time and clamping on to Peter's skull. The frustrated creature shrieked after Peter and then tore its leg from the dead crow-thing's mouth, leaving deep and bloody slashes in its own flesh. But it was oblivious to the pain, as it flung itself back into the chase.

Peter threw his forearms up over his face as he crashed through a wall of crisscrossing dead branches that blocked his path. He felt his exposed skin tear, but when his feet hit the pavement beyond, he didn't slow to inspect his wounds, he just charged right out.

Moving across the open road, he looked left, seeing Jakob standing in the flatbed, aiming the big M249 light machine gun toward the woods, where Peter had exited. As Peter dove into the woods on the far side of the road, he expected to hear the cacophonous roar of the big weapon, followed by the groaning impact of a slain ExoGen, but neither of those things happened.

Peter climbed to his feet and stepped back into the road, eyeing the forest, where Jakob kept the weapon trained.

Where the hell did it go?

"Where the hell did it go?" Jakob shouted, channeling his father's thoughts.

Then Peter saw it.

The long beak slid out of the forest, looking almost like just another branch, slowly positioning itself to strike, fifteen feet above Jakob.

THREE

Ella Masse had experienced moments of heightened awareness. When the blood is pumping double-time and oxygen saturates the mind, the world seems to slow down. Things become clearer. Colors appear more vivid. Smells develop more layers. And sounds become more crisp. In her old life, she had experienced this phenomenon on the cusp of discovery. Most people picture science as a dull, laborious job of endless repetition. To a degree, it was true. But after months, or even years, of hard work, that moment of breakthrough, of Earth-changing discovery... There are few other rushes that compare. She'd felt it when she first laid eyes on the initial results for RC-714. The test corn not only grew in the harshest of environments, it had also spread aggressively. They were going to feed the world.

Instead, they'd made the world hungrier than ever before. They gave humanity an endless food supply that had made everyone, and everything, that ate it, ravenous for flesh. Any flesh. The smallest animals were affected first. Species of rats, squirrels, rabbits and mice had turned on each other in great bloody wars. Then they had attacked other species, including people, and then each other. And it wasn't long before larger mammals, including people, joined the fray. As the Pandora's box of ancient genes became available, evolution, spurred by ceaseless hunger, mutated nearly every living thing into something monstrous.

Only those who managed to not consume the ExoGenetic crops had remained unchanged, and of them, only those prepared for the violence to come, had survived.

Since leaving the safety of the ExoGen facility in San Francisco, Ella had experienced several more moments of heightened awareness. At first, they had left her feeling shaken and disturbed. Adrenaline did strange things to the body and left most people shaking as its positive, life-saving effects wore off. But she had come to embrace the feeling, knowing it made the difference between life and death, for herself and her family, which now included Peter...and Jakob.

The boy wasn't exactly keen on her yet. She understood why. She was his father's former mistress. Loyalty to his mother made her the antagonist, and she wouldn't argue against it. Had Peter chosen her over his wife all those years ago, Ella wouldn't have tried to change his mind. But Jakob's mother had also tried to eat the boy. Ella, at least, hadn't done that.

And now, as the oxygen pumped into her brain by adrenaline-fueled blood sharpened her sense of the world around her, she saw a chance to win the boy over, by saving his life.

She twisted her shotgun up, aiming into the tree branches above the truck, where a triangular spear was aimed at Jakob's chest. The Apex bird had given up chasing Peter and was now poised to strike his son.

Unless she could stop it.

But she couldn't.

With the shotgun still in motion, she shouted, "Jakob!"

She couldn't see how the boy responded to her warning, because she didn't take her eyes off the creature above them. When its head exploded from the trees and stabbed its spear-like beak toward the truck, she had no idea whether the strike found Jakob's body. She didn't hear a scream, but then, the strike was so fast and powerful she didn't think the boy would have time to scream.

The bird's head came up for a second strike at the same time Ella's shotgun finished swiveling upward.

God, that thing is fast, she thought, and then she pulled the trigger.

The shotgun roared, firing a storm of 12 gauge pellets into the large target, just ten feet above her. The blast would have shredded most living things on the planet a few years ago, but now, the pellets simply embedded themselves in the monster's thick skin.

Closer, she thought. *Point blank will—*

Her thoughts locked up when the bird turned its head and killer beak toward her. Instead of killing the creature, she'd managed to seal her own fate.

An arrow whistled through the air, striking the beak and deflecting away. The massive, featherless bird paid it no heed.

Ella heard Peter shout her name, but she didn't turn. If this was her end, she would face it head on. She pumped the shotgun and saw the bird's eyes flicker slightly wider. It was going to strike faster than she could pull the trigger.

A loud boom hiccupped a shout from her mouth, but her fright was as short-lived as the bird's predatory confidence. A small implosion punched a red hole into the creature's chest. It was quickly followed by a much larger explosion from the bird's back. She heard the burst flesh slap against the trees and leaves behind the creature, and then a series of booming reports erased all other sounds. A line of bullet holes stitched its way up the creature's writhing body. The final round punching into one eye and out the other, came from a different direction. The bird fell in a heap, crumpling in a bloody mass of chewed-up avian meat.

Ella turned right, from where the final shot had come, and found Anne clutching a handgun in her small hands, the barrel smoking.

The girl looked Ella up and down, her forehead twisted in worry.

"I'm okay," Ella told her daughter, and she knew who she had to thank for that. Jakob stood in the back of the armored pick-up truck, still holding the M249 machine gun mounted in the bed. Blood trickled down his right arm, revealing just how close he had come to being impaled...before saving her life.

So much for scoring brownie points, she thought.

She was about to thank him when he beat her to it. "Thanks, Ella. If you hadn't shouted..."

She smiled and replied with a genuine, "Thank *you*."

"Everyone okay?" Peter charged around the back of the truck, nocked arrow aimed at the very dead ExoGen. Upon seeing the creature, he slowly removed tension from the bow string and removed the arrow. He scanned the group, eyes lingering on Jakob's arm for a moment before moving on. "Where's Alia?"

Fear flickered into Jakob's eyes for a moment, but then Alia slid out from beneath the truck, a pistol gripped in her hands. Despite being four years older than Anne, Alia lacked the younger girl's experience and defiant bravery. They had been training Alia while on the move, but she was a slow study. Jakob had struggled at first, too, but a few weeks in the wild had done a lot to boost his confidence and quell his fears. Ella saw more and more of Peter in the boy with every passing day. But Alia...she was still a liability. So when things got crazy, her job was to get out of the way, and this time she'd chosen to hide under the truck.

"FYI," Alia said, a quiver in her voice, "under the truck isn't the best place to hide."

Jakob glanced down at the truck bed, his eyes widening. "Holy shit."

A six-inch wide hole had been punched in the floor—one of the few outer surfaces that didn't have extra layers of armor plating welded to it.

Luckily, the strike that had sliced Jakob's arm and hammered through the floor had missed anything important, above and below the truck bed's surface. The look in Alia's eyes as she squirmed out from beneath the truck, said it had been a close call though.

"Everyone in," Peter said, climbing into the driver's seat.

No one complained or argued. This wasn't a family vacation. All of the sound would have attracted the attention of any Apex ExoGens within earshot, and once they were close enough to smell the massive amount of blood from the two dead birds, they'd be whipped into a frenzy. Ella had little doubt that the scene would be littered with more dead bodies before the sun set.

The faster they left the area, the better. There was still a chance they would run into an ExoGen while fleeing the scene, but better to deal with problems head on than linger around and face three hundred and sixty degrees of trouble.

As the kids slipped into the back seat, Ella climbed into the front, feeding a fresh shell into the shotgun. They had found and raided a National Guard Depot, pilfering guns and ammo, just a week ago. Ella had claimed an M4 assault rifle, which she used most often, but in the close confines of a thick forest or a building, she preferred the shotgun. They'd also managed to find a good amount of 5.56×45 mm NATO rounds for the machine gun. If they hadn't, she would have become an ExoGen shish kabob.

Peter pointed at the first aid kit beneath Ella's legs and snapped his fingers twice. The first aid kit had been heavily customized over the past few weeks, containing supplies that made it closer to a mobile surgical suite than something you could pick up at a grocery store. She handed the box to him and he held it back over the seat.

"Anne, patch him up."

"Seriously?" Jakob said. "She can't sew a straight line."

"You'd rather Little Miss Barf's-A-Lot puke in the wound before stitching it?" Anne asked, taking the kit and popping it open.

Alia raised her hands. "I'm not touching it."

"See?" Anne said, removing a hooked needle from its sterile packaging and handling it with her grimy fingers.

"Anne," Peter said. "Your dirty fingers are nearly as bad as Alia's fictional puke. Keep it clean. Do it right."

Anne frowned and sighed, but her attitude quickly shifted to something resembling professional discipline. She had come to respect Peter over the past few weeks. When he spoke in that deep, serious tone, she listened. And learned. She had become quite deadly during her time in the wild, with just Ella. But they had survived mostly through an almost cruel cunning. Now she was disciplined. Learning to keep her cool and react with her brain as much as with her instincts.

Jakob calmed when he saw the shift in Anne's attitude. He lifted his short sleeve up over his shoulder and stayed quiet as Anne began to clean the arm with alcohol.

With everyone settled, Peter started the truck. The engine roared to life, making Ella flinch. The truck always felt too loud, but once it was moving, the sound was minimal. Anything able to hear them, would likely see them anyway. They had talked about ditching the truck, but it got them where they needed to go faster, could outrun some enemies and provided hard-hitting protection in the form of armor and a light machine gun. Their route east had become circuitous thanks to broken bridges, blocked roads and dangerous territories, but they were still making better time than they would have on foot.

Instead of heading directly northeast for Boston, as intended, they had been forced southeast, all the way down through Charlotte, North Carolina, and into South Carolina. The plan was to hit I-95 and follow it north, all the way to Boston. If the road was clear, they would make the trip in a day. If it wasn't, and they were forced to follow more winding back roads, they might have a few more weeks on the road. But before that happened, they had one last stop to make—at Little Hellhole Bay. It didn't sound like a nice place to visit, before or after the Change, but it was one of many locations Ella had helped build a biodome farmstead. She felt the occupants might be able to help her work at George's Island...if they were still alive, and if she could convince them to leave.

As dangerous as life in a biodome could be, it was still a lot safer than trekking through the wilderness in a truck.

Jakob hissed as Anne slipped the needle into his skin and pulled the two-inch-long slice together. The wound would heal and Jakob would live, but Ella was under no illusions. They were hunted by nearly everything left alive in the world, including her former employers, who wanted them for far worse reasons than satiating their primal, unceasing hunger.

FOUR

"What do we think?" Peter asked, looking out the windshield at what looked like a busy supermarket.

There were cars still in the lot. The day was clear and warm. The corn growing on the large flat roof looked like a neat haircut, but there was so much growth covering absolutely everything that Alia Rossi filtered it out. If not for the stench of their odor-masked bodies, she might have been able to convince herself that the nightmare had come to an end...that the Change had never occurred...that her father had never gone mad and her mother was still alive.

But she couldn't even pretend, because if she felt just a hint of her previous life, she would cling to it like an addict.

Except that it's gone, she told herself. *This is the world now.*

She tried to be strong for Jakob. Modeled herself after Ella, and Anne, and Peter. But she was no good at it, really. And when push came to shove, and then teeth and claws and twisted freaks of nature, she cracked. Hiding became her specialty. No one judged her for it, or complained. Better that she was out of the way, rather than in it. But that didn't stop her from feeling useless.

So when Peter posed the simple question about what looked like an untouched oasis from the past, she thought, *I can check expiration dates on food,* and said, "Let's do it."

"Well, if Princess Pouty-Pants is in, I'm in." Anne smiled at Alia.

Alia couldn't tell if the younger girl was really mocking her or engaging in some kind of playful banter. Anne was a mystery to her. Funny, but jaded. Young, but somehow older than her and Jakob. Their relationship was rocky at best. Anne took every sarcastic potshot that presented itself. Alia came to the conclusion that the girl was trying to thicken her emotional skin. Maybe because she cared about Alia. Maybe because she cared about Jakob and didn't want to see him hurt. He was doubly at risk because of Alia. He took risks protecting her, and if he ever failed to protect her, the fallout might be enough to break him, too.

Jakob was adapting. Learning. Growing stronger, tougher and more resilient. He was a far cry from Peter, Ella and Anne still, but he was cruising ahead, while Alia was standing still.

But I can read labels, she thought, and opened her door first.

After a brief and cautious walk, they stood in front of the grocery store entrance. The doors were shut and the interior was dark, far more ominous than Alia expected. "So...we can't break a window, right? That would be too loud."

Peter's response was to step up to the automatic door, grasp the metal handle and pull. It resisted for a moment, but then the gears that hadn't moved in a long time, gave way, whirring as the door opened.

Before entering, Peter said, "Lights on. We'll do a sweep of each aisle and then break into two groups."

After turning on their headlamps and chambering rounds in their silenced weapons—Alia had a handgun but she couldn't remember what kind—they crept into the store. Peter took the lead, followed by Jakob, Alia, Anne and Ella. This was their usual formation, and Alia understood the point of her position. There were two layers of people who could fight on either side of her.

Protecting her.

They moved across the front of the store, which faintly smelled of rotted food, but more like dust. They paused for a moment at the cereal aisle, where a heap of dead bodies lay between the Cocoa Puffs and Cinnamon Toast Crunch.

"There was either a really good sale, or these guys got a hankering for fresh meat all at the same time." Anne seemed unfazed by the mound of death, but Alia thought...hoped...it was just an act.

When the Change started affecting humanity, people resisted their growing urges. At first they ate more meat. And then only meat. And then raw meat. Eventually, someone would succumb and take a bite out of a neighbor, family member or total stranger at the grocery store. And once the smell of fresh blood filled the air, it triggered a response in everyone nearby. Alia had no trouble picturing that here. One of these people, probably someone buried beneath the rest, had snapped and attacked. Then everyone in the store on the fringe of changing had lost the battle against it and had joined in.

She shivered as her imagination took over, replaying scenes of spraying blood, gnashing teeth and tearing fingernails. It would have been like some kind of zombie apocalypse, but worse. Because people weren't just killing each other, they were changing as they did, growing more efficient and deadly and hungry with each kill. Whoever walked away from this feeding frenzy probably didn't even look human anymore.

"Okay," Jakob said. "Cereal was never on the list anyway." As one of the most genetically modified and processed foods available before the Change, cereal was generally off limits. But it had remained popular even after ExoGenetic crops sprang up everywhere. Everyone was fed during those days, but that didn't stop people from wanting their microwave meals, instant puddings and chocolate-dipped donut bites. Fresh produce was no longer sold in stores, but processed food never went out of style.

"Looks like this store is a mixer," Jakob said. He'd coined the term at the last grocery store they had visited. Mixers didn't separate organic food from regular food, but shelved them together, making their best bet at finding safe food a little bit harder.

After finishing the sweep, they split into two groups—adults and kids—but Anne wandered off within thirty seconds of the split. "You guys need some smoochy time," she said as she wandered away, scanning lines of boxes. "Just like Mom and Dad."

Alia didn't think that was true about Ella and Peter. They hid their affection for each other during the day, but Alia wasn't deaf. She heard them on occasion during a sleepless night. She never got up the nerve to peek, but it didn't sound like they were having thumb wars.

But for her and Jakob...time alone was at a premium, so Alia didn't complain when Anne walked away.

And neither did Jakob.

They didn't speak for a few minutes as they scanned the shelves, but they grew steadily closer. When they stood shoulder to shoulder, Jakob leaned closer and said, "You smell horrible."

She laughed and said, "And together, we're like a bouquet of shit."

He put his arm around her and squeezed her close.

As she turned to kiss him, her eyes locked onto a jar on the far side of the aisle. She stopped mid-pucker and said, "Whoa."

It was peanut butter.

Organic peanut butter. *Chunky* organic peanut butter. The holy grail of post-apocalyptic treats. Peanut butter had a long shelf life. Back when there was still an Internet, she'd watched a video of a man eating sixty-year-old peanut butter rations from the Korean War. If the expiration date, which was more of a suggestion to keep food moving off the shelf, was early enough, there would be no fear of ExoGenetic contamination. They could eat it. *All* of it. And there were at least thirty jars.

Jakob picked up a jar, twisted it in his hand and smiled wide. "Jackpot." He lifted the jar and looked inside. "It's separated—"

"Organic peanut butter is always separated."

"Well then, it's perfect." Jakob looked up and down the aisle. "Now we just need to find some coconut oil and dark chocolate and we'll be in business."

Both items, when organic, were on Ella's safe list. Coconut was not an ExoGenetic crop, and organic, free-trade chocolate was one of the last crops to be overrun. They also had very long shelf lives. If the dates were right, they could have the makings of an epic snack, unlike anything she'd had in two years. Her mouth watered, but the food took a sudden back seat when Jakob, in his excitement, wrapped her in his arms and kissed her.

They had kissed before. A lot. Their awkward first kiss had been back at her farmhouse, in the biodome, just a few feet from where her mother had been buried. They had never met, but shared a kiss that expressed their elation at finally meeting. There had been many more kisses, snuck in during brief private moments. In the darkness of night. When Anne fell asleep in the truck and the parents were looking out the front. But this...this was different. This was passionate.

When they separated, Jakob looked bewildered. "I guess peanut butter is an aphrodisiac."

Alia said nothing. She just took him by the hand and led him away. "Where are we going?"

"Bathroom," she said. "I saw them in the corner of the store."

"Why?"

"I have to pee." That was the truth, and she never passed up a toilet, whether or not they flushed. But that wasn't the whole truth, and as Jakob's hand grew sweaty in hers, he knew it, too.

When they reached the door to the women's room, she put her hand on his chest and said, "Wait here."

He looked a little surprised, but said, "You really do have to pee. I thought that was like code or something."

"Real and code," she said.

"Hold on." Jakob pushed the bright blue door open slowly, aiming his rifle inside the room, scanning it from side to side. With no signs of danger or even a bad smell, he stepped aside and held the door open for her. "Your throne awaits."

"Be just a minute." Alia said and stepped inside. When the door was closed, she tried to let herself feel normal. *It's just a bathroom.*

She opened the first stall. The toilet was pristine and empty. There were few things more disappointing than a post-apocalyptic toilet that hadn't been flushed.

Just pretend the power is out, she told herself, dropping her pants and sitting on the cool seat. When she was done peeing, she reached for toilet paper and smiled. It was a simple thing, but she'd gone without it too many times. Once was too many times. It was a stupid thing, but it brought her joy, and as she wadded it up, wiped and then stood to pull up her pants, she was lost in the moment. Her hands moved on muscle memory, first buckling her belt, and then reaching back and pushing the small metal lever.

Her mind woke up as the lever shifted downward. She flinched her hand away, but it was too late. Water pressure that had been contained for years exploded into the toilet with uproarious urgency.

The bathroom door burst open. "Alia!"

She stepped out of the stall, face twisted in concern. "I flushed. I didn't mean to. It just—"

The wall between them shook. A long hooked talon punched through, separating them. Alia screamed and reeled back. The hard shell was green, and its bottom side was serrated like a massive knife.

Jakob fell back out of the bathroom, raising his rifle to fire. A second exoskeletal appendage slammed through the wall and struck the door, slamming it shut.

Alia scrambled away, slipping on the smooth tile floor, grasping for the silenced handgun she had holstered before sitting on the toilet.

The massive limbs moved in and out, sawing through the wall with frantic jerking motions. Alia's screams were drowned out by a loud chirping that tore through the air like an alarm. It was the most noise she had heard since the battle at her parents' farmhouse, and if anything else was around, it would already be on its way.

The wall gave way, coughing a cloud of drywall into the room. Support beams bent and broke. And then a head slid into the room, insect like, but unidentifiable. It had massive oval eyes that shimmered under the glare of Alia's headlamp. Three sets of mandibles opened and closed, while smaller grinding mouths twitched. The thing lacked any kind of expression, but exuded menace, and hunger.

Alia drew her weapon and pulled the trigger. The first three rounds missed, despite the creature's size. But the rest struck the oversized insect's head and forelimbs, ricocheting into the ceiling and walls. The 9mm weapon, about all she could handle, was ineffective.

Through the frenzied chirping, she thought she heard voices. The bathroom door shook from the far side. It opened an inch, but when it struck the creature's leg, it was pushed back, sealing predator and prey in a fifteen-foot-long space with no other exit. Not even a window.

A claw snapped out and cracked the tile floor, just missing her legs. She pushed back further, but stopped when her back struck the wall.

The insect pushed deeper into the room, incensed by its failure.

Alia tried to reload her weapon, but she only managed to drop it and the spare magazine.

When the creature struck again, so fast that the limb looked like it had teleported from one spot to the next, Alia pushed herself up onto her feet. She screamed, again and again, but the sound was lost in the insect's chirping, a symphony of life and death.

With nowhere else to run, Alia dove into the stall, yanked the door shut and twisted the lock. She huddled atop the toilet, clutching herself, sobbing.

The metal walls vibrated. The tip of a claw stabbed through. It pulled free with a shriek of carapace on metal. The next strike would be hard enough and deep enough to find her.

A cacophonous boom shook the air.

The floor trembled.

A second boom rang out.

The chirping fluttered and stopped.

In the silence that followed, Alia wept. Then something moved.

It's coming back!

Walls crumbled. Tiles crunched. It was right outside the stall.

The door shook.

She heard voices shouting her name, but she couldn't hear who, over the sound of her own ragged screams.

The door was torn open.

It was Peter, shotgun in hand, face covered in white gore.

She fell into his arms, vision fading. She remembered being carried. She saw a large number of empty shells lying on the hallway floor as she was rushed out of the bathroom. Peter had resorted to using the loud shotgun when normal bullets had failed. The rest of the retreat from the grocery store, and then the area was a blur. Somewhere along the line, she fell asleep.

When she woke up again, everyone was quiet. She said nothing, but started crying when she found a jar of peanut butter in her lap. She could have gotten them all killed, but they were still showing her kindness. Alia wondered how long that would last. Sooner or later, she was going to get someone killed.

Sooner or later, she was going to have to leave.

FIVE

"Are we there yet?" Anne asked. It had become a running gag and was usually good for a chuckle, harkening back to a time of normalcy, when driving across the country with siblings was considered mind-numbingly boring. But now, with the possibility of every turn revealing a new horror, crossing the country was far from dull. They rode mostly in silence, each of them keeping watch in a different direction.

Jakob had told Anne about how, when he was younger, he used to imagine a man running in time with the truck, leaping from building to building, or trees, or whatever else they passed. She thought it was strange at first, but sometimes caught herself imagining a giant sword extending from the side of the truck, cutting down all the trees and endless fields they passed.

Instead of laughing, Ella replied, "Almost," which killed the joke and put her fellow backseat riders on edge. So far, the two biodomes Anne and her mother had visited had been left in ruins. Lives had been lost or uprooted. Jakob and Peter had nearly died on multiple occasions, and Alia had lost her father. The man had already been out of his mind, but he was still her father. Anne was still getting to know her father, but already she couldn't picture a future without him in it. He was brave, and strong and disciplined. While the world had fallen into chaos, he brought order and balance, even to her mother, who had become somewhat savage to survive. Anne didn't hold that against her mother. They'd both survived only because they were willing to do horrible things, and Peter was equally willing, but his strategic mind was better at avoiding trouble, or getting out of it without losing a piece of his soul in the process.

Or maybe he just lost less of it. He'd seen combat before, and not the kind where people were killing ravenous monsters. He had fought and killed other people. Normal people. And it had left scars on his body and psyche. He had told her about it one day while foraging. At first, it seemed like he was just shooting the breeze, telling stories to his daughter. But then she understood that it was a morality lesson about the horrors of war. A warning to not get lost in the killing and death and non-stop adrenaline. "It can change the way you see the world," he had said. "When you become numb to death, you become numb to life, and it's a lot easier to lose something you can't feel."

"Like I might cut off a finger if I can't feel it," she had said.

"Mmm," he had agreed, "except that losing your finger only affects you. If you were to die..."

She had thought his concern was about how Anne dying might affect Ella. But when he turned away from her, hiding his face and whatever emotion was going on there, she understood that he was becoming as fond of her as she was of him.

Since then, she had fully embraced the idea that she now had a complete family unit. Maybe the only one left on Earth. And for that, despite all the death and violence and horrible monsters trying to eat them, not to mention a good deal of the numbing he had warned her about, she felt blessed.

And now, as they approached another biodome, she couldn't help but feel a growing sense of impending doom. Would they be welcomed? Would they face yet more monsters? Would a member of her family— even Alia, who sometimes irked Anne—be in mortal danger? And how could Anne's parents not see these risks? Why not just drive around and keep on going? Could the people holed up there be that helpful? They probably weren't even alive.

"You've got to be kidding me," Jakob said, looking out the side window opposite Anne. She blinked out of her thoughts and understood her brother's disheartened tone. The roadside for miles had been flanked by unending fields of what looked like miniature trees with green, orb covered stalks topped with lettuce heads. Her mother said they were Brussels sprouts. Actually, she had said, "Brassica oleracea var. gemmifera," but Anne knew what that meant...somehow.

But now the Brussels sprout plants were giving way to lush, swampy land. It wasn't the terrain itself that was frightening, but the kinds of creatures that once might have populated the area, and what they might have become since the Change.

"Aww, geez," Alia said, leaning over Jakob, her body nearly lying on top of his. Was she really afraid or just copping a feel? *Teenagers*, Anne thought with a roll of her eyes. She hoped she'd never be one. Not that she wanted to die, she just hoped she could skip past that stage of life. From what she could tell from Jakob and Alia, not to mention her own mother's monthly cycle, hormones were hell.

"Did you see the name of the street?" Jakob asked.

While street names weren't very important to Anne's day-to-day life, she often read the signs anyway. She made a game out of guessing why the name had been chosen. Was it random? Did it describe the terrain? A person who lived there? The funniest she'd seen was French Hussy Road. She had been tuned out for the past few minutes and missed this sign.

"Alligator Road," Jakob said. "*Alligator*. They were bad enough before. What could—"

"Hey Jake," Peter said, sounding calm. "Do me a favor?"

"Uh," Jakob said. "Yeah?"

Peter glanced in the rearview, making eye contact with his son. "I think you know."

"Right," Jakob said. "Sorry. I'll try not to point out what a bad idea this is."

Anne cracked a smile. Jakob had been picking up some of her biting sarcasm. She liked it.

A wooden sign on the side of the road read, 'Alligator Creek Ahead.'

"So am *I* allowed to say what a bad idea this is?" Anne asked. Peter just smiled. He wasn't stupid. He knew they were entering dangerous territory. But really, everywhere was dangerous territory.

This just *sounded* worse.

The small two-lane road was framed by lush trees and wet ground, full of ferns and moss and surprisingly few ExoGen crops. The already aggressive swamplands had maintained some of their territorial grip. But not all of it. A mixture of crops grew in patches. Anne whispered their names as she spotted them. "Beta vulgaris. Brassica oleracea var. botrytis. Brassica oleracea var. capitate. Oryza sativa." Otherwise known as Sugar Beets, Broccoli, Cabbage and rice, which grew right out of the water.

She wondered again how she knew all these strange scientific details, but her line of questioning was cut short by yet another sign, this one for "Little Hellhole Bay."

"Okay, seriously," Jakob said. "Little Hellhole Bay? Did you search the map for the most ominous sounding stretch of road on purpose?"

Ella looked back over the seat, a slight grin on her face. "Actually, that's where we're headed. That's where the biodome is. Just because it doesn't sound safe, doesn't mean it's actually unsafe."

"Pretty much does these days," Jakob said. "If things like lemon trees can dissolve people from the inside out, and suck them dry for nutrients, then a place like Little Hellhole Bay can live up to its name."

"Only one way to find out," Ella said.

"Are the people there really worth the risk?" Alia asked.

"One's a geneticist. The other is a computer scientist. So, together, they're like a replacement me."

"I thought *I* was the replacement you?" Anne asked, a spark of anger creeping into her voice. She still hadn't really come to grips with the idea that she'd been grown, in a lab, as some kind of better version of her mother, with all of her mother's knowledge stored on a USB drive embedded in her skull. How numb did her mother have to become to make decisions like that? What kind of person steals DNA from a long-lost boyfriend, engineers a daughter and implants tech into her head? Anne had no memory of the surgery, so they must have done it when she was young. Anne had wondered how old she really was, but didn't ask. Her oldest memories were hazy, and *felt* really old, but that didn't mean they weren't manufactured or implanted. Maybe she was ten years old, or three. Either way, she didn't want to know. It made her feel less human. Less alive.

Less...loved.

Sadness swept over Ella's face. "Anne, you're—"

"Better," Anne said. "You've said. The best of you both. I know. That doesn't mean...forget it. Also, people with guns at two o'clock."

Peter hit the brakes and brought the truck to a jarring stop, angling the vehicle, so that if bullets started flying, they'd hit him first. Three men dressed head-to-toe in black military uniforms stepped onto the road, assault rifles aimed at the truck.

"Three more in the trees," Ella said.

Anne saw them a moment later, perched on hunting hides mounted to trees, partially concealed by the lush, green foliage. All weapons were trained on the vehicle. If these people wanted to, they could riddle the windshield with holes and kill them all far more efficiently than a lone ExoGen. Even in a world full of rapidly evolving death machines, the human race could still get the job done when they banded together.

Peter rolled down his window and extended both hands, showing that he wasn't armed. His assault rifle was just below his hands, easily within reach, but the message was clear: We aren't looking for a fight.

The three armed men strode toward the car, but only one of them kept his weapon turned on Peter. The other two started scanning the surrounding swamplands.

The nearest of them, leaned in and peered through the windows, his eyes hidden behind a mirror-lensed face-mask. "Well, gol-dang. Y'all out for a Sunday drive?"

Is it Sunday? Anne wondered. She'd stopped keeping track of days a long time ago.

"We're here to visit some friends," Peter replied, his voice calm and neutral.

"That so?" the man said. "What're their names. Might know 'em, seeing as how these are my stompin' grounds."

Ella leaned toward the window. "Bob and Lyn Askew."

"Bob and Lyn..." The man cocked his head to the side. "Oh, right. Yeah, I know 'em. They're back inside the compound."

"Compound?" Peter asked.

"Up the road a ways," the man said, motioning back behind him. "Safe place, if y'all want to kick up your feet for a spell."

Anne squinted at the man's reflective face and saw Peter's skeptical reflection.

"You know," Peter said. "I think we'll just—"

The man pulled his facemask up to reveal a gaunt face covered in random patches of hair. He grinned, revealing a gap where his front teeth had once been. "Well now, I'm going to have to insist. Folks round here don't take too kindly to people refusing our hospitality. Best you all step out of the vehicle, slow and steady, like that turtle that beat Bugs Bunny in the race."

Peter glanced at Ella. She shook her head slowly, almost imperceptibly. Anne couldn't discern if she was telling him to not act, or to not listen to the man. Then Peter raised his empty hands a little higher. "We don't want any trouble."

"Listen to what I'm tellin' you and you won't find none," the man said. "Name's Boone."

Peter offered his hand, and the man shook it. "Peter."

"Why ya'll shave your heads?" Boone asked.

Really? Anne thought. *That's the first question he has to ask?*

"Lice," Peter said, and Boone quickly withdrew his hand.

Anne nearly laughed, but held it in.

"Fair warning," Peter said. "There is an M4 between me and the door. I'm going to have to catch it, so it doesn't fall out."

Boone took a step back and aimed his weapon at Peter's head. "Like a turtle."

"Ayuh," Peter said, apparently imitating the cartoon turtle. He got a laugh out of Boone and then opened the door slowly, lifting the M4 by its handle in the most non-threatening way possible. He then placed the weapon in the truck's flatbed.

When he lifted his empty hands again, Boone lowered his rifle. "You all seen some shit."

"Shit's seen us," Anne said, and got a laugh out of the man.

"Well, all right then. If ya'll wouldn't mind stepping out, one at a time, I'll take you to Bob and Lyn. Can't say whether or not they'll be happy to see you, but I'll take you to 'em, just the same."

Ten minutes later, they were completely unarmed and headed down the road on foot, while a few of the men stayed behind and rummaged through *Beastmaster*.

Anne glanced back at the men, taking stock of them, wondering which of them they might have to kill first. She wasn't sure if her parents were buying into Boone's Southern charms, but she doubted it. Boone, on the other hand, exuded confidence and an air of cockiness that made Anne want to kick him square in the nuts. But she'd hold back until the time was right. Until *Peter* said the time was right. And then she would kick, scratch, bite and stab her way to freedom. She hoped Boone wasn't stupid enough to try to prevent them from leaving, but she had a strong hunch he was far stupider than that.

SIX

"Open up," Boone shouted at the twenty foot tall gates that looked like something out of King Kong. The two massive doors had been constructed from tall tree trunks, sharpened at the top. The poles were bound by a mishmash of ropes, nailed planks and screws. Not the work of a master builder, but sturdy nonetheless.

Peter took note of the dark brown stains marring some of the sharpened tips. The wall had stood up to attacks from something large enough to impale itself atop the twenty-foot-tall spikes.

Several dull clunks sounded out as the doors were unlocked from the inside. They opened slowly, revealing two men and one woman. They were dressed in dirty shorts and T-shirts, lacking all of the military garb worn by the men outside. The only obvious feature they shared with Boone was a lack of hygiene and the weapons they carried. The woman held a hunting rifle and the two men carried AK-47s, the preferred weapon of terrorists, back when there was such a thing. The weapons had been legal in the United States when converted to semi-automatic. A quick glance at the weapons revealed a third pin hole, meaning these had either been purchased illegally, or converted after the world went to hell. Laws didn't matter anymore, but the first option—illegal arms dealing—spoke to these people's character, which was called into question the moment they threatened his family. He didn't care how subtle or polite Boone was acting. The man wasn't fooling anyone. They were in mortal danger, and walking deeper into a shit-storm with every step. The problem was that Peter hadn't seen a way out of it without getting his family killed.

So he waited, and watched, taking in every sight, sound and smell that might provide him with the key to their salvation.

While Boone and the other good ol' boys outside the gates were dressed like military, their swagger, grungy appearance and lack of discipline marked them as weekend warriors who got the chance to go full time when civilization came to an end. Peter suspected they might have even enjoyed the end of the world and the new status it brought them in this small community of survivors. It was impressive, to be sure, but Peter wasn't sure if the horrors inside the fence would be any better than those outside it.

"Marcus, Stevie," Boone said, pointing at the two men with the muzzle of his AR-15 assault rifle.

Definitely not military, Peter thought.

"Lock up behind us, and quit gawking. These people are my guests."

Marcus and Stevie both turned their eyes down to the ground. They hadn't really been gawking, just taking in the newcomers with interest, maybe even a hint of hope.

Boone was either the leader here, or at least someone of authority. Perhaps they operated on some kind of caste system. Peter had a strong suspicion that life inside the gates was only slightly more tolerable for Marcus and Stevie, than life on the outside.

"Hey, baby," Boone said to the woman, who was dressed in a dirty flannel shirt and short shorts. Peter guessed she was of Cuban descent. She looked like a too-tan Daisy Duke: a little too short, a little too chubby, and sporting a smile so phony it broke Peter's heart. While some of the people here were having the time of their lives, it seemed that just as many lived in fear, despite the weapons in their hands.

"Hey there, Boone," the woman said. Even her Southern accent sounded forced. "You make some friends while you were out?"

"Well," Boone said, "that has yet to be determined, but they seem like nice folk. Don't want no trouble."

"No, sir," Peter said with a nod and a fake grin that was far more convincing than the girl's. He held his hand out to her and said, "Name's Peter."

There was momentary light in faux Daisy's eyes. She started to lift her hand, saying, "Isabe—"

Boone cut her short by placing the rifle muzzle atop her hand and slowly easing it back down.

"Now, girl, don't forget yourself." Boone, a foot taller, stood over the girl, still acting casual, but exuding menace. Marcus and Stevie paid the scene no attention, closing the gates and sliding several long metal beams back in place across the seam. Peter gave them a second look, trying to find common ground between them and the girl, whose full name he guessed was Isabel. While her skin was deeply tanned, the two young men were almost pale white. Marcus had freckles and red hair. The other had flat brown hair.

Upon seeing Isabel, Peter thought the caste system might be racial, but the two gate guards were as white as white got.

"Sorry, Boone," the girl said, deflating, eyes on the ground.

Boone hauled back and slapped Isabel's backside. On the surface, it looked almost playful, but the impact drew a pained cry from the girl's lips. Her smile became even more forced, as tears began to well.

Ella took a step forward, but Peter gripped her forearm, holding her back. If Boone attacked the girl with deadly force, they would act, but not until then. And hopefully not before fully understanding what they were up against.

"Go tell Mason we got visitors," Boone said, not noticing Ella. "I'm gonna take 'em to see Bob and Lyn. Then we'll be up."

Isabel looked confused by this last bit, but scurried away with a nod. "Will do, Boone."

Boone cupped a hand around his mouth and called after the girl. "And I reckon I'll be callin' on ya this evening. Finish what we started here, aight."

The girl's quick walk turned into a jog.

Boone flashed a smile at Peter and winked, clucking his tongue. "Girl is dumber than a sack of rocks, but rides my..." His eyes turned to Anne, then moved back to Peter. "Well, you know what I mean."

"I think I do," Peter said.

"Well, all right then." Boone started walking backward deeper into the camp, extending his arms out to either side, "Welcome to Hellhole Bay, bastion outpost of humanity's only surviving population. Well, until you all showed up. Been a while since anyone came a-callin'."

Peter ignored Boone's theatrics and scanned the area. The massive fence was really a wall stretched out in either direction as far as he could see. Just inside the fence was a twenty foot stretch of water, like a moat on the wrong side. The waterway narrowed as it cut across the path ahead, where a log bridge, just wide enough for a vehicle, but maybe not strong enough for one, allowed them passage. Peter looked down into the water as they crossed, half expecting to see alligators writhing about, ready to devour intruders. But the water was clear and fresh. A slight current moved toward the far end of the site.

"Water flows in on one side, from a crick," Boone said, noting Peter's attention. "Out the other side. Metal grates keep the critters out. Gives us fresh water for the crops."

The word crops turned Peter's attention forward. The outer fringe of the strange complex ahead of them was basically scorched earth. There were nubs of things that had grown and been burned. "You burn the crops that grow?"

"Yep," Boone said. "Anything green outside the domes is toast."

Domes, Peter thought, looking beyond the scorched earth, confirming Boone's use of the plural as accurate. Like all the biodomes Peter had seen, there was a farmhouse providing access. But extending from the backside of the glass biodome was a second, and a third. There were five biodomes in all, and what looked like a sixth under construction. These people had taken Ella's design and duplicated it. With the Southern climate, sunny weather and a plentiful—and filtered—water source, they could grow enough food to support a village, which was precisely what they were doing.

A small town of ramshackle homes, constructed from sheets of stainless steel, PVC pipes and plastic siding, filled the space between them and the farmhouse. Each single-story structure looked just big enough for one or two people, and Peter suspected they were really just for sleeping. Most didn't even have doors. Privacy would be hard to come by in a place like this. There were a few ragtag people milling about. An older woman swept trash from the grid of dirt paths between the homes. A few men carried supplies here and there. But most of the village's residents were somewhere else.

"Where is everyone?" Jakob asked.

Peter flinched when his son spoke, but it was a harmless question.

"Either outside the wall doing what needs to be done, working on the new dome or serving inside with the others. Most people think tending the crops is the sweetest gig. Fresh air, fresh food. And yeah, they're not supposed t' eat that food. S'posed to get rations like the rest of us. But we all know they're skimming. Who in their right mind wouldn't? I mean, me and the boys maintain our musculatures by foraging what we can out in the swamp. We don't share none, either. If yer lucky, and don't fuck around, you two—" He pointed at Peter and Jakob. "—might find yerselves back outside the fence. Reunite you with that sweet ride. Goin' on supply runs. Shootin' up critters. Shit is a good time. I'm tellin' you. I'm *tellin'* you."

When Boone faced forward again, Peter felt a tug on his shirt. Anne walked behind him, swirling an index finger around her ear and rolling her eyes in the universal symbol for: 'He's nuts.'

Peter gave a subtle nod and faced forward again, taking in every nook and cranny of the strange amalgam of medieval and futuristic worlds. Is this what the future of humanity would look like, even if they could eat ExoGen crops? *Probably*, he decided, but hopefully without the kind of abuse he suspected was the norm at Hellhole Bay.

Boone led them through the maze of small shacks and then toward what looked like short lean-to stables. Maybe for goats. Unlike the small homes now behind him, the six units, stretched out in a row, all had doors. Chain link doors. And concrete floors. As he got closer, he could see that some of the cells were occupied—by people.

"Now," Boone said, turning around again, walking backward. Peter noticed the man's index finger had slipped around his weapon's trigger. Whatever they were about to see, Boone expected it would get a negative reaction out of them. "Ya'll keep in mind that there are reasons for everything here. It's like what Einstein said, equal and opposite reactions for every action. Aight?"

Peter slowly took Ella's hand. She was trembling with rage, close to unleashing that savage fury that had kept her and Anne alive in the wild. But this was not the right place. If they were going to stay alive, they also needed to stay calm. To play along. He gave her a squeeze, and she responded with two of her own. She got it.

And she proved it by saying, "Not a problem." She hadn't spoken much at all, and she let a slight Southern drawl trickle from her lips. "We all like Einstein."

Boone looked like he'd tasted something sour for just a moment. Peter thought he was trying to figure out if Ella was really on board or mocking him. But he apparently couldn't figure out which was the truth. He shrugged his eyebrows and twisted his lips, turning back to the cages. Then he thrust his arms out like a conductor. "Welcome to the coop. It's where all the Questionables go."

"For how long?" Jakob asked.

Boone grinned. "'Til there ain't no doubt about their loyalty. To Hellhole. Our way of life. And Mason. Really, it's up to him."

"This is where Bob and Lyn are?" Ella asked, working a little too hard to sound casual.

Boone stepped to the side, motioning to the next chain link gate. "In there."

Ella took a step closer, and Boone stopped her with a raised hand. "Remember..."

"I remember," Ella said with a nod. Then she and Peter looked through the chain link fence together. When Peter saw what was inside, he took Ella's hand again. She squeezed hard, digging her nails into his palm, channeling her rage. He accepted the pain without flinching. He barely noticed it.

Inside the cage was an emaciated woman. She looked eighty years old, but Ella had said Lyn was forty-five. The woman's blue eyes glanced in their direction, but she remained in place. Beside her lay her husband, Bob, whose white, withered eyes were motionless.

Bob was a corpse.

SEVEN

"Ya'll have had your curiosity satiated, yeah?" Boone had taken a few steps back, rifle raised. Peter couldn't tell if the man was expecting trouble, or hoping for it. Either way, they weren't going to give him an excuse to pull the trigger.

"What did they do?" Peter asked.

"Insurrection," Boone said, and then spat on the ground by his feet. "Tried to change the natural order of things."

"This was their land," Ella said, showing some of their cards. "Their home."

"No such thing as land ownership anymore. World went and changed. Only the fittest can survive. Some of the weak, too, I s'pose, if they don't question things. Plenty of unfit people still living inside these walls on account of what the strongest of us provide."

"Makes sense," Peter said. The words were hard to say, but sounded believable. "Like having kids." He motioned to Jakob, Anne and Alia, who had yet to see what remained of Bob and Lyn.

"Hey," Anne complained. She fell silent when Jakob gripped her shoulder.

But she didn't go unnoticed.

"I reckon you're right about that," Boone said, leaning down to Anne's height. "You're a feisty one, yeah?"

"You have no idea," Anne said, the words nearly a growl.

Boone chuckled. "Looks like you're made of good stock. White, but not like them two Cat-lickers." He looked the group over. "Naw. Not a Fire Crotch among ya."

It took Peter a moment to decipher what Boone was saying, but he came to the conclusion that Marcus and Stevie were Catholic, and that 'Fire Crotch' was a reference to Marcus's red hair and Irish ancestry. *The caste system isn't just racial,* Peter thought, *it's also religious and ancestral, focusing on old prejudices.*

Boone clucked his tongue and gave Anne a wink. "Too young yet, but time's still moving forward, ain't it?"

That last comment shocked a strange kind of stillness into the group. Boone had just revealed the stakes. If they didn't get out of here—or got killed in the attempt—life would become a nightmare, especially for the girls.

"So Mason did all this, then?" Peter asked, redirecting the man the way a parent would a child in the throes of a tantrum.

Boone stood up, looking a little more relaxed after his revelation of Bob and Lyn, not to mention his not so veiled sexual threat to a twelve-year-old girl, didn't incite violence. "Yes, sir. Well, he organized it. Was a contractor before things went crazy. Built the first of these here domes." He raised his chin toward Lyn and Bob's corpse. "For them. Found out what it was for and took matters into his own hands. Had three of 'em built before the world turned to shit. Most of us working on the outside have been here since the beginning, though we sometimes bring in new blood." He nodded at Peter. "Something you might cotton to, if you're still around tomorrow."

Peter heard the threat. If they weren't around tomorrow, it wouldn't be because they were set free. "Imagine I would," Peter said. "We've been living in the wild for so long, I'm not sure I could stand more than a few days inside these walls without getting blood on my hands."

Boone gave a gap-toothed smile, clearly hearing Peter's threat as comradery. "We are speaking the same language, my friend." He pointed to the cell at the end of the row. "Now, yer rag head's gonna have to sit things out for a bit. Kids, too, though I don't think them two will be there long." Boone raised a hand when he looked at Ella. Her anger was bubbling to the surface. "I know they're your kids an' all, but we got rules, and kids can't go inside the house. And since yer new, I can't let 'em have the run of the place, neither. Soon as Mason says ya'll aren't Questionables, we'll assign shelters and jobs. Till then, you best do as I say."

"I have a name," Alia said, her voice jolting tension through Peter's body. *Why couldn't she have just stayed quiet?*

Boone squinted at her. "That so?"

"Alia," she said with a raised chin.

Peter half-expected Boone to backhand her, which would set off Jakob and then their chances of escape would evaporate. But Boone's reaction wasn't violent.

It was worse.

He looked the girl up and down. "Well now, Alia, I reckon you're of age."

"Of age...for what?"

Alia had led a sheltered life before the Change, and a hermit's life after it. Her only relationship with a boy was with Jakob, and the pair hadn't been alone since their first kiss in Alia's father's biodome. Her innocence was on full display now.

"Marriage," Boone said. "I ain't never been with a rag head before. Course, I ain't sure I want to marry one neither. Course, I ain't got to marry you to pork—"

"Hey, Boone," Peter cut in, sensing things were about to go downhill. Jakob's fists had clenched and his eyes followed Boone like a bird of prey preparing to strike. And since Peter had been training his son for the past few weeks, Jakob might even be capable of...what? Killing a man? An ExoGen creature was one thing. Killing a human being left a mark on a man's soul. He didn't want that for his son. He motioned to Anne. "Young ears."

The fiendish look in Boone's eyes melted into a lop-sided grin. "Right you are." He sniffed and rubbed his nose with a dirty finger. "Follow me, then."

He led them to the last cell in line. Peter counted three people already inside, barefoot and hidden by the slanted roof's shadow. He could see them shifting about, though. *At least they're not corpses.*

Boone twisted a key in a padlock and popped it free. The chain link gate creaked open. The people inside withdrew deeper into the shadows.

Boone motioned inside the cell. "Welcome to Casa de Questionable."

Anne looked inside, but didn't step closer. "Why are *they* in there?"

"Stealing. Lying. General disregard for the status quo. Don't you worry none. Not a one of them is prone to violence." He gave her a wink. "Not like you, anyhow."

Anne sighed and stepped inside without any further protest. Alia hurried after, the prospects of staying free with Boone worse than being locked up with strangers. Jakob paused by the gate, looking back at his father. Peter just gave the boy a silent nod, and Jakob returned it. That nod, simple as it was, said a lot. Promises were made. Trust sought and given. One way or another, Peter was going to return for the kids, and leave this place.

Jakob stepped inside the cell and pulled the gate shut behind him. He even put the latch back in place.

"Much obliged," Boone said, slipping the padlock into the latch and locking it once more. "Ya'll ready?"

Ella crouched by the gate, fingers hooked around the chain link. She whispered to Anne, who nodded a few times and then said, "Love you, too," loud enough for Boone to hear. Peter doubted the pair were sharing typical parting words between mother and daughter. But there was no way for Boone to know that. In part, because they'd spoken softly, but also because he was a few bricks short of the world's smallest chimney.

"Ready," Ella said when she stood back up.

Boone led them back toward the farmhouse. It was three stories tall, white and in a very simple sense, it reminded Peter of his own home, before he blew it up. But there were a few obvious differences that stood out. The windows were barred on the lower floors. Peter wasn't sure if that was to keep monsters out, or to keep people in. Maybe both. But with the twenty-foot wall and armed guards, keeping monsters out was a solved problem.

Maybe the bars came before the walls? Peter wondered, but he knew he was just being hopeful, and that could be a fatal mistake. He chided himself for trying to find the best in the people who lived here. He should be on the lookout for the worst. Presently, that was Boone.

"Be polite," Boone said, as he led them up the farmer's porch stairs toward the front door. Peter imagined the door had once been solid wood, but it was now a slab of steel. "Tell the truth. He can always tell when someone is fibbin', and there ain't no faster way to wind up in the Questionables. If he offers something, accept it. And if he asks you to do something for him, only appropriate answer is a 'Yes, sir,' and a nod."

Peter was surprised by Boone's aid. The man had grown more friendly since taking them from the truck. He'd made some threats, sure, but most of them, aside from the sexual allusions directed at the girls, also included ways to avoid unsavory outcomes. Peter had gone out of his way to be agreeable, and it seemed to be winning Boone over. He doubted the man who'd organized this outpost of humanity would be as unperceptive, but maybe there was a way to avoid violence?

There I go hoping again, Peter thought.

Boone thumped his fist against the steel door three times. "It's Boone. Here to see Mason."

The sound of locks snapping open came from the other side.

Boone motioned to the door with his head. "Takes 'em a while. Not sure why, but Mason keeps the place locked up tighter than a nun's poontang."

The opening door kept Peter from having to come up with a reply. A black woman dressed in a traditional maid's uniform bowed as she opened the door. "Mistuh Boone," she said in an old-fashioned, Southern accent, stilted and unnatural. "Massa Mason is expecting you. He's in the study."

Massa? Peter thought. *Did I hear that right?* Peter went rigid as his eyes shifted from the uncomfortable maid, to the foyer wall where a large Confederate flag hung. A hint of music wafted through the air. It sounded pleasant enough on the surface, but in the current environment it felt more like acid in his ears. He heard the lyrics, 'With a holy host of others standing 'round me, still I'm on the dark side of the moon,' and he recognized the song as James Taylor's *Carolina in My Mind*.

Mason, whoever that was, had a deep love affair with all things Southern: good, bad, the ugly and probably even worse. The poor woman at the door was the last straw for Peter. He no longer wanted to just escape this place alive, he wanted to stage a coup in the process. There were good people here, people who deserved better lives, free of subjugation to racist assholes. Leaving them like this...

He just couldn't.

As Peter followed Boone down the hallway, old wooden floorboards creaking underfoot, he came to the conclusion that he was, without a doubt, a Questionable. But the real question was, could he keep that from Mason long enough to kill the man?

EIGHT

Eddie Kenyon had gone native. With the exception of eating ExoGen crops, he had completely abandoned civility and decorum. He rode bareback upon a massive wooly steed, like something out of the last ice age. The brutes could travel for days without food or water, though both were plentiful. Their powerful bodies and rhino-like horns that split at the ends into an array of sharp, scooped blades, fended off all manner of creatures. Alone, the creatures might fall to an Apex predator, but their strength was in numbers, like the tribe's.

They called themselves Chunta, and they had a kind of language. Most was grunts and shouts, but there were words and phrases spoken by the males. Still, this was a matriarchal tribe. The three women stood a foot taller than Kenyon, who was just as much taller than the other males. The males were mostly covered in hair, ran with a sideways galumph and attended to the females' every need.

Kenyon, while male, held a position of prestige. The matriarch, Feesa, who spoke stilted English, understood that Kenyon was smarter than the rest of them. And *he* understood that she could rend his arms from his body as easily as he could petals from a flower. He had become an advisor, helping them defeat enemies, find sufficient food and shelter and most importantly, track their prey.

While Kenyon was still fully human, and he managed to remain so by foraging non-ExoGen foods, his thirst for vengeance matched the feral woman's. The Chunta were fiercely loyal to each other. Kenyon suspected that the Change had happened late in these people, when most everything else had already turned into ravenous killing machines. They'd banded together in the early days, forging a bond that remained, even after the Change. Instead of evolving into individual monsters, they had evolved as a group. As did their steeds, which Kenyon thought might have been bison from a farm. Copulation was frequent and polyamorous, often devolving into sweaty, hairy orgies that Kenyon had trouble stomaching. But he did his part, using his knowledge of female anatomy to help maintain his high stature.

Over the weeks, he had shed his clothing, and thrown himself into tribal living. There were times he even enjoyed the primal comradery. But he never forgot the reason for his devolution and long sojourn across the country: Ella Masse. She had used him, betrayed him, broken his heart and left him for dead. She could have returned to ExoGen with him and Anne. Could have been safe. Could have made things right. Instead, she chose a life on the run, in the wild, with the fucker who had nearly killed him. Peter Crane.

When Kenyon caught up with them, he was going to kill Jakob, Peter's son. Make his father and Ella watch. Then he'd do Ella. Make the bitch pay. He'd kill her, but not Anne. That was Ella's deepest fear, that her precious Anne would have to live in this screwed-up world without a mother. And then it would be Peter's turn. But Kenyon wouldn't get the pleasure of taking that asshole's life. That fell to Feesa, the matriarch, who had been close to the previous matriarch, known as Kristen in her life before the Change. She had been Peter's wife, whom he killed in front of his son, and the tribe. It was an offense that Feesa would not forgive, and the others followed her lead.

Kenyon appreciated that about Feesa, and even believed that should he be slain, she would seek vengeance for his life. He wasn't sure he would do the same, but he had grown fond of her, as much as a man could for a woman like her...if she could really be considered a woman still.

Calling her ugly was an understatement.

Her bottom teeth, like all Chunta, were long, curved and pointed. They jutted out from her pouty lower lip, curling upward several inches before punching back into the skin of her face. The wounds were really just deep, hard scars now, but it was still disturbing to look at. Her nose had evolved to deal with the teeth, pulling back into the face, so that there was barely a nose at all. The only bearable trait about her was that unlike the men, and to an extent, her female companions, the hair on Feesa's body was fine and soft, and her breasts were ample. Kenyon had become somewhat fond of her, more because of her powerful spirit than any kind of physical attraction, but the parts of her that remained feminine helped make his more visceral duties bearable—and if he was honest with himself, sometimes fun. The Chunta lived without inhibition. He'd never felt such freedom, but he would risk it all for revenge. As would Feesa.

He stood in a tree, looking down at the men below, all of whom were oblivious to his presence. Feesa was perched on a branch beside him, cocking her head to the side, while the men escorted a familiar armored truck down a long dirt road.

He sensed Feesa coiling to strike. Seeing the vehicle enraged her, and her simple mind no doubt linked these strangers to Peter. But now was not the time to strike. These men had clearly encountered Peter and Ella, and would know their fates. There was intelligence to be gathered. Plans to make. But these concepts were beyond Feesa, who was guided primarily by instinct.

But not completely.

Kenyon reached out slowly and tapped her forearm. When she looked at him, he shook his head. Then he raised his hand and made a gun shape with his fingers. She shook her head at this, frowning so deeply that the teeth embedded in her cheeks strained against the skin. Kenyon tapped his head in a gesture that she understood was him telling her to think, that this was a matter of strategy, that she needed to trust him.

And she did.

Her face scrunched, but her muscles relaxed.

When the men were a hundred feet beyond them, Kenyon and Feesa climbed down the tree into the foot-deep swamp water. Kenyon's instinct told him to be wary for snakes, turtles and gators, but in the new world, most of those things had already eaten each other nearly to extinction. Those left alive wouldn't be hard to see coming. Not in shallow water, anyway.

But when Feesa raised her flat snout and sniffed the air, he remained still and vigilant. She hooked her fingers and raked them through the air—the Chunta sign for an Apex. Then she shook her head and pointed in the direction from which the men had come. Whatever it was, it was far enough away to not concern Feesa much. But Kenyon didn't share her confidence. If there was an Apex hunting in these swamps, it might already be tracking these men. If that was true, it wouldn't be long before it was tracking him and Feesa, too. And that was a problem.

While the Chunta were ExoGenetic creatures, they weren't Apex. As a group, sure, but individually, they didn't stand a chance against a super-evolved predator.

Kenyon pointed to Feesa's eyes, ears and nose, and then back down the dirt road. She nodded and said, "Careful. Yes." Her voice rumbled out of her throat, sounding more like Barry White than a woman—or even a monster who used to be a woman.

Then they started off through the swamp, following the oblivious men. If the men didn't lead him to Ella or to one of her group, he could interrogate them. If that didn't work, he'd let Feesa interrogate them. Either way, he was going to find out where Ella and Peter had hidden themselves. If they were dead, these men would pay for stealing his vengeance. If they were alive...the swamp was going to run red.

NINE

Mason was a soft man—not at all what Ella had been expecting. The palpable fear emanating from Hellhole Bay made her think the man in charge would be tyrannical in action *and* appearance. But the man sitting behind the mahogany desk, peering over the top of a pair of thin reading glasses, looked more like a turtle without a shell. He was dressed in white slacks and a short-sleeve, white, button-down shirt, both of which matched the wispy hair poking out from the sides of a gray Ascot cap. He flinched at their entrance, pale blue eyes squinting at Peter. But when he looked at Ella, those eyes widened. He reached out to a CD player, turning down the music, stood from his seat and tipped his hat like a true Southern gentleman.

"Ma'am," Mason said, looking her up and down. "It's an unusual pleasure to welcome someone such as yourself into my humble abode."

"It's equally unusual to have my children locked up in a glorified chicken coop," Ella said, flashing a smile as phony as Mason's, though she thought he did a much better job.

Or maybe he really is happy to see us?

So far, the man had no real reason to dislike them, other than the fact that they were traveling with a 'rag head,' but maybe that prejudice was Boone's alone? *No,* she thought, remembering the maid at the door. Her ridiculous outfit and forced accent harkened back to darker times for anyone not wealthy and white, a role Mason seemed to be enjoying.

The office was lined with book shelves. Most of the tomes were popular novels. The dog-eared book resting on his desk was titled *The Dirge of Briarsnare Marsh.* They weren't exactly the books of a thinking man...but they were literature nevertheless. Memories of Bob and Lyn Askew flitted to the forefront of Ella's mind. Bob with his action and horror novels. Lyn teasing him about it. These were Bob's books. Bob's office.

Bob the corpse.

Mason cleared his throat and widened his smile. "I am sorry about that, truly. But I assure you, there is method to the madness. With the future of mankind at stake, and our food source at constant risk, we've been forced to take drastic...sometimes cruel, measures to ensure our survival." He motioned to the two antique chairs opposite the desk. "Please, sit."

Ella didn't feel like sitting, but when Boone gave Peter a nudge in the back, she realized it wasn't a request. When Peter motioned to her chair and said, "Go on," she realized he was still playing along. Still thinking with his head instead of his heart, and right now, that's what would keep them alive. So she smiled and took a seat, knowing the other two men, gentlemen both, wouldn't sit until she had. Peter sat down next, followed by Mason, who looked pleased by the way the ritual had progressed.

"Now then," Mason said, leaning back in Bob's office chair. "You all have been living out there for how long now?"

"A few weeks," Peter said before Ella could even think to answer. And it was just as well. Peter was the better liar. If Mason really was good at detecting untruths, it was better if Ella kept her mouth shut.

"And I hear tell that you arrived in what, some kind of tank?"

"A technical," Peter said.

"Technical," Mason repeated. "Can't say as I'm familiar with the term."

"Military jargon," Peter said. "Just means it's a truck with a big gun mounted to it. In this case, a Dodge Ram with an M249 light machine gun."

"Uh-huh..." Mason twiddled his fingers together. "Sounds like you know your way around guns."

"Served in the U.S Marine Corps," Peter said.

He's being honest, Ella realized, *but leaving out details.* Telling the man he was a Marine would explain Peter's knowledge of weaponry, and help validate the story of their survival. But leaving out the fact that he'd been a Critical Skills Operator would make him seem less dangerous. Peter wanted the man to see him as a potential ally—another gun-toting grunt—but not a threat.

"You look a might too long in the tooth for active duty," Mason observed. "What was your rank when you left the corps?"

"Sergeant Major," Peter replied. It was a demotion from Captain, but high enough and said with conviction. "Served two tours. Afghanistan."

"And you left because..."

"PTSD," Peter said, still being honest. "That's Post Traumatic—"

"I know what it is," Mason said. He leaned forward, elbows on the desk, hands clasped. "So how does a man with PTSD survive the wilds of the new world?"

"I worked through it, sir. A long time ago." He reached out and took Ella's hand, his affection catching her off guard. "I had help."

"You're a whole man again, then?"

Peter nodded. "Yes, sir."

Mason looked them both over for a moment. "Since neither of you are wearing wedding bands, am I to assume you're living in sin? Had the boy and girl out of wedlock?"

Ella glanced at the window behind Mason. She could see the Questionable cells in the background. *He was watching.*

"No, sir," Peter said, pulling Ella's attention back to the polite interrogation. "Wearing rings in the field is a bad idea. Might end up with a ring avulsion—what happens when your ring gets caught on something and yanks the finger out of joint, or clean off." He reached into his shirt and pulled out a silver chain with two rings dangling from it.

Ella tried to show no reaction that Peter kept his and Kristen's wedding bands around his neck. She wasn't surprised. Peter was an honorable guy like that, and he had loved his wife. Why not remember the time they had by keeping a memento of their marriage? What she was, was jealous. But that was ridiculous. Kristen was dead, killed by Peter's own hand.

"And I don't think we've been properly introduced. I'm Peter Crane, and this is my wife—"

"I think it's time I heard from the lovely lady herself." Mason turned to Ella, his gaze friendly, but discerning. Peter had apparently passed the man's truth test, but Mason wasn't fully convinced. So it was Ella's turn to endure his scrutiny. "Your name, ma'am?"

"Kristen," Ella said. "Kristen Crane."

"Doesn't exactly roll off the tongue, does it?" Mason chuckled at himself.

"My father always said it sounded like a Marvel Comics super hero name," Ella said. In truth, it's what she had thought about Kristen, when she heard about Peter's wedding plans. "You know, Peter Parker. Jessica Jones. Kristen Crane."

"Mmm," Mason said, his smile wavering. She was failing his test. Forcing her words. "An unfortunate amalgamation of names, then."

"Yes...sir," she said, and nearly said more, layering on phony quips about something as insignificant as their names. She stopped herself, clearing her throat and then waiting for Mason to continue.

The man sat in silence for a good ten seconds and then asked, "How did you survive the Change?"

Peter opened his mouth to reply, but Mason held his palm up, "Let the lady answer."

"Well, we had the truck," Ella said. "And a lot of—"

"I don't mean the past few weeks in the wild," Mason said. "I have boys that can do the same. What I'm wondering is how, when the rest of the world started eating itself into oblivion, you all remained..." He swept his hands out toward Ella and Peter. "...as you are. Human. I know how my people survived, but you are the first outsiders we have encountered that are not..."

"Evolved," Ella said.

Mason grinned. "That's a word for it, I suppose, if you believe in such things."

Ella smiled and followed Peter's lead of near complete honesty. "We had a biodome. Like yours. But just one of them."

"I see," Mason said. "And how did you acquire said biodome?"

Ella let her discomfort over the subject show. "From Ella Masse."

"The very same woman who provided the former residents of this home with their biodome. How fortuitous for you. The very same woman, if I recall, who created the crops that led to the unhinged *evolution* of all life on Earth."

"She tried to warn—"

Peter was silenced once again, this time with a harshly raised index finger.

"Tell me, Kristen," Mason said. "What made you worth saving, while the rest of the world went to hell?"

For a moment, she was worried that he recognized her. Before the Change really took effect, she had been on TV several times, warning people about the dangers of ExoGen crops. That was before the company caught up with her, kidnapped her and threw her in a cell until she agreed to stay quiet and continue her work for them. At first, she had wondered why they hadn't simply killed her, but later she had realized it was her mind they wanted. The genetic tinkering they had done, for reasons that still evaded her, was just the beginning. Despite having been a somewhat public figure for a few weeks, she was now far skinnier, had a clean-shaven head and was covered in grime. Her own parents might not recognize her.

Ella looked at the floor, and then glanced at Peter. "He did." She met Mason's eyes. "She wasn't interested in saving me. Just him."

Mason waited for more.

"They had an affair. Had been childhood friends, and then more than that for a while. We ended up back in the same town with that bitch, and he..." She shook her head at the very real memories. "He couldn't say no to her. Never could."

"And yet here you are," Mason pointed out. "Together, and by all accounts, in love."

"He...made the right choice in the end. Chose his wife and children over something...shallow. She was nostalgia. A reminder of younger days. I have struggled to forgive the choices he made. I've hated him for it. God knows, I have. But in the end, he chose his family, and that...that is a man worth loving, despite his faults."

Mason gave a nod and leaned back in his chair. "Takes a strong woman to forgive such grave misgivings."

"Wasn't easy," Ella said.

Mason gave another nod. "Now then, near as I can tell, the Askews were friends of Dr. Ella Masse. Like-minded science-types, whom you asked for by name, yes? Given your husband's adulterous past, I'm surprised you accepted such a generous gift."

"There isn't anything I wouldn't do to protect my children," Ella said. "That woman...she was a lot of things I didn't like, but she was also brilliant. When someone like that tells you the world is coming to an end, you listen, even if it means accepting help from someone who hurt you the most."

"And the Askews?"

"There was a list of names and locations," Ella said. "Of biodomes around the country. Eighty-seven of them. Bob and Lyn were on the list. It's why we came here."

"And where is this list now?"

Ella shrugged. She'd thrown the list away long ago, and really didn't know where it was. "I memorized it."

"Uh-huh. And how did you come upon it? The list."

Ella took in a deep breath and let it out as a sigh. "She came to our house."

"When?"

"Five weeks ago."

"Where is she now?"

"Dead," Peter said. "I put a bullet in her."

Mason's eyebrows crested high on his forehead. He appeared to be enjoying the story now.

"She came to us seeking shelter," Ella said. "It's why she paid for the domes. So she'd have places to hide. But when she came to us, she brought trouble in her wake. Stalkers. Horrible creatures with tails that look like wheat stalks. Hard to see in the tall crops. They hunted in a pack. And we...Peter, had to destroy the house to escape."

"And Dr. Masse? She died at the house?"

Ella nodded, and then spoke to Peter. "But it didn't need to be done in front of the kids."

"Couldn't have been avoided," Peter replied, anger creeping into his voice.

"Now, now," Mason said. "I am not a fan of lover's quarrels."

"Sorry," Peter said. "It's all still...raw."

"What about the girl with you?" Mason asked, shifting subjects.

"Sir," Boone said, speaking for the first time since entering. "I was wondering if I might—"

"Let them answer, Boone," Mason said. "Be polite."

"Her name is Alia," Peter said, and when Mason didn't shush him again, he continued. "Daughter of Brant and Misha Rossi, owners of the first biodome we reached. I promised I'd look out for her."

"What happened to the parents?"

"We were attacked."

"More of those Stalkers?"

"ExoGen," Peter said. "They were looking for Ella. They had a Black Hawk and two Apache helicopters."

"And yet you survived," Mason said.

"Not all of us," Peter replied.

"And have you seen these helicopters since?"

Peter shook his head. "I told them she was dead. I think they believed me, but they tried to kill us anyway. The leader, a man named Kenyon, I think he had feelings for her."

"Sounds like Dr. Ella Masse was a knockout." He held a hand out to Ella. "No offense to you, Mrs. Crane. A woman with that much control over the opposite sex tends to bring trouble wherever she goes."

Ella grinned. "I couldn't agree more."

A knock at the door turned everyone around. Boone opened it, revealing a nervous looking Stevie.

"Better be important," Boone said.

"Gunshots," Stevie said. "Three of them. Distant. Perimeter guards haven't seen anything, but Roy and the others aren't checking in. We've tried calling them a bunch of—"

Boone unclipped a handheld radio from his waist, flicked it on and spoke into it. "Roy, this is Boone, come back?" He lifted his finger and waited, listening to static. Then he pushed the call button again. "Roy, quit fuckin' around. If you're hearing me, you best answer. Over."

When no reply came, Boone just looked to Mason.

"Go ahead," Mason said. "But take Mr. Crane with you."

Peter grew tense, but didn't complain.

"Sir, I don't think taking this—"

"Nonsense," Mason said. "I believe Mr. and Mrs. Crane have been forthright in their answers to me, and while I still have questions that need answers, I don't see any reason to refuse this man's help...if he's willing to provide it."

There was no mention of the children, but everyone in the room knew Mason had them as collateral.

Peter stood. "I'll do my best."

"Very good," Mason said, standing and offering Peter his hand. When Peter shook it, the older man added, "And don't worry about your wife none. I'll entertain her in your absence."

Peter smiled and withdrew his hand. "Thank you." He turned to Ella and said, "Be back soon." Then to Boone, "Lead the way."

When the two men had left, Ella turned back to Mason, whose smile had widened enough to reveal teeth as white as his clothes. "Well then, Kristen, what am I going to do with you?"

TEN

"Don't look at them," Jakob whispered to Anne, who was staring at the people sitting on the far side of the cell. He didn't fully understand what made someone a Questionable, but he guessed they'd done something wrong to end up here. Sure, the people who ran the place had an obviously skewed sense of right and wrong, but that didn't mean they only locked up nice people. Murder and theft were probably still jailable offenses, even to the morally ambiguous.

"They're not going anywhere fast," Anne said, not averting her eyes. "*Look* at them."

Against his own advice, Jakob followed Anne's instructions. She was a lot younger than him, but when it came to the wild world, she was far more experienced. That included dealing with people. While Jakob had spent two years holed up in a farmhouse with his father, Anne had lived in a large community, and then fled across the country with a group of people, including Eddie Kenyon, a man who turned out to be a little psycho. So he trusted her judgment. Not of their cell-mates' character, but of their ability to cause him harm.

The three people sharing the concrete floor with them—two men and one woman—were in various states of living decay. The oldest of them, a skinny man with wispy gray hair, looked the worst off. He stared back at Anne with defiant eyes, as though he resented her assessment, but was still unable to prove her wrong. The second man and the woman, were huddled up together in the back corner, clutching each other, more afraid of Jakob than he was of them. They had the wide-eyed look of people who expected the worst to happen at any moment, probably because it often did.

Jakob's fear turned to pity. What had these people endured? None of them looked dangerous, not even the defiant old man. They looked...normal. Emaciated and hungry, but normal.

"I'm Jakob," he said to the group. When no one replied, he motioned to Anne and said, "This is my sister, Anne. And my..." he glanced at Alia. They had been romantically involved, to be sure, but they'd never had a discussion about official titles. What were they? Friends with kissing benefits? Girlfriend and boyfriend? Would they become more? Were they already? Maybe romance was accelerated at the end of the world, when there was no one else left? He decided to jump to the logical conclusion. "...my girlfriend, Alia."

Relief flowed through his muscles when she smiled and gave a slight wave. It was corny, he knew, to be concerned about his relationship with Alia while they were being held prisoner inside a hostile compound, separated from his father and Ella, but... Well, hormones paid the apocalypse no attention. And with the whole world out to eat him, a little bit of teenage affection—Anne called it 'obsession'—kept him sane. And that was a good thing. One of the few left in the world from his point-of-view.

No one replied. Blank eyes stared back. For a moment, he thought the three of them might actually be dead. Then the woman blinked.

Jakob focused on her. She had ratty-looking blonde hair that hung in clumps over her dirt-covered face. He'd seen the look before. Hell, he emulated it. "Were you living on the outside?" he asked. "In the wild?"

The woman's eyes twitched.

"We were, too," Jakob said. "At least, for the past few weeks. Our farm was attacked." He hitched his thumb toward Alia. "Hers, too. Now we're here."

"And here you will stay," the old man said, his voice rattling like he'd enjoyed a few too many packs a day. Jakob reassessed the man. Was he starving or just miserable from nicotine withdrawal?

"H-how long have you been here?" Alia asked.

The old man turned toward the couple. "Two years in the camp. About a week in the cell?"

"For what?" Jakob asked.

"Well," the old man said. "I took too long with the lemonade. These two were caught...well, doing what men and women sometimes do. And if that sounds ridiculous to any of you, the only men and women allowed to engage in such activities are those approved by Mason, and that is generally relegated to Mason himself and a handful of his most trusted hands. Mason's got himself a real harem inside that house. Most of them want no part in it, but they don't really have a say anymore."

Anne clenched her fists. "Why doesn't anyone help them?"

The old man grunted like a cantankerous horse. "Most people living outside the house never see them, let alone communicate with them. I only know them because I worked inside, too. I'm a handy kind of guy, and I know my way around a kitchen. Was a line cook in Philly, for a while. Aside from his motley gang of enforcers and guards, I was one of the few men let inside the house. Mason believed I was too old to fraternize with his wives." The man tapped the side of his nose with his forefinger. "More than a few of them know that's not true. I might have twenty years on Mason, but the plumbing is still good, and I've spent more than a few nights tending to wounds inflicted by that man."

He took a deep breath, and as he let it out, the fight that had been building in his voice seemed to melt right out of him. "This place could have been a blessing. There's food enough for everyone in those domes. The walls provide safety. The human race could have begun again, right here. Instead, he took Hellhole Bay's name to heart. Brought his own kind of hell to Earth."

Anne seemed unfazed by the man's doom and gloom. She nodded her head at the woman. "Why aren't you, you know, in the house? Looks like you might be pretty under all that dirt."

The woman's eyes flicked to the man beside her, with whom she'd apparently had an unsanctioned relationship.

"You don't need permission to speak," Anne said. "From him or anyone else. At least, not while you're already locked up. What more can they do?"

The old man guffawed. "I'm going to walk out of this cage. So will she, despite the scarlet letter Mason's branded on her chest. His boys can still have their fun with her. But him..." He pointed at the younger man. "He's either going to wither and die in this cell, be thrown out against the next monster that comes looking for trouble, or be used for target practice. Whatever the case, his end won't be—"

"Shut-up," the woman said.

"Carrie," the young man chided.

"No reason to keep quiet," she said, her Southern accent far thicker than the old man's. "He's right. They won't do anything more to me, and there ain't nothing I can say that will make things any better or worse for you." She turned to Jakob. "John, here, thinks old Willie in the corner there, is a spy for Mason, on account of his life in the house. But he's just as hungry and dirty as the both of us."

"Why would Mason want to spy on you?" Anne asked.

"On account of him fearing a rebellion. Mason and his men make up roughly thirty percent of the compound's population. The rest of us are kept hungry, weak and separate. Took me a while to figure out why, but it's because he's a paranoid man. A little food and respect would have made loyal servants out of us all, but he chose the alternate route, and now he fears us. Maybe even more than we fear him. So every now and again, he conjures up a reason to deem some of us Questionables. Throws us in here. Less frequently, he puts someone to death, and I reckon ol' Willie is right about John's fate."

John, a twenty-something year old man who looked like he'd stepped into a hurricane and walked out the other side with a story too horrible to tell, let out an anguished sigh, but said nothing.

"They caught us screwing, dead to rights, but we're just friends."

Ouch, Jakob thought. *Post-apocalypse friend-zoned. Harsh.*

"Was just letting off some steam," she continued. "And it's not like anyone else was having a go. One case of the creeping crawlers and those boys had no interest in dipping their wicks. Good for me they didn't know the difference between crabs and them little red spiders. Sprinkled 'em on and presto, I was a free woman. For a time, anyway. Now I'm here, still not planning an insurrection."

"Maybe you should," Anne said.

The three captives on the far side of the cell tensed.

Jakob almost shushed Anne. For all they knew, their cellmates could be there to determine whether or not newcomers were a threat. If they spoke of rising up against Mason, maybe these three would tell him? Even if they weren't spies, they might tell him with the hopes of gaining his favor. Of course, Willie and Carrie had already confessed to several other infractions that Jakob could trade for favor.

When he saw fear creep into Willie's and Carrie's eyes, he realized that they were thinking the same thing. The duo had let their guard down, probably because they were speaking to three kids they'd never seen before, but now they had that terrified look of children caught looking at pornography.

Jakob held up his hands. "We're not here to spy on you, either, I swear."

"Why's she talking about rebellion?" Carrie asked.

"Because I don't like being caged like an animal," Anne said, "and if there were a few more people willing to help, our Dad would—"

"Ignore her," Jakob said. "She has an inflated opinion about what our father can do. You know how kids are."

Anne kicked him, but didn't say any more.

"Your father the big fella Boone was talking to?" Willie asked. "And that tough looking lady with him...that your mother?"

"Yeah," Jakob said. It was far more complicated than that, but Jakob didn't want to explain.

"Certainly looked as capable as the girl claims," the old man said. "But if he's a smart man, he'll join up and do Mason's bidding. Only real way to get the lot of you out of this cage." He pointed a shaky finger at Alia. "Except maybe her. Racism runs deep in these parts. Only a few people with skin darker than a sun given tan are here, and that's because they're useful. Used to be more at the beginning, but these Questionable cells have seen a lot of use over the years. So my advice to you, young miss, is to make yourself useful."

"B-but, I'm just a kid," Alia said. "I don't know how to do anything."

"Better learn quick," Willie said, "or lie and then learn quick."

"It won't come to that," Jakob said to Willie, and then turned to Alia. "My father won't let it happen."

"Sounds like you have a little more faith in your old man than you wanted us to know, eh?" Willie tapped his nose again and gave a nod. "You have nothing to worry about from any of us. We're already up shit's creek. Might as well be in cahoots, too." Willie leaned forward, elbows on knees. He moved faster than Jakob would have thought, more aged than emaciated. "Your daddy trust you?"

"Yeah," Jakob said.

"How much?"

"As much as anyone can," Jakob said.

"And he's a good man?"

"The best," Anne said.

"Says his daughter."

"I only met him five weeks ago," Anne said.

Willie grunted and met Jakob's eyes. "She telling the truth?"

Jakob returned Willie's gaze, trying to get a read on him. Was he crazy? Was he a spy? Was he exactly what he seemed to be—an old man sick of living in a literal hell hole without much left to lose? "Yeah. He's honorable, if that's what you're asking. Nothing like that Mason guy."

"That's exactly what I was asking," Willie said. "Now then, let's talk insurrection."

"Thought you said there wasn't one," Anne said.

Willie grinned and looked to John, then Carrie, who returned his smile and nodded. "Well, there is now."

ELEVEN

To Peter's surprise, the search-and-rescue party sent after the missing group of men was composed solely of Boone and himself. That told him a few things. First, Boone had no fear of what might be hunting him on the outside, which meant he was supremely stupid, or genuinely good at surviving—but still stupid in most regards. Second, it meant that the majority of Mason's most skilled and loyal men were currently outside the gates. Sure, there might be armed guards watching the walls, and some of them were probably hardliners like Boone, but Peter guessed most of them were more like Stevie and Marcus.

He couldn't be sure, though, and until he was, playing along was the safest option—until the kids were set free.

Or was it? Boone had the keys. Peter had no doubt he could take them by force. But would the gates be opened to him if he returned alone? And if they were, would he be greeted with a bullet? Even if he could take the keys, re-enter the camp, free the kids, retrieve Ella and leave again, without waging a one-man war, something still nagged at him. Hellhole Bay, perhaps the last bastion of humanity outside a scattering of biodomes and ExoGen themselves, was a corrupt, evil place.

Could he just leave? Even if they reached George's Island and altered the human genome so that ExoGen food didn't turn people into rapidly evolving eating machines, what good would that do if their fellow survivors were still monsters at heart?

"Sure you don't want to wear something a little more protective?" Boone asked. He was dressed in black military clothing and body armor. It would stop a bullet, but wouldn't do a whole lot of good against an Apex predator, or a knife for that matter. It looked cool, but had limited mobility. If they were walking into a conventional battle, he'd have taken Boone up on the offer, but out here in the wild, he was happy with the dirt-covered tan cargo pants and equally soiled black t-shirt. Not only were they a natural-looking camouflage, but they also smelled like the outdoors.

"I'm good," Peter said. "Thanks for the offer, though."

Boone stepped over a log, gripping his AR-15, back to Peter. It was the thirteenth time the man had left himself completely open to attack. Peter couldn't decide if it was an intentional test, or if the man simply had no combat awareness.

Neither, Peter decided. *He trusts that I care about Ella and the kids, and won't endanger them by doing something stupid.*

"Your funeral," Boone said.

The swamp around them was still, lacking the non-stop sound of birds and insects normally present in such locations. Peter eyed the water, half expecting something to burst out and snatch one of them. But Boone moved with more confidence, following a worn path through clumps of moss covered islets. ExoGenetic crops grew around them, protruding from the water and from the mounds of land scattered around them. They mixed in with hearty plants and ferns that hadn't retreated from the ExoGenetic advance. But the path ahead was clear. Maintained. This wasn't just a jaunt through the wilds in search of missing men.

"Where are we headed?" Peter asked.

Boone waggled his hand forward, indicating the winding path that disappeared behind a stand of short, twisting trees. "The lot. Where we keep vehicles."

"Why don't you keep them at Hellhole?"

"Firstly, the bridge at the entrance ain't big enough for a vehicle."

"That's the only way in?"

"Yep. And secondly, it keeps the degenerates and unknown Questionables from stealing them."

"They'd have to be pretty desperate to leave the safety of Hellhole, don't you think?"

Boone shrugged. "People do stupid things. A few have tried leaving on foot. Sure you can imagine how that ended."

Peter could, but his mind's eye didn't conjure images of ExoGenetic creatures hunting down those poor people. He saw Boone looking down the sights of that AR-15 in his hands, pulling the trigger with a smile on his face. "Sure can."

"None of them was like you and me, though."

"How's that?"

Boone looked back with a lopsided grin. "Killers. Men who do what it takes to survive, eternal soul be damned."

Peter gave a nod. "I suppose you're right."

"Glad t' hear it."

You shouldn't be, Peter thought. Then he asked, "And the men we're searching for?"

"More of the same," Boone said, trudging through foot-deep black water separating one islet from the next. "Dangerous men. Survivors."

"You all have a name?" Peter asked.

Boone looked confused. "We all have names."

"I mean as a group," Peter said.

"Like a nickname? Naw. Seems kinda cheesy if you ask me."

"More like a callsign," Peter said. "All the most elite units in the military have them. Have for thousands of years. The Persians had The Immortals. King Arthur had the Knights of the Round Table. The Paladins fought for Charlemagne. In the Marine Corps, I was a member of the Raiders. Groups of fighting men deserve a name. Helps form bonds in battle. Unity." He was pouring it on a little heavy, but he wanted Boone to start feeling that sense of comradery with him. Naming this group of men would be a step in the right direction.

"Huh," Boone said. "S'pose there is something to it."

"Something like Mason's Devils," Peter offered.

"Not bad, I guess," Boone said, pondering the issue he'd never before considered. "How 'bout Redneck Rampagers?"

It was a horrible name. Not even grammatically correct. But it *was* accurate and revealed that Boone was not only aware of his backwoods nature, but proud of it. "Perfect," Peter said.

"Redneck Rampagers it is, then." Boone froze in his tracks, eyes focused straight ahead, like a cat who'd just spotted prey.

Peter looked past him, searching for what had the man spooked, but he saw nothing. The idea that Boone's attention to detail or ability to detect danger was beyond Peter's irked him. *The man had no formal training,* Peter thought, *but he did grow up here. He knows the smells, sights and sounds. If something is off, he'll know about it long before me.*

The realization made their prospects of a simple escape less likely. Boone would be able to hunt them down, which meant he would have to be dealt with first. But that was the brewing plan anyway. Peter, in good conscience, couldn't abandon the large number of people living under Mason's oppressive rule. It had been a while since Peter had assisted in a regime change, and he didn't always agree with it, but in this case, with the future of humanity at risk, he wasn't going to look the other way.

"What is it?" Peter whispered.

"Should be a guard up ahead." Boone pointed to a tree, where a perfectly camouflaged hunter's tree stand was mounted, twenty feet off the ground. Boone let out a bird call, which sounded convincing, but in this lifeless swamp, it would attract the same kind of attention as shouting. Peter kept that to himself, though. If the guard was missing, or dead, they could be in trouble. But what kind of trouble?

"The stand looks intact," Peter said. "No claw marks. No blood."

"Uh-huh," Boone said. "Wasn't one of them mutates. That's for sure."

"Maybe he heard the men at the Lot were missing and went to check?" Peter asked.

"If he did, he's gonna get throttled." Boone crept forward, heading for the stand. When he reached the tree, he slung the AR-15 over his shoulder and gripped the coarse bark on either side. Then he shimmed up, scaling the fifteen feet in seconds. He slid over the camouflaged wall and into the hide.

"Sombitch," he muttered.

"He dead?" Peter asked.

"Surely is." Boone emerged from the hide and slid down the tree. Peter had never seen someone move through a tree with such ease. Boone hadn't just been raised in the swamp, he'd become one with it. "Dumb shit's neck is broke."

Peter eyed the tree stand. "You know what that means, right?"

Boone nodded. "Some*one* killed him. For sure weren't no mutate."

How had someone scaled the tree, entered the stand and broken the man's neck?

"Was he armed?" Peter asked.

"Sheeit." Boone spat at the tree, and Peter wasn't sure if he was cursing the dead man or whoever it was that killed him. "Yeah, he was. Hunting rifle with a scope. Sidearm, too. Can't remember what kind."

"So the men at the Lot have gone silent and your lookout is dead. Weapons missing. You're under attack."

"Sounds 'bout right."

"Should we get reinforcements?" Peter asked.

Boone sniffed and shook his head. "Redneck Rampagers don't need no reinforcements. Whatever this is, I can handle it."

Peter suspected Boone's decision had more to do with a lack of reinforcements rather than an absolute faith in his abilities. If someone had come through here and killed his men, they might have done Peter a favor. Then again, he might just be trading one Devil for another. Until he knew, Boone was the closest thing to an ally he had.

"Can I have a weapon?"

"You shittin' me?" Boone said. "This all started not too long after y'all showed up. For all I know, you're in cahoots with whoever is out here."

Peter frowned. "Good point." And it was a good point. Had they been followed? And if so, by whom?

"Thank ye," Boone said, starting down the path once more. "Lot's a quarter mile ahead. Follow close, but not too close, and keep your trap shut."

"You got it," Peter said, eyeing Boone's sidearm. It was a Heckler & Koch P30 with .40 caliber rounds. Not heavy enough to do serious damage to an Apex, but heavy hitting enough to drop a human target with one shot to the right spot. He resisted the urge to take the weapon, fell in line behind Boone and followed him down the path.

He wasn't sure what they would find, but he suspected there would be bodies. The question was, would Peter and Boone join them?

TWELVE

"Sweet tea?" Mason asked, leaning against the side of the wooden desk. He'd been polite since Peter left with Boone, but he had a gleam in his eye that made Ella uneasy. He had the cocky arrogance of a high school football star, but if he had trophies, she suspected they'd be something closer to heads mounted on stakes.

She wanted to dive over the desk and bury her nails in the sides of his neck. She could do it. As deadly as he might be, it wasn't because of his own prowess, but rather the men who followed him—and at the moment, none of them were present. But neither was Peter, or the kids. So she stifled her urge to channel the primal instincts she'd discovered in herself over the past few months, and tried her hand at charming the man in return.

"Sweet tea?" she said, smiling. "God, yes. Don't tell me you have ice, too."

"In cubes. Yes, ma'am." He picked up a small bell from the desktop and gave it a shake.

The door opened and the black woman wearing the maid outfit took a single step inside before bowing her head. Her eyes flicked toward Ella, making eye contact for just a moment before returning to the floor. Her face was hard to see, but Ella felt the woman's embarrassment. Or was it shame? "Massa Mason. What can I do for you?"

"Sweet tea for two," he said.

"Yes'ah." With another quick bow, she turned around and scurried away.

"Won't be a long wait," Mason said, "but how about a tour in the meantime?"

"Absolutely," Ella said, standing. Despite her willingness to play along, her body still burned with tense energy, looking for an outlet. "I'd love to see the biodomes."

"Sure you would," Mason said, "but as a former biodome resident, you know that can't happen in your..." He looked her up and down. "...current state."

Shit, Ella thought. She'd set herself up for what was coming next, and with enough enthusiasm to ensure that backing out would look suspicious. Still, she had to try. "Another time, then."

"Nonsense." Mason stepped around her, and entered the hallway. She noted the lump on his back where a gun was hidden, tucked into his gleaming white pants. "Once you're cleaned up, I will personally escort you through the biodomes. We've managed to accomplish a lot. I think you will be duly impressed."

Ella smiled and said, "I'm sure."

Mason stopped at the end of the hall, resting a hand on the polished banister and calling through the formal dining room, into the kitchen. "We'll take that tea upstairs, Charlotte."

"Upstairs?" She sounded nervous.

"That's what I said, indeed."

"Yes, massa."

He grinned at Ella and motioned to the hardwood staircase. "Now then, ladies first."

"A true, Southern gentleman," she said.

"One of the few left on Earth, I'd guess."

"Perhaps even the last," she said, stepping by him and heading up the creaky stairs. She could feel his eyes on her, watching her shifting backside as she took each step. She was covered in dirt and dressed in unflattering cargo pants, a black tank top and a green, plaid flannel shirt, but men sometimes saw reality and fantasy at the same time. To Mason, she was a world of new possibilities. *More than he knows,* she thought, and she continued up the stairs, putting a little extra thrust into her hips.

The second floor felt much like the first: old wood, white walls, and the gentile décor of a middle-aged Southern woman. Still life paintings hung on the wall. A small table cloaked in a doily held a vase of wild flowers—freshly picked by the look of them.

Ella flinched as a door to her left swung open. A woman dressed in a maid uniform, similar to Charlotte's, but far too tight, stepped into the hall. "Something I can get for you, Mister—" Her eyes registered surprise at seeing Ella, then a flicker of something else, like pity, before turning toward Mason as he crested the staircase. "Something I can get for you, Mister Mason?"

"Not right now, Shawna," Mason said, taking her hand and kissing the back of it. "Perhaps later. In the meantime, heat up a towel for our guest."

Shawna feigned an 'aww shucks' kind of smile. It was a noble effort, but her jaw was clenched tight. She was pale white, like she hadn't seen the sun in a long time, with straight black hair and a curvaceous, almost plump body. *Locked inside, but well fed,* Ella thought, *like cattle.* But there was something about her, in that clenched jaw, that said she wasn't quite as docile as a cow. *That's what Mason likes,* Ella thought. *What gets him off. Breaking defiant women.* She didn't look like Shawna or Charlotte, but she had defiance in spades, and he had no doubt taken note.

Ella took a small measure of comfort in the fact that Mason had requested only one towel, and that he seemed interested in Shawna's... services...later on. He might be interested in Ella, but he wasn't ready to be overt about it. Ella thought he was still evaluating whether or not she was his type, and no doubt trying to conjure a way to get Peter out of the picture—or perhaps just hoping that would happen while he was out with Boone. Had the two men shared a signal that she missed? Was there really an emergency, or was Boone taking Peter into the swamps to execute him? If that turned out to be the case, Mason would find out that Peter wasn't the only member of their ragtag, post-apocalyptic family worth fearing.

"Of course, sir," Shawna said with a strained giggle. "Anything for you."

They're living out his fantasies, Ella thought. *Role playing.* The vivacious, slutty maid. The old-world, Southern, black maid. She wouldn't be surprised if the next maid she met wore a short skirt, held a feather duster and spoke with a French accent. *Maybe that's what he has in mind for me?*

And if not, maybe that's where I can get his mind.

When Shawna headed downstairs, Mason snuck around Ella and opened the next door on the left. Inside was a large bathroom with a claw-foot porcelain tub, a white tile floor and marble countertops. Mason flipped the light switch turning on a row of large bulbs mounted over a massive, wall-sized mirror that reflected the bathroom. *And everything that happens in it,* Ella thought.

"Bathroom is one of the rooms I upgraded after resettling Hellhole. It's a far shade more luxurious than it was before. Hot water, soap, shampoo and conditioner are at your disposal—not that you'll have much use for the latter two, but your hair will grow back in time." Mason grinned. "Shawna will stop in with a warm towel and some fresh clothes. I'll come to collect you in what, twenty minutes?"

"Sounds divine," Ella said. "The bath, clothes and towel, I mean."

"Not the company?" Mason said with a faux pout.

"That has yet to be determined," she said. "But you're off to a good start."

He flashed a sly grin and tipped his Ascot hat. "Best I can ask for. I'll leave you to it."

Ella stepped inside and offered Mason a parting smile as he closed the door behind her. Her smile dropped into a grimace. She rolled her neck, hearing her vertebrae pop from the tension. Then she looked at herself in the mirror and froze. It wasn't that her reflection was almost unrecognizable—she was too skinny, covered in dirt, and had a few fresh scars—it was how the mirror itself was constructed. She looked it over quickly, inspecting the side closest to her, and then the top and bottom. It was five feet tall, rising up from the bottom of the sink, all the way up to the ceiling, and it stretched the twenty foot length of the bathroom. She looked for clips holding it in place, but there weren't any. The mirror wasn't mounted to the wall, it was part of it.

Her eyes widened for a brief moment, but then she forced a casual smile back onto her lips, the kind of smile a woman thinking about a man might have. The kind a man hoping for something more might want to see. Then she leaned in close to the mirror like she was inspecting her face and placed her finger tips against the glass like she was holding herself up.

She turned her face side to side, looking it over, glancing at her hand against the glass just once. But it was enough. Ella had worked in enough labs, in her long years of schooling and outside it, to have been on both sides of an observation mirror. There were two dead giveaways that a mirror was two-way, designed for spying. First, the mirror was part of the wall, not hung on it. The second was called the 'finger test.' A finger placed up against a normal mirror can touch its own reflection. A finger placed up against a two way mirror was separated from its reflection by the thickness of the glass, in this case, a quarter inch.

Mason was on the other side of this mirror, watching. Observing. Waiting for a show. And if she didn't give him one...

She stared into her own eyes for a moment, picturing Mason on the far side of the mirror, looking back. *If it's a show he wants...*

She lifted her shirt slowly, bunching the fabric beneath her breasts. She'd lost a lot of weight and dropped a cup size while living in the wild, eating a diet of foraged food. If she wore a bra, it was a sports bra, but the tank top had enough support built in, so she'd opted to go braless. And today, that worked in her favor. She let her breasts fall out of the shirt together, smiling beneath the fabric as she lifted it away. If Mason was watching, he was already entranced.

She walked to the tub and turned on the hot water. As steam wafted into the air, her smile turned genuine. She could, at least, enjoy this. Before they went back into the wild, she'd have to wallow in mud again like a pig. But for now, she'd enjoy the bath, and the notion that it would completely disarm the man behind the glass. Thinking of her hands around his throat, she pulled down her pants.

THIRTEEN

"So, let me get this straight," Anne said. "No one has tried to break out of these cells?"

"I think it's generally assumed that escape would be worse than being caged," Carrie said in dismay. "Besides, the gate is chain link."

"And the floor is concrete." Anne rolled her eyes. "I can see. I have eyes. But I'm starting to wonder if you guys need glasses. Or maybe new brains."

She looked at old Willie, then Carrie and finally John. The first two seemed befuddled. John seemed almost uninterested, resigned to his fate at the end of the hangman's noose, or whatever these people did to execute people.

A groan rose from Anne's throat when Jakob seemed equally baffled.

"Seriously?" she said to her half-brother. "Have you learned nothing?"

"What?" he said. "No one knows what you're talking about."

And no one is taking me seriously, because I'm twelve. "Ask a question. Observation. Hypothesis. Test. Repeat—if necessary. And when that's all done, take action."

Jakob sighed. He'd heard her modified version of the Scientific Method, which she called the Survival Method, more than once. She tried to teach him. Tried to make him memorize it and use it the same way Eddie Kenyon had taught her. He turned out to be a bad guy, but the method still made sense. Still worked. But Jakob resisted learning from his little sister. In the safety of *Beastmaster*, with her mother and father, it hadn't bothered her much. But here and now, with their lives on the line, she wished he'd taken the lesson more seriously. Especially now that she had to convince a bunch of adults that she wasn't a foolish child.

"Question," she said, "Can we escape? Observation. One, the floor is concrete. We're not digging out. Two, the gate is chain link, padlocked shut and screwed into a sturdy wooden beam. It's not going anywhere. Three, the ceiling is made of corrugated metal held together by bolts."

All eyes turned upward. The waves of metal siding, used for a slanted ceiling, were indeed held together by bolts.

"Holy..." Jakob reached up and tried to twist one.

"Observation," Anne said. "They're rusted. It's humid as a fat man's ass crack here."

Jakob grunted, trying to twist the bolt. He hissed in pain, withdrawing his hand and shaking it.

"Hypothesis." Anne raised a finger. "Humidity affects wood, too. Rots it. Especially when the lumber isn't pressure treated." She patted the wall behind her. "Like this wood. So, the cell's weakest point is the exterior wooden walls." She pointed to the front gate, the side wall behind Carrie and John, and the back wall behind Willie. "There, there and there."

"How do you *know* all this?" Carrie asked.

Anne shrugged. "I read a lot." It was true. Before her life in the wild began, she didn't do much more than read and cause mischief in the

ExoGen facility, pulling pranks and spying. But there were a lot of subjects Anne knew a lot about that she couldn't remember learning. Like with pressure treated wood. Everything back in San Francisco was metal and glass, built to survive the end of the world.

"Continuing hypothesis," Anne said, but was interrupted by Alia.

"The roof overhangs in the front and back, so those walls probably stayed drier during rainstorms." Alia crawled across the cell, stopping short when she noticed the five-gallon bucket. She winced and reeled back.

"Found the shitter," Willie said, leaning up. He took hold of the bucket's handle and dragged the concentrated filth to the back of the small cell. "Might seem gross now, but sure beats soiling yourself."

Alia just scrunched her nose and continued on her way, a little bit slower now, carefully picking the spots she put down her hands. "Hypothesis," she said, upon reaching the side wall beside Carrie and John. "Of the three outside walls, this one will be the weakest."

She reached out and pushed on one of the vertical planks. It bowed, but held strong. She moved down the line toward Willie, testing each plank.

"Not that way," Anne said. "The other way. Specifically, behind him." She pointed at John, who looked more annoyed than surprised.

Carrie shifted away and swatted John's shoulder. "Move out of the way."

John obeyed, but didn't move far. Alia had to partially lean over his cross-legged knee to reach the wall. She probed the middle and then moved down.

"This feels wet, still. I think—" Alia let out a yelp as the wooden plank folded outward at the bottom. Without the wall's support, she fell forward, face-planting. "Oww!"

Alia reeled back from the impact, sliding back across the floor, hand to her face, into Jakob's arms as he rushed to meet her.

"You all right?" Jakob asked, trying to look past the girl's hand.

She took her hand away from her face to reveal a bloodied nose. "How bad is it?"

Anne leaned over the girl, reached out and squeezed her nose between her thumb and index finger.

"Oww!" Alia said, flinching back.

"What the hell was that for?" Jakob asked, glaring at Anne.

"She's fine," Anne said. "Just pinch it."

Jakob motioned to Alia's face. "Her nose could be broken."

"If it were broken, she would have screamed instead of saying 'oww.'" She took hold of Jakob's arm and squeezed it hard. "And we have bigger problems."

The intense pressure on his arm and Anne's deep, threatening voice, which he had learned to never ignore, freed him from his mind-numbing concern for Alia. Jakob had overcome a lot of his weaknesses over the past few weeks, but his girlfriend had replaced them all. She distracted him. Put him in danger, and by extension, put the rest of them in danger.

"The hole in the wall?" Jakob asked.

Anne shook her head and sang, "One of these things is not like the others."

Jakob looked confused. "Sesame Street?"

Anne shared his expression. "What?"

"That song is from Sesame Street," he said.

"People on a street sing that song?"

"It was a TV show. For little kids."

"I spent my 'little kids' days in a tube," Anne said. "I've never seen—" But then she remembered it. The people. The strange fuzzy creatures. *What the hell?* "Tell me how to get to Sesame Street."

"Exactly," Jakob said.

"Brought to you by the letter H," Anne said, her mind drifting, and then snapping back to reality. "H for hypothesis. One of these things is not like the others." She left out the sing-song tune and looked at Carrie and John. Then turned to Willie. "How badly do you want your freedom? And I don't mean just from this cage."

The old man squinted at her. "What exactly are you asking me, kid?"

"Before we talk about getting out of here, and about who will help us once we're free, and about how Mason and his pals can be...usurped, we need to make sure that only the right people hear the plan."

"No one here but us," Willie said. "And they only check on us twice a day with food and water."

"What I'm asking you, Willie..." Anne said, leveling her most intense gaze into the man's eyes. He was old enough to be her great grandfather, but was listening carefully. "...is this. To regain your freedom, for however few years you have left, are you willing to listen to me?"

"I'm listening now, aren't I?"

"Are you willing to fight?" she asked.

"Much as an old man can."

"Are you willing to kill?"

"Anne," Jakob said.

"Same question goes for you, Jakey boy." She turned to Carrie. "And you."

Silence settled into the cell, squeezing her eardrums until John leaned forward and spoke. "And what about me?"

"I already know about you," Anne said. She pointed at the ring on his finger. "School ring, top of the class, worn proud. Don't recognize the school name, but you're not stupid." Her finger rose to his hair. "That haircut makes you look handsome to the ladies, but it was also done with a sharp pair of scissors, by someone else."

Carrie leaned away from John, looking at his hair. It wasn't exactly styled, but the cut was even, bordering on professional. Carrie's scrunched up forehead said she hadn't noticed the hair before, but she did find it odd now that it had been pointed out.

"Seriously?" John said. "You don't like my hair?"

"I don't like your face," Anne said, "but that's not really the problem."

"Then what is?" John asked.

"The knife strapped to your right leg."

All eyes shifted to John's right leg, which was covered by dirty jeans. The fabric was wrinkled, but among the folds was the slight outline of a thin blade, easy to miss when someone was sitting cross-legged.

John leaned forward quickly, hiking up the pant leg and reaching for the now exposed blade. It was flat and black, the handle and blade all one piece of forged metal. It looked like a throwing knife to Anne, but that didn't mean it had to be thrown to be deadly. In the tight confines of the cell, the young man, easily stronger than all his cellmates, could probably kill every one of them. But Anne had planned ahead for this moment.

Just as John slipped the knife from its sheath, a large booted foot collided with the side of his head. John flopped to the side, unconscious, the knife clattering to the concrete floor. Anne winced at the sound. If anyone was within earshot, it would undoubtedly attract attention. She scurried across the floor and snatched up the blade.

John groaned, dazed, but still conscious.

"Still dangerous," she said, closing on the man, knife in hand.

"Anne," Jakob said. "Don't!"

"We can't risk him living," Anne said. "Even if we knock him unconscious, he'll give us up the moment he wakes up."

"It's murder," Jakob said.

"It's a revolution," Anne said.

"We just got here," Jakob argued. "They might even agree to let us go!"

Anne held the knife above John's heart, but kept her eyes on Jakob. "You know our parents. You've seen enough of this place. Do you really think they're going to just sit back and do nothing? How long do you think it will be before someone comes for us? Before someone uses us for leverage?"

Jakob said nothing, but she could see he agreed.

Part of her wished he didn't, that he'd talk her out of what she was about to do. But he couldn't, and he wasn't hard enough to do it himself, so...

She pulled her hand back, ready to thrust the blade into John's chest. But before she could, John was lifted up by two gnarly hands, one under his chin, one supporting the back. With a quick jerk, John's head snapped too far in one direction, the sound of snapping vertebrae opening his mouth in a silent scream. Then his head twisted in the opposite direction, again too far. The second crack made John's body fall limp, leaning back into Willie's arms.

"No way I'm going to sit back and watch a little kid kill a man for me," the old man said, dragging John into the cell's back corner and positioning his corpse so it looked like he was sleeping. When he turned back around, he grinned and said, "Viva la revolución. Let's get the hell out of here."

FOURTEEN

"That's the Lot," Boone whispered, lying in foot-deep muddy water, peering out between the ExoGenetic rice stalks that had claimed this portion of the swamp. A hundred feet ahead, on the far side of a paved road, was a combination gas and service station with a large, fenced-in parking lot for cars being worked on.

Peter took a deep breath through his nose, smelling earthy decay and something sweet that he thought must be the rice—most likely engineered to smell and taste like it had been dipped in maple syrup. He remembered hearing about this strain on the news when people first started eating the out-of-control crops. Boiling it and eating it plain was supposed to taste something like rice pudding, without the cinnamon and raisins. The thought made his stomach rumble loud enough for Boone to hear.

"When was the last time you ate something?" Boone asked. "Sounds like you got an angry coon in your gullet."

"Early this morning. Bunch of leaves and mushrooms." The displeasure in Peter's voice was genuine. Eating vegetarian was hard enough. Eating foraged foods... It just wasn't enough, especially split between four people. At least Anne could eat the ExoGenetic crops, but the rest of them were getting skinnier and weaker by the day.

Boone lifted himself part way out of the muck, unzipped a pouch on his chest and pulled out a Slim Jim. "We got a shit load of 'em. Old enough to eat. Enough preservatives to keep a zombie fresh."

Peter accepted the dried meat snack with a nod. He peeled the wrapper open and devoured the food in three bites. It wasn't much, but the simple act of kindness gave Peter a flicker of hope that Boone wasn't as sinister as he appeared. *Of course,* he thought, *he could just be trying to keep my stomach from giving away our position.*

"Why is there a gas station way out here?" Peter asked, looking at the place, which was surrounded on all sides by swamp. The sign by the road read: 'Gas and Gears.'

"Nearest town is a few miles down that way," Boone said, nodding his head to the right. "Next nearest town is a few more miles that-a-way. Fastest way 'tween here and there is this stretch of road. It's a little out of the way, but most people pass by it eventually. Plus, Austin, the previous proprietor, kept his prices low. Course, he sometimes put saw dust in the gears, too, but that don't matter none now. His corpse is rotting away in the swamp out behind the garage."

"What's his body doing out there?" Peter asked.

"It's where I dropped him, after putting a bullet in his head."

"He changed?"

"If that makes you feel better, sure." Boone pushed the rice stalks further apart. "Ain't nobody here."

"Wait," Peter said, but it was too late. Boone stepped out into the road, weapon ready, but totally exposed. If someone had been out there, or some*thing,* he'd be a dead man. But nothing happened. They were alone. And once again, Peter couldn't tell if Boone was lucky or had an exceptional knack for being in tune with this environment.

Feeling vulnerable without a gun, Peter stepped from the water, dripping wet. He hurried up behind Boone.

Half way across the road, Boone's foot fell just short of the yellow line, and he stopped. He looked like a runner, taking his mark. Then the rest of his body went rigid. "You smell that?"

The same mixture of sweet rice and decaying swamp filled Peter's nose as he breathed deep. Then something else. He winced. "Smells like shit."

"And a lot of it," Boone added, starting across the road again, angling for the service station's entrance.

The glass door, stenciled with the same Gas and Gears logo as the sign out front, opened without a sound. *Boone and the boys have been keeping the place up,* Peter thought, *probably treating the Lot like a home away from home, free from the authoritative gaze of Mason.* A piece of paper taped to the inside of the glass held a chicken-scratched message: No shirt, no shoes, you better have tits.

Peter smiled at the sign, but only because Boone was watching him.

"Me and the boys like to hang here on occasion. Not nearly as safe as Hellhole, but a good place to blow off steam." Boone stopped Peter just outside the door. "You ain't gonna be tellin' Mason, are you?"

Peter could see that the countertop had been converted into a bar, complete with stools. The shelves behind it were covered in bottles of various liquors and wines, probably old enough to be safe. Maybe old enough to be spectacular. "You have bourbon?"

"Blanton's," Boone said, a grin creeping up one side of his face.

"Then your secret is safe with me."

"Well, all right then." Boone stepped inside, and Peter followed, letting the door close behind them.

The fecal smell disappeared. *Whatever it is,* Peter thought, *it's not coming from in here.* The smell had him on edge, but the prospect of tasting Blanton's bourbon again... "Mind if I get a glass now? You know, in case we die?"

"Now that's a good toast if there ever was one." Boone took two shot glasses from the shelf. They were smudged with fingerprints on the outside, no doubt used and reused multiple times without a wash. But the alcohol would kill whatever germs the previous users had left behind. Boone snatched a round Blanton's bottle from the shelf, gripped the small horse and rider mounted atop the cap, and pulled the cork. Peter caught sight of the date written on the label. It was twelve years old and very safe to drink.

Boone poured two shots, right to the rim and slid one to Peter. They downed the alcohol in unison, neither man showing a reaction to the burn. Peter put his glass down and relaxed.

"One more for the road?" Boone asked, about to pour another shot. He stopped short when Peter put his hand over the glass.

"While there isn't much more in the world I would like to have at this very moment, than a second shot of that liquid gold, it's been a while since I had a drink. I can already feel it."

Boone scoffed. "Wouldn'a figured you for a lightweight." He refilled his own glass and downed it before Peter could remind him that something outside smelled like sundried shit.

"Gal dang," Boone said. "At least you have good taste in drinks." He put the bottle back on the shelf, carefully, almost reverently. To Boone and his good ol' boy buddies, this was a sacred place: like ten-year-old boys with a fort in the woods with nudie mags hidden in a buried safe. "Now," Boone said, "let's ferret out the source of that smell. And let me tell you this, if it's something my boys did, you're going to see exactly how this fella—" He tapped an index finger against his own chest. "—keeps his men in line. I ain't no stranger to the fine arts of corporal punishment."

Peter gave a fervent nod, but stayed quiet. Boone was more of a lightweight than he thought, or wanted Peter to think. The alcohol had loosened him up, and fast. And while that might help Peter subdue the man if necessary, if things went sideways as they often did, he'd prefer the man fighting by his side to not be three sheets to the wind.

Boone led him through the office-turned-bar and into the garage, which had been converted into a real man-cave. There was a pool table, several dart boards and a collection of antique chairs. It actually looked like a place Peter would enjoy kicking back in for a few drinks with his friends. If his friends were still alive. And though Boone seemed a little more human now, it was unlikely. *When pigs fly,* Peter thought, and then he shook his head. It was fairly likely that a flying pig existed someplace in the world.

"Get the door, would'ja?" Boone lifted his AR-15 to his shoulder, ready to fire.

Peter unlatched the door and then yanked it up, the clank of metal wheels sliding through the guide bars making him wince. *Too loud,* he thought, wondering how this place had yet to be overrun by an Apex predator.

Boone paid the loud door no attention and stepped out into the paved lot, scanning back and forth with the weapon. There was an assortment of vehicles, mostly trucks and SUVs. There were also a few cargo vans, and at the back, a large moving truck. Between the vans and truck was *Beastmaster,* parked in line with the rest, but not in the same condition he'd last seen it in. The armored pickup truck had been shot up, beaten and abused over the past few months, but it had never been...violated.

This is personal.

Boone saw it, too, and he made his way toward the truck, aiming between the other parked vehicles as they passed. But they were alone. Whoever had defaced the car was long gone.

Boone stopped in front of *Beastmaster,* cocked his head to the side and read the message, written in shit, smeared on the windshield. He added his own inflections to the message, written in perfect English. "'Peter, Peter, Kristen beater, gonna find yer girl and eat 'er.' Am I reading this right? Kristen is yer wife. And yer girl is Anne? If my boys—"

"Your boys didn't know our names."

"Well then, ain't this something." Boone swiveled around, leveling the assault rifle at Peter's chest. "Seems you haven't been completely honest with me, have ye? Who's with you?"

Peter ignored the weapon, focusing on the message instead. "Why would anyone with me threaten my family? Why would they expose themselves like this?"

"Then who is it?"

Peter's mind raced for an answer, but before he could find one, a *thunk* from the back of the nearby moving truck made both men flinch.

"Someone's in there," Boone said, adjusting his aim toward the back of the truck.

Peter placed a finger to his lips and crept toward the large sliding door. He put one hand on the latch and counted down from three on the other, dropping one finger at a time. At zero, he unlatched the door and threw it up.

The sight inside the truck stumbled Peter back, as a wall of old-penny smell rolled over him. The inside of the truck was floor to ceiling gore. Bodies lay mangled and torn apart. It was hard to tell where one man ended and another began. But there was no blood outside the truck, meaning the men had been herded inside and then slaughtered. But who could do that? Or what? These men had been armed. But here in their secret fort, their guard might have been down. They might have been drinking. And whoever did this...they were good. And ruthless. And apparently, they had a grudge against Peter.

A man near the door shifted as the late day sun bathed him in light. He was missing both legs at the knees and pretty cut up.

It's a miracle he's still alive, Peter thought. *Must have just regained consciousness.*

Boone rushed over to the man. "Who did this, Ty? Tell me!"

The man named Ty, covered in blood and chunks of human meat that did not come from his own body, struggled to speak. "T-t-tweren't h-human. Cept for one f-fella. Big b-big...hairy..." His eyes rolled back and he fell limp.

"Ty!" Boone shook the man. "Ty!" Then he dropped his friend back, and without checking for a pulse, declared, "He's gone."

All of Boone's confident bravado drained from his body. His limbs went slack. He stumbled back until he bumped into the hood of a BMW and sat. Tears welled in his eyes. Boone, like everyone still living on Earth, had no doubt seen his fair share of death, gore and inhumanity, but these men—his men—might have been the last thing in the world that brought him any kind of joy. And he lost all of them at once.

He's breaking, Peter thought. *He's no good to me broken.*

"Ty was murdered." Peter wasn't sure if Ty was really dead or just unconscious, but it didn't matter. He'd be dead soon, no matter what they did for him. And since the man was already unconscious, he'd pass in relative peace. What did matter was the description. A man among big, hairy non-human creatures. "Someone did this to him."

Peter saw a flicker of light in Boone's eyes.

"You mean some*thing*," Boone said.

"ExoGentic creatures don't simply slaughter men," Peter said. "They eat them. And they damn well don't herd victims into a moving truck first. Ty said one of them was human." He gripped Boone's arm, squeezing his own sense of urgency into the man. "Your men were murdered, and their killer is still out there."

The spark ignited. Boone's jaw clenched. He stood, ready for action, but still unsure about what to do or where to go. But Peter had ideas about both.

"How many good men are defending Hellhole?" Peter asked.

"Most of them were here," Boone said, his voice shifting from quiet to grave anger. "Maybe a handful. Fifteen, if you count the bunch who will turn tail, first sign of danger."

"Won't be enough," Peter said.

That got Boone's attention. He turned to Peter, eyes wide. "Enough for what?"

"I need a weapon," Peter said. "And this time, I'm not asking. Because if I'm right, Hellhole is about to live up to its name like never before."

FIFTEEN

The strange lopsided grin stretched across one half of Mason's face left no doubt that he had been entertaining himself by watching her bathe. *How many women has he watched through that one-way mirror? How many of them have ended up in maid's uniforms as a result?* It occurred to her that the whole, 'take a bath' routine might be a tried and true vetting system Mason used to select which women worked on his staff—pun intended. She smiled back, but only because she pictured the kids' reaction to her mental pun. The way Anne and Jakob had bonded, like lifelong brother and sister, gave her hope. It also gave her more than enough reason to plunge her thumbs into Mason's eye sockets. But not yet. She wanted to learn more about Hellhole and the people in it first.

"That was the second most pleasurable experience of my life." Ella stood from the King size bed where she had been sitting, and stretched, letting the clean white blouse hug her chest a little tighter. The bedroom was clean and fresh, with white walls, curtains and a canopy over the bed. The furniture was solid cherry, gleaming with a fresh polish. A faint lemon scent hung in the air. None of it had any effect on her, but she did her best to look as comfortable as the bedroom was designed to make women feel. When she relaxed again, she took note that Mason's eyes, like the Grinch's heart, had grown two sizes. The man's libido was in full swing, despite his age.

She glanced down and saw more evidence of the man's still raging hormones. "Your zipper's down," she said.

Mason looked caught off guard for the first time since they'd met. He staggered back a few steps, smoothing his shirt for a better look at his crotch. He fumbled with his fly and zipped it up. "So it is," he said, fixing his shirt. "How embarrassing."

Ella shrugged. "Nothing I haven't seen before."

"I'm sure," he said, the smile returning. "Do your clothes fit?"

She looked down at the white blouse and flowing white skirt fringed with what looked like a doily at the bottom. A real Southern belle's outfit, so clean and gleaming that out in the wild, she'd stick out like a fluorescent fishing lure in a pond, attracting ExoGenetic monsters with every shift of her body. Like albino animals born outside of captivity, she wouldn't survive long. And perhaps that was part of the message: you're only safe inside the walls. But Ella thought that Mason just liked it. In fact, the only major difference between her outfit and the maids' was the color. White and black.

Oh God... Ella fought to keep the disgust from showing on her face. *He's treating the dress like a wedding dress. White, because he hasn't had me yet.*

It was just a guess, but it made a sick kind of sense. Mason had managed to lead all these people through the Change, had built multiple biodomes and had a true Southern gentleman charm about him. But he was also, quite clearly, a sexual predator. And perhaps always had been.

She smiled wide and ran her hands over her hips. "Everything fits perfectly." *And you're never going to see me in black,* she thought.

"Good," he replied. "Very good. Now, if you'd still like a tour—"

"Love one," she said, and there was nothing phony about her earnest desire to see how this man—a contractor in the world before—had taken her design for a self-sustaining biodome and turned it into a series of interconnected domes.

"Then I would be delighted to provide one." Mason tipped his Ascot cap and motioned to the door. "Ladies first."

She stepped into the hall, headed for the stairs and descended slowly, searching the first floor for any signs of trouble. The house décor was a mix of old and new. Antique furniture, also perfectly polished, filled the living and dining rooms. But the paintings on the walls...while some were older, boring examples of Southern landscapes, others looked more modern. Then she saw a painting she recognized and paused in front of it. The style was modern, but the painting was at least seventy years old.

"You have good taste," Mason said, stopping in front of the Picasso painting. "It's titled 'Head of a Woman.' The palette is rather subdued, don't you think? But I feel it is a good representation of mankind's dual nature. She looks frightened, but not of something external."

"Of what she is becoming," Ella said. The broad strokes cleaving the woman's face into odd shapes was distinctly Picasso, but the inhuman visage it created really did resemble some of the half-human monsters roaming the world now.

"He painted this in France. 1943."

"During the German occupation?"

Mason grinned. "A woman who knows her history... You are better educated than I would have guessed."

She waved off the compliment and hoped to hide her intelligence. "Discovery channel."

"Mmm." Mason reached out and traced the black line curving down through the woman's face with his finger. "Dora Maar. That was her name. Picasso didn't get along with her. I sometimes wonder if all these lines represented some inner desire to...cleave his subjects with a different kind of utensil. Of course, the brush is the gentleman's preferred tool."

"You know a lot about Picasso," Ella noted.

Mason shrugged. "The boys were smart enough to steal the placards with the art."

"These aren't prints?"

"Procured them a few months back. From the Ackland Art Museum in North Carolina. Not too far. Four hours by truck."

"Not too far? A lot can happen in four hours. Your boys are lucky to be alive."

"You survived a *much* longer journey."

"I had Peter."

Mason scrunched his lips, twisting them side to side. "You have that much faith in his abilities?"

Ella paused before answering. Would intimidating Mason with Peter's prowess make the man afraid to overstep, or would it solidify his resolve to have Peter killed? *He's going to kill him either way,* she thought, and decided to put the fear of God into him. "He's seen and done things that most people can't even imagine."

"I'm not so sure about that." The grin on Mason's face was more convincing than his words. This was a brutal man. But what he didn't know was that surviving in the wild had turned her into a brutal woman. He wore his savagery very close to the surface, but he still had no idea who she was, or of what she was capable.

"The world has made us all do...unsavory things," Ella said. "But my husband's long list of violence started long before the Change. Killing monsters is one thing, killing people..." She shook her head in faux disgust. "That takes a different sort of man."

"That it does." Mason started down the hall toward the kitchen, a spring in his step. "Peter sounds like the sort of man I need. Think he would be interested in staying on? All of you could stay, of course. Even the...girl traveling with you. Unless you have someplace you'd rather be?"

Mason paused by the kitchen door, motioning for Ella to once again take the lead. "I know the Askews were your friends, and I regret the condition in which you found them, but I think you'll agree that this oasis is worth saving, no matter the cost."

Ella couldn't hide her anger over Bob's passing and Lyn's deplorable condition, but she also couldn't blatantly disagree with him. While Bob and Lyn's fates were deplorable, and something Mason would pay for, she couldn't deny that this last colony of humanity outside of ExoGen needed to be protected. "I do. Agree. But I don't like it."

"No one does," he said. "Not at first. But a few nights without fear of being consumed tends to alter perspectives."

Ella stepped into the kitchen.

Three women turned to greet her. She recognized Charlotte, who was rolling out what looked like a pie crust. Shawna was there, too, chopping apples.

Apples? Ella peered at the bright red fruit. *There must be an old, non-ExoGenetic orchard nearby.* Her mouth watered at the prospect of eating an apple again.

The third woman was blonde and aquiline, her features sharp and defined. Where Shawna was curvy, this woman was thin, almost frail. "Salut," the woman said in French, confirming Ella's fears about maid choice. But if this was the French maid, what did Mason have in mind for her? She determined to never find out.

"Hello," Ella replied, and then to the other women. "Hello again."

Forced smiles were the only replies before the women returned to work, their eyes evading Mason's.

They were terrified of him.

"Sabine," Mason said. "This is Ella. Could you prepare her something to eat?" He paused, thinking for a moment. "And have the same brought to the children with the Questionables."

Sabine gave a curtsy, her movements fluid, almost poetic. "Oui, Monsieur Mason."

She was a dancer, Ella thought. *Before the Change. A ballerina.* But was she even French? Ella didn't think so. She spoke French, that was clear, but the accent didn't sound authentic.

"Thank you, kindly," Mason said, as he breezed through the kitchen and into the back room. Once upon a time, the space might have been a mud room, where tired farmers, or a family's children, would have kicked off dirty shoes and boots. Now it would lead to a very modern door, offering passage to a biodome.

As Ella followed Mason toward the back of the kitchen, Sabine's hand snapped out. The woman's movement was so fast that Ella nearly punched her, but when she saw the look in the woman's eyes, and felt the steady grip on her hand...

It was a warning.

She's telling me to get out, or maybe to make myself undesirable somehow.

Ella returned the squeeze, offered a grin and gave her a knowing nod. The woman let her go, but took no solace in the message being received.

Are they really just concerned about my wellbeing? Or is there something else? Something I'm missing?

The hiss and pop of a decontamination room coiled Ella's insides. She'd heard the familiar sound all too often in her life, and during her time with ExoGen, after the Change, it served only to remind her that she was a prisoner. That was, until she had escaped. And here she was, about to walk through another decontamination chamber. *One that I designed,* she reminded herself, *but a prisoner once more.*

For now.

She stepped into the chamber and waited as Mason closed and sealed the door behind them.

"Removes any and all particulates from bodies and clothing. So if—" He waved his hand dismissively. "What am I saying? You already know all this. You recognize the design, of course?"

Ella nodded slowly. "It looks the same as ours."

"The one provided by your husband's mistress..." He shook his head like he still couldn't believe Peter's betrayal, like he was stung by it himself.

"I hated the bitch," Ella said. "But she also saved my family's life."

"Interesting perspective." The decon fans kicked on, filling the chamber with a tumultuous, roaring wind that shifted direction every few seconds, nearly tearing the skirt from her body. There was nothing she could do to keep it from lifting up, revealing the lacy white panties she'd been provided. But Mason had already seen a lot more. It didn't keep him from leering, though. He was so intent on looking, that he didn't see her own gaze, leveled at the thick vein on the side of his neck, or her hooked fingers, a twitch away from tearing into him.

Then the fans fell silent, the pressure equalized, and the door on the opposite side of the chamber unlocked. Mason opened the door, flooding the small space with the fragrant smell of growing things. The odor nearly brought tears to her eyes, and Mason did notice that.

"It's moving," he said, "for everyone. The first time they come here. And smell this. See it for themselves. *Taste* it. But to truly appreciate it all, you need to see the macro view. Lead the way."

The layout of the biodome hadn't changed from her original design. There were twenty raised rectangular garden beds. Each fifteen feet long and seven wide. A central aisle divided the space into even sides with walkways between the beds and along the walls. A network of water pipes crisscrossed overhead, with three nozzles positioned over each garden, providing an even spread for the plants growing below.

And they were growing.

Whoever was in charge of the dome had a green thumb. But right now, she and Mason were alone. She'd expected to find people—more women—tending the gardens. *It can't be just Mason and the maids. Not with five functioning domes.*

He sent everyone away, she thought. *Wanted the place to himself. Away from prying eyes or judgmental glares.* He might have already visited the self-service station while she was in the bath, but he apparently had vigor to spare. In fact, now that she could see him up and about, he looked bigger and fitter than she would have guessed. But was he a threat—aside from the gun tucked into the back of his pants? That would be determined the moment he tried anything.

"What do you think?" Mason said, walking the long way around the room, admiring the crops. "Take a closer look."

Ella obeyed, crouching down beside a row of carrots. The stems were lush and green. Fragrant, too. Her stomach growled.

With a chuckle, Mason said, "I heard that from here. Take one. Try it."

That was an invitation Ella couldn't pass up, and doing so would be supremely suspicious. She uprooted a carrot, surprised and delighted to find its bright orange body a full foot long. She stood, wielding the carrot the way an actor might an Oscar award, and she carried it to the sink mounted to the side wall. She looked at the root vegetable, almost glowing in the bright sunlight beaming through the glass dome above, protecting this oasis from the deadly crops outside.

"Daucus carota ssp. Sativa. It's perfect," she whispered, and then took a bite.

Flavor exploded with each chew. It was distinctly carrot, but almost like carrot concentrate, enough to make her pucker, salivate and crave more. She took a second bite without swallowing, chewing vigorously as the sweetness hit her. The flavor, on par with the best cake she'd ever eaten, was followed by a realization. She'd gotten the carrot's identify-cation wrong.

This is Daucus carota ssp. Sativa variant RC-714.

This is an ExoGenetic carrot!

Her jaw stopped moving, the toxic food frozen in her mouth and stuck between her teeth. *Did I swallow it? Oh god, I swallowed it!*

"Too good to be true," Mason said, slowly moving toward her. "Right?"

She pushed the carrot chunks out of her mouth, letting the food fall to the concrete floor. She spat a few times and then used the sink to rinse out her mouth.

Mason stopped ten feet way. "Didn't your parents teach you not to waste food, Ella?"

Her mouth was full of water, ready to spit into the sink, when the last word of his sentence sank in.

'Ella.'

He knows.

He knows who I am!

Ella turned toward Mason, fists clenched, but he'd already closed the distance.

SIXTEEN

"I can't do that," Boone said, taking a step back from Peter. "Not until I get Mason's say so."

"Your men are dead." Peter motioned to the back of the still-open moving truck. The gesture was unnecessary. Boone knew what Peter was talking about. But it got the man to take another sobering look. The absolute carnage filling the inside of the truck—and only the inside—revealed an attacker, or attackers, who were incredibly strong and smart. And if Peter was right about who that was... "We're running out of time."

Boone stared at him, no doubt weighing the dangers of trusting Peter and betraying Mason's orders. And while he was doing that, Peter was gauging the likelihood that he could subdue Boone and take the weapons he needed. He hoped he wouldn't need to do that. Weapons weren't any good without people to aim and fire them.

"Don't try it," Boone said, taking another step back and bringing his AR-15 up a little. It wasn't quite aimed at Peter, but the threat was clear.

"Damnit, Boone." Peter gripped the sides of his head, trying to contain his building anger. "You don't know what—"

A loud *thunk* against the outside of the moving truck interrupted and pulled Peter's eyes toward it. A spear protruded from the metal side. The tip was stone, but it had been thrown with the incredible force of someone no longer human.

When Peter turned back to Boone, the man held a hand up to his cheek, where it had been sliced open. Blood flowed into his beard. The spear throw had been meant for his head, a realization that slowly crept into Boone's eyes.

Too slowly.

"Down!" Peter yelled, diving into Boone. He shoved the muzzle of the AR-15 down and tackled the man to the ground as a second spear sailed past, puncturing the truck's large tire.

Peter scrambled back to his feet, yanking Boone up with him and searching their surroundings for attackers. The fenced-in lot was clear, but they were surrounded by swamplands. The spears gave him a direction, though—across the street, in the trees through which they had come. *They're blocking the path back to Hellhole.* Peter glanced at his truck... *If we go on foot.*

"Where are my keys?" Peter shouted.

"In the garage," Boone replied, stumbling forward as Peter shoved him toward the garage door. Movement atop the chain link fence surrounding the lot caught Peter's attention and confirmed his fears. It was a hair-covered Rider. The creature, who had previously been a man, was a foot shorter than Peter, but it would be far stronger. And the long, curved teeth protruding from his lower jaw and curving up into the skin of his cheeks, were a formidable weapon, not to mention the long, black fingernails turned into claws.

Peter yanked the spear from the truck's tire, triggering a loud hiss of escaping air. He lobbed the spear at the Rider about to leap into the lot. The spear missed its target, but it forced the man-beast to lean out of the way. He lost his grip and fell away. It was a momentary reprieve, but it gave Boone time to reach the garage.

Boone turned in the doorway, dropped to one knee and brought his weapon up. Peter flinched when he looked down the weapon's barrel. The rifle coughed. Bullets buzzed through the air. There was a shout of pain and then a thud of flesh hitting pavement.

Peter spun around to find a dead Rider laying behind him, three rounds stitched up its chest. Even as blood pooled around it, the creature still reached for him, black claws flexing. Peter had saved Boone's life and Boone had returned the favor.

"Move it!" Boone said, his shock giving way to the confident actions of a man who had seen action in the past and come out on top. But how many men had Boone had by his side during those encounters? And how many monsters were out there now?

Only one way to find out, Peter thought, as he charged for the open door. *The hard way.*

Boone closed and locked the door behind Peter, watching through the glass. "The hell are they? You know, don't you?"

"We call them Riders."

"Riders? What do they ride?"

"Woolies, but I didn't see any out there, and that's a good thing."

"But..." Boone looked stymied. "They're working together? Like people?"

"Most ExoGenetic creatures became solo predators, hunting each other toward the mass extinction of all life on Earth," Peter explained. "But the last creatures to turn during the Change—some people and some herd animals—adapted into packs. And in this case, they evolved as cooperative species. Almost symbiotic."

"Symby-whatic?"

"Means they need each other to survive."

"Seem to know a lot about this stuff," Boone said, suspicion creeping back into his voice.

Peter moved to the front office, ducking low as he looked out the window. "Also means the Woolies won't be far." He snuck back into the garage. "Now would be a great time for those weapons we spoke about."

Boone hesitated for just a moment and then kicked open a chest against the wall. Inside was a collection of weapons that looked like they might have been taken from previous captives. Atop the haphazard mass of metal was

Peter's own rifle. He picked up the weapon and ejected the magazine. It was full, but he didn't see any spares in the chest, or ammunition. He looked out at the lot again. *Beastmaster's* back hatch was down. His cases of supplies and ammo still surrounded the mounted machine gun. Boone's men had been interrupted before they could fully pillage the vehicle. "We need to get to my truck."

"These walls are concrete," Boone said. "Safer in here."

"Against spears maybe," Peter said, and then as though to prove his unfinished point, the garage's side wall folded inward, vomiting concrete blocks as something massive plowed through.

Peter and Boone both dove for the pool table, sliding beneath the solid sheet of slate. The table shook as chunks of wall toppled into the room, but it withstood the assault. Before the last blocks hit the floor, Peter poked his head out and saw the ugly face of a Woolie pulling out of the newly formed gap. The creature looked like a cross between a hairy rhino and a buffalo. The single horn on the tip of its nose split like an antler, ending in razor sharp scoops. Tendrils of brown hair hung in clumps, matching the drool dangling from its mouth, sweeping back and forth across the floor, like a lazy janitor's mop. Its jaundiced eyes twitched toward Peter, but it made no move to attack. It just lumbered back.

Making way, Peter thought. "We're about to have company!" He pulled himself out from under the table, climbed to his feet and chambered the first round. Before he could aim the weapon at the massive hole in the side wall, the window beside him shattered inward. He twisted toward the sound and caught sight of a male Rider curled up in a ball, unfurling his body as he catapulted through the air.

Peter tried to fire his weapon, but it wasn't designed for close quarters combat. The Rider struck him in the side. Man and beast went down together, sprawling across the concrete-littered floor.

A spear tip stabbed toward Peter's throat before he could get back to his feet. He caught the shaft, stopping the blade just an inch from his throat, but he only managed to delay his death. The male Riders, while smaller than Peter, and the females of their ExoGenetic species, had powerful muscles. Like apes, who could out-muscle a man more than twice their size.

When the tip of the spear met Peter's skin and began slipping through it, he nearly lost his grip. And as a shout of pain and emotional agony at failing his family rose up in his throat, the blade sank deeper.

And then, with a blast of noise, the blade slipped out.

Peter's chest heaved as he watched the Rider fall to the side, an arc of blood flowing out behind its head, while a plume of gore sprayed out in front of it. He stared at the creature, as its body struck the floor, kicking up a cloud of powdered concrete. Its lifeless eyes looked back at him.

Then a voice cut through the shock. "Get the fuck up, man!"

Peter gasped a deep breath and adrenaline carried the oxygen straight to his brain, sharpening his senses and speeding up his reaction time. The effect, which he'd felt before, was that time had suddenly slowed. In reality, he was simply processing the world around him much faster.

A shadow moved in the open wall. He gripped the spear lying next to him and hurled it toward the opening without fully registering what was there. By the time he saw the Rider, it was already falling back, the spear planted firmly in its sternum, its long-toothed lower jaw slack in surprise.

Thumps echoed down from the ceiling. Shadows shifted in the swamp outside the ruined wall. A Woolie bellowed from the street, its call like a fog horn. *That's going to attract a lot of attention,* Peter thought, but maybe that was the idea. If the man accompanying these creatures was who Peter feared it was, they might be calling reinforcements.

Peter hauled himself up, and shouted at Boone. "Keys!"

Boone gave a nod and made for the front office.

Movement outside the garage door spun Peter around. A Rider had leaped down from the roof and was coiled to spring. As the creature dove into the garage, Peter pulled the trigger and held it, putting six rounds into the

Rider's head. The first shot killed it. The force of the remaining five stopped its forward momentum and deposited the body at Peter's feet.

Boone stumbled back into the garage, stepping over debris and jingling the keys. "This them?"

Peter snatched the keys from Boone's hand and turned for the ruined door. "The moment we're out in the open, they'll be on us."

"Ayuh."

"Don't stand your ground, Boone. Don't even slow down. Just get in *Beastmaster* and—"

"Beastmaster?"

"The truck."

Boone flashed a grin. "Well, all right then. Let's kick this in the nuts and get 'er done."

"I'll take point, you cover our six," Peter said. "Steady pace. Stay close."

"Copy that."

Peter stepped through the ruined door, leading with the assault rifle, sweeping back and forth, looking for targets. The lot appeared empty, but he could hear movement just beyond the fence. *Riders hiding behind the cars,* he guessed. Boone shuffled out behind him, walking backwards, aiming up at the garage roof at first, and then in all directions.

"Don't see nothing," Boone said.

Peter ignored him and kept moving. They were fully exposed now. It wouldn't be long before they proved too irresistible a target.

The attack came just three steps later, but the Riders were done throwing spears and attacking one at a time. A fog-horn blast bellowed from the swamp across the street. It was followed by the rumble of heavy bodies charging across the pavement. Six Woolies, three with Riders, three without, burst from the trees, headed straight for the lot.

"Run!" Peter shouted, tugging on Boone's shoulder. He pressed the 'unlock' button on the key fob and was happy to see the tail lights flash on twice. The doors were unlocked.

As they reached the truck, the first of the Woolies reached the lot, plowed through the chain link fence and slammed into the truck parked there. The smashed vehicle shot across the lot and crashed into a second with tremendous force.

The second Woolie did the same. They were turning the parked vehicles into massive projectiles, while simultaneously blocking off any chance of retreat back to the garage.

Peter put the key in the ignition.

A third truck careened across the lot, followed quickly by another.

The gear shift clunked down into Drive.

A pickup truck whooshed past, directly behind them, clipping one of the spikes welded to the back of *Beastmaster*. The flung pickup sprang into the air, slamming down on the open moving truck, further violating the corpses.

Peter shoved the gas pedal down. The big Dodge Ram roared forward, striking the chain link fence with a clang and peeling it away from the metal support poles. The fence stretched out, trying to hold them in place like a spider web clinging to a bird. The truck pushed forward until the fence slipped up and over the roof and sprang back toward the lot, just as the last Woolie struck, closing the gap where they had been just moments before.

Peter peeled hard to the left, flinging mud as he avoided a drop off into the swamp. Tires squealed as they reached the road.

"That way!" Boone shouted, pointing to the right.

As its windshield wipers and cleaning fluid attacked the excrement-soiled windshield, the truck roared away from the scene. But it wasn't alone. The powerful Woolies and their Riders were unfazed by the impacts with the vehicles. Peter and Boone weren't more than fifty feet away by the time the creatures turned to follow them.

Peter glanced in the rearview, expecting to see the Woolies fading in the distance. *No way those big things can keep up*, he thought, as the truck moved past fifty miles per hour. But what he saw in the mirror reminded him that making assumptions about creatures who could rapidly evolve and adapt was often a fatal mistake. It had been weeks since he'd seen these things, and while fast and powerful then, they'd obviously evolved some speed since. The Woolies weren't just keeping up—they were gaining.

"Get back there," Peter said, hitching his thumb toward the truck bed and the machine gun mounted there.

Boone turned to climb over the seat, but stopped short, head turned out the passenger side window. "What in the—aww shit!"

Peter glanced out the window in time to see a massive pair of jaws, filled with foot-long conical teeth, explode from the swamp, reaching out for the side of the truck. Before he could take action or even shout in surprise, the open maw snapped closed.

SEVENTEEN

Ella saw the incoming attack too late to do much about it. The punch was aimed at her temple. If she tried to lean back, the fist would connect with, and most likely break, her jaw. Dodging Mason's broad-knuckled fist was impossible. But she could make him regret it.

She turned to face the blow and tilted her head down, shifting the impact from her temple—which would have knocked her out cold, if not killed her—to her forehead.

His fist full of old phalanges struck hard, colliding with the thickest part of her skull.

Two shouts of pain echoed off the curved glass ceiling.

Ella's was cut short by a flicker of unconsciousness. The solid strike had snapped her head back, mashing her brain into her skull. She toppled backward into a raised garden of potatoes, regaining consciousness on impact.

Mason's yelp of pain became a hiss. He shook his right hand, and then held his index finger in his left hand. He squeezed hard, unleashing a muffled pop that was followed by another yelp. She didn't know if he was trying to set a broken bone, or fix a dislocated joint, but when he was done, he didn't try bending the finger.

Ella blinked and tried to get back to her feet, but she felt like she'd just woken up from a long sleep after a night of binge drinking. Her limbs were not fully obeying her commands yet.

Mason looked down at her, but didn't take a step closer. "You're a crafty bitch, aren't you?"

"At least I'm not a geriatric rapist," Ella said. Each word sent a pulse of pain through her head. She tried to hide it. To look strong. But she knew her squinting eyes and downturned lips were projecting her vulnerability.

"You are far worse than that," Mason said. "The Bhagavad-Gita and Oppenheimer both got it wrong. The world wasn't brought to its knees by a multi-armed Vishnu, or the atomic bomb. Civilization was destroyed by *you*, Dr. Ella Masse. Seems only fitting that someone bring you to your knees."

Despite the pain in Mason's hand, a hungry look returned to his eyes. It lingered on her face for just a moment longer, before traveling down to her skirt, which had been flung up, exposing her legs.

"You were a mess when you first entered the camp. And to be honest, the shaved head still isn't working for me. But it's different. And different is fun. Despite the grime and old blood and whatever else you'd been rolling through out there—" He waved his hand toward the wall, indicating the world outside. "—I saw your potential. I've been with all manner of women, but they were all...soft. In body, mind and spirit. But not you. You are a hard woman." He raised his injured hand. "And you have not disappointed."

He took a step closer, but not too close.

"The problem is, we're under something of a schedule. Your friends are on their way."

"Peter will—"

"I'm not speaking about your counterfeit husband." Mason leaned his head to the side, eyes traveling up Ella's exposed thigh.

She pulled the skirt down, and shuffled back. Her head throbbed, stopping her short. It hurt like hell, but not quite as bad as she made it seem. She groaned and held her head, rolling her eyes for a moment before gripping the potato bed's plastic edging.

"I'm talking about your employers."

Ella held her breath, the shock on her face genuine.

"Yes," Mason said. "ExoGen is on their way here. Just for you. And your daughter."

"W-what? How?"

"We installed a HAM radio just a week ago. I'm not sure why, but we never thought to try it before. S'pose we just assumed there was no one else out there to talk to. Imagine my surprise when I heard a message broadcast by the harbingers of doom themselves. They were looking for the one and only Dr. Ella Masse, and her daughter—both of whom were hiding the secrets to preventing the Change from taking place. Tsk, tsk, Ella. I don't know what your motivation for destroying civilization was, and I can't even say I don't appreciate this new world you've created, but if turning you over to the company you duped means a future beyond these walls, I have to do my civic duty."

"They're trying to *stop* me from fixing the problem," Ella argued.

"Says the architect of hell."

"I tried to warn people," she said. "I built these domes to save people. And you've done that like no one else."

"My vanity cannot be fluffed, but other things... Well, perhaps we can arrange your escape."

Ella glared at the man. Was he offering her a chance to escape in exchange for a sexual favor? Was he really that preoccupied by the exploits of his manhood? As the first repulsive notion of considering Mason's offer entered her thoughts, Ella's hand felt a large lump just beneath the soil's surface. She dug her fingers down and lifted a dirty, football-sized potato from the soil. "These are Solamum tuberosum, variant RC-714. They're ExoGenetic. Is this what you're eating?"

Mason grinned. "It's what we're all eating."

"For how long?"

Mason took a deep breath and let it out slowly, counting on his fingers and wincing when he moved the injured index digit. "Thirteen months. Are you impressed?"

Ella *was* impressed, but not with Mason. "The Askews. They did this."

Mason nodded. "The crops, as you noted, are still ExoGenetic, but the RC-714 gene that unlocks millennia of dormant adaptations, has been blocked. The crop's adaptations remain intact, but they no longer modify the DNA of those who consume it. Lyn said they had rusted the revolving door shut. The problem, of course, is that these crops can only co-exist with the crops outside. They can't replace them. Which means that these biodomes are still required. We have more than enough food, but remain prisoners of Hellhole."

"The Askews fed you, and you repaid them by locking them up? By starving Bob to death?"

"They questioned my authority."

"Because this was *their* home."

He shrugged. "There are no governments. No laws. No land rights. Who is to say what is right and what is wrong? *I'm* writing history now. Whoever comes next will remember me as humanity's savior."

"Did you tell ExoGen?"

"They're on their way. Were surprisingly close. Tracking you, I suppose."

"Not about me," Ella said, shaking the potato at Mason. "About this?"

The trace of doubt on Mason's face came and went like a Formula 1 race car zipping past, but it was enough to confirm Ella's fears.

"Mason, listen to me." She held the potato up. "This is a gift. Not just to you. But to the world. It's not a solution, but it's big. You can feed people. Really *feed* people."

"I've heard similar words come from your mouth before," Mason said. "That was on TV, and you had nicer hair then, but you were a snake oil salesman then, and you're a snake oil salesman now."

"I didn't know," she said between clenched teeth.

"Mmm." Mason took a step closer, leering again.

"Mason, they are going to kill you and everyone here. They told you the truth about my work. I am working on a cure. On a way to alter the human genome, so we can eat any ExoGentic crop without fear of mutation. The human race can have a future. But that's not what they want. That's not their design."

"Why would they want to stop the human race from being able to eat?"

Ella sat up a little straighter, her head clearing. "For the same reason you hold back this bounty from most of the people in this camp."

That seemed to sink in.

"Control," he said. "To what purpose?"

She wanted to grill him about *his* purpose. About his sick preoccupation with having a house full of fantasy maids. His motivations were as base as they come, without unlocking a single prehistoric gene. But that would only incite him and cloud the rational thought slowly pushing against his aging, but raging, libido.

"I don't know yet," she said, and it was true. She'd never been part of ExoGen's inner circle. She knew some of them. Even liked some of them. But the reason why they released the ExoGenetic crops, even after they understood what would happen, or perhaps because of it, was still a mystery. She had always assumed it was a more complex version of Hellhole Bay. Mason had remade this small part of the world to suit his every desire. And it was only possible because the old world had died. ExoGen was no doubt doing the same, but on a much larger scale.

A worldwide scale. With a longer endgame. And whatever that was, it still required that the remnants of humanity, including Mason and every living soul in his Hellhole, to be changed into monsters or slaughtered. "But they have control. Absolute control."

She pushed herself up a little higher. "You're right. There are no governments. No laws. No right and wrong. Society is being rewritten, but by whom? Not you. Have you considered how ExoGen survived the end? How they have helicopters en route? They're located in San Francisco. You know that, right? And yet, here they are, on the East Coast, looking for me. How many people are living here? A hundred? Do you know how many people, loyal to ExoGen's future, are alive and well on the far side of the country?"

He just stared back at her. He didn't know. Hadn't thought to answer any of these questions.

"Thousands," she said. "The cradle of humanity's future isn't here in Hellhole, it's in San Francisco. With ExoGen. *Unless*...unless I can set the rest of us free. They're coming here for me. And for Anne. That's true. But once they have us? You and your harem are dead. These domes will be reduced to rubble. You will not be remembered in anyone's history books."

Mason grinned. "A riveting speech."

"It's the truth."

"Perhaps," Mason said. "Perhaps not. Either way, my earlier offer still stands."

"Oh my God, are you serious?" Ella gripped the potato tightly, lowering it back toward the soil. "Don't you get it? Whether or not I degrade myself for you, they *know* where you are. You are going to die."

He sighed, but it sounded more like a growl—exasperation mixed with primal desire. "And what are you suggesting we do?"

"Fight!" she shouted, and lobbed the massive potato at him.

EIGHTEEN

Peter swerved hard to the left, tires squealing as he nearly drove headlong into the swamp on the left side of the road. He cut the wheel back before plunging into the inky black waters, and since they were still on the road, and not being crushed by monstrous jaws, he assumed his last ditch maneuver had worked, pulling them just out of the creature's reach.

He looked in the rearview and saw the last of it career over the far side of the road. The massive beast was a blur one moment, and then concealed by an enormous splash that hid its dark body from view the next. Peter didn't see much of it, but what he did see urged his foot to push on the gas pedal a little harder. Not that it did much good. He already had the pedal pushed against the floor.

"What in the name of St. Peter's shit was that?" Boone shouted, eyes wide with surprise, a hint of a grin on his lips. Peter understood that the smile wasn't some kind of mania or psychotic thrill-seeking rush, but a genuine delight at still being alive.

Peter was smiling, too. A brush with death, and the adrenaline that brings, can leave survivors feeling elated for a bit. The numbing shock, body shakes and sleepless nights of fear-induced sweat would come later. "Apex."

"That worse than those hairy things?" Boone looked up over the seat through the rear window. "Which, by the way, are still on our tail."

Peter looked in the rearview again. Four of the six Woolies and two of the Riders had already passed the creature in the swamp, cloaked in shadow. If the Riders were operating under the normal guiding force that drove most ExoGenetic species—insatiable hunger—they would have turned on the newcomer. Instead, they'd continued pursuing Peter and Boone, which meant they had objectives. They were coordinated.

Thinking. Evolving intelligence that could guide their hunger. But more than all of that, it meant the attack was something else. Something that confirmed Peter's fears.

It was personal.

This wasn't random.

Wasn't hunger-driven.

This was revenge. Against him. Against his family.

He pushed the pedal even harder, but it still did nothing to help. The Dodge Ram was a powerful vehicle, but weighed down with armor, weapons and ammunition, it was closer to a tank than a dragster. Acceleration was a slog, but once it got going, there wasn't much that could stand in its way. Unfortunately, both a Woolie and whatever had lunged across the road, were big enough to stand up to the truck. Fortunately, they were all still in the rearview. But Peter suspected there would be more between them and the camp.

That's where Ella is, he thought, *that's where Kenyon will be.*

"There it is!" Boone shouted. "I see it in the swamp! Keeping pace with the stragglers!"

Peter glanced from the rearview to the side-view mirror. He flinched when a massive shape exploded from the swamp, clutched the last Woolie and Rider in its jaws and plunged back into the water on the far side of the road. The fifty-foot-long creature was easy to identify this time. The long body and ridged tail were familiar to anyone who had spent time in the swamps of the South.

"Gall dang, that's a croc!" Boone's smile had faded. He'd spent enough time in the swamps to have a healthy fear of the average American alligator, which grew to a maximum length of fifteen feet and weighed five hundred pounds. They were man-eaters capable of dismembering, consuming and crapping out even the largest and strongest human male. But this thing...it was worse. And not just because it was larger.

"It's coming back!" Boone shouted.

Peter watched the action in the mirror. Trees burst and toppled over, giving way to the largest ExoGen Apex he had ever seen, larger and more intimidating than even the matriarch Stalker. It didn't have a pack to add to its strength, but it didn't need one. The jaws were large enough and powerful enough to snatch up a Woolie the size of *Beastmaster* and kill it with a quick squeeze. Alligators can bite down with the force of 2125 pounds per square inch, strong enough to flatten a human skull or shatter the intensely strong shell of a snapping turtle. The Nile Crocodile can take down even tougher prey with its 5000 PSI bite, but even that monster, at 20 feet long was dwarfed by the Apex surging back onto the road. It probably could crush down with 30,000 PSI—more than enough to mash the armored truck, but that, at least, would be a merciful end. Anything human caught in those jaws would be instantly reduced to paste. There would be no pain, just an immediate lack of existence.

The ExoGator hit the pavement running.

Not running, Peter thought, *galloping.*

Alligators were one of the most perfectly evolved species on the planet. They'd been around for a hundred and fifty million years without needing to evolve. While other species came and went, alligators and crocodiles, dominated their habitats. They were already Apex predators when the Change began, and even with RC-714 unlocking their genetic potential, they didn't have much need to evolve. That was, until food became scarce and they had to move over land. So this alligator reached back into its past, found an ancestor with long limbs, and evolved to run. Fast.

The second Woolie was snatched up from behind, mewling briefly as its backside was flattened inside the mighty jaws. When the hairy beast fell limp, the alligator gave two shakes of its head, severing its prey in two. While still running, the creature tipped its head back and swallowed the Woolie's ass-end whole. Then it set its sights on the rest of them.

"Here!" Boone shouted. "Here, here, here! Turn left!"

Peter slammed the brakes and turned the wheels. Tires squealed out a high-pitched staccato rhythm as they bounced over the pavement. A lighter vehicle would have flipped. Facing the wide dirt road, Peter accelerated, kicking up a cloud of dust that would let their pursuers know exactly where they'd fled.

The cabin filled with the grinding rumble of loose rocks beneath the tires. Peter's hands tingled as the steering wheel shook in his iron grip. He twitched the wheel back and forth, eyes glued to the winding dirt road, delicately balancing between speed and control. One wrong move and they'd slam into a tree or plunge into the swampy waters. Whether or not they perished on impact, stopping would be a death sentence.

When Boone climbed into the back seat, Peter tried his hardest to not look at the man. "What are you doing?"

"Manning the big gun, right?"

Peter's instinct was to argue. To call it what it was: too dangerous. But Boone wasn't his family. The man was a fighter and, if Peter was honest, expendable. They had bonded as warriors in the heat of battle, but family still came first, and a hail of 5.56 X 44mm bullets spraying from the backside of *Beastmaster* would increase his odds of reaching them. "Do it."

The rear window slid open just in time to allow a pain-wracked bellow to fully permeate the cabin. They'd just rounded a bend and couldn't see the ExoGator or the Woolies, but it sounded like the alligator was continuing its mobile smorgasbord. On one hand, Peter was glad for the help, on the other, he knew the line of entrées ended with him and Boone.

Peter focused on the wheel, slowing a bit as they approached a sharp turn. Boone was half way through the small opening in the back window, worming his way into the truck bed. If the truck turned too hard, the man might fly off the side. Peter wished he'd had time to explain the rubber band system he'd repaired with Jakob. Once strapped in, the machine-gunner could be jounced around without fear of falling away. But there wasn't time.

Peter heard Boone chamber the first round. A few seconds after rounding the bend, the machine gun beat a rhythm in the air, keeping time with a frenetic metronome. Fifteen rounds later, the weapon went quiet, replaced by a string of curses.

"What's happening?" Peter asked. The side-view mirror revealed three Woolies still in pursuit, two with riders. They were a hundred feet back and gaining with each thunderous foot fall.

"I can't hit shit while we're moving around," Boone called, his voice nearly inaudible as wind whipped the words away.

"You want me to stop?" Peter asked with a grin.

"You shitt'n me? Fuck no!"

Soldiers joked. In the quiet times. In the face of bullets. Even in the face of death. Humor kept them human. Kept them sane. At least until they went home. Humor tended to stay behind, on the battlefield.

A second blast of machine gun fire ripped through the air. The lead Woolie twitched, stumbled and then kept on coming. But its rider, flailed back in a burst of red, toppled through the air and rolled to a ragdoll stop in the dirt road. The man-thing lay still for just a moment before the last thunderous shaggy beast crushed him beneath its feet, leaving a trail of gooey red in its wake.

Peter shouted in surprise as the alligator catapulted out of the swamp beside the road and snapped at the Woolie, which leaned to the side, evading the bite. Then, instead of continuing the pursuit, the Woolie turned to face its adversary and charged, its deadly, scooped horn leading the way. The horn was no doubt sharp enough to pierce the gator's thick flesh, and the Woolie powerful enough to drive it deep, but would it be enough to kill the monster?

Not even close.

The ExoGator twisted its head around toward the Woolie. Instead of plunging the horn into the gator's side, it ran headlong into those gaping jaws. Teeth impaled flesh. Blood sprayed. And with a quick upward snap, the Woolie was sent cartwheeling through the air, dropping back down far out of sight.

Boone adjusted his aim.

Puffs of dirt raced up the road, making a line toward the gator and then striking it. The struck flesh rippled like water, but there were no holes. No spurts of red. No explosions of gore from the far side. The gator flinched, but was not injured. It clamped its empty jaws together, the clomp loud enough to hurt Peter's ears. Then it was up, resuming its horrible gallop.

As Peter followed the bending road to the left, he saw the ExoGator run straight, plunging back into the swamp. While *Beastmaster* and the short-legged, hairy Woolies were confined to the road, the gator moved freely through the swamp, instinct guiding it to follow the old adage: the fastest route between two points is a straight line.

"Hang on!" Peter said, pushing the truck toward unsafe speeds and then beyond. The curving road took them directly into the gator's path, and he didn't want to be there when it arrived.

The roadside crumbled as the truck skirted the edge. The rear tire slipped over the side for a moment before jouncing back up, nearly knocking Boone from his post. He shouted a string of Southern obscenities, most of which Peter didn't understand, but he held on. When the road straightened out, they picked up speed, and just in time.

"Here it comes!" Boone shouted. His voice was followed by the machine gun's roar. Peter looked out the side window. The gator was lunging toward them, mouth open, loping through the four foot water like it was a road. Small red spots pocked its pink tongue, the bullets punching through, but doing nothing to slow the behemoth.

Movement in the side-view got Peter's attention. Two Woolies and a single Rider were right behind them. The Rider was on his feet, legs bent, clutching handfuls of clumpy hair.

He's going to jump, Peter thought.

But then the view became a mass of tangled and tumbling limbs. The croc missed the truck and slammed into the two Woolies. All three beasts went down in a writhing mass of angry limbs. The impact and subsequent battle would give Peter and Boone time to escape, or at least increase their lead. Peter focused once more on the road ahead, until he heard thumping in the back.

"You okay?" Peter shouted back over his shoulder.

There was a thump and a gasped shout. "H-help!"

The rearview showed Boone in the clutches of a Rider, its arms wrapped around his back, squeezing him tight. The hairy man-thing had its mouth open so wide that it looked dislocated, the hooked four-inch-long spears it had for lower teeth just inches from Boone's neck. The only reason it hadn't taken a bite was because Boone had both hands on the creature's face, holding it back, but inch by inch, he was losing ground with each beat of his heart. The man had just seconds to live, and then Peter would be next.

NINETEEN

Eddie Kenyon was impressed. After seeing the number of still-human men at the gas station, he suspected one of Ella's biodomes would be nearby. Sure, the swamps could be scavenged for food, but the men had looked well fed. And he'd seen some of their stomach contents spilled out on the floor of the moving truck. The men were eating vegetables, and not the kind that could be foraged. His suspicions were soon confirmed when the men spilled their guts, literally and figuratively. He learned the location of the camp, known as Hellhole, and that Peter, Ella and the kids had been taken there as captives. Easy pickings.

After leaving a contingent of male Chunta and their steeds behind to watch the gas station, Kenyon, Feesa and the other female warriors had trudged through the swamps, moving slowly and quietly, until they spotted the twenty-foot-tall wall that looked like it could take a beating. They wouldn't be forcing their way inside, though he suspected the large gates might eventually give way to a persistent assault from their steeds.

But the wall wasn't what had him on edge. From his perch in a tall tree, he looked out at what might be the last vestige of civilization outside San Francisco.

The camp was vast. More like a small town. There were five bio-domes. He could see the lush plant life growing within them. Enough to feed dozens of people. The shanty town surrounding the farmhouse at the camp's core looked like it could house a hundred people. And there were signs of activity everywhere he looked. Everything was maintained. Footprints were scattered about the barren earth. And the land itself was completely clear of ExoGenetic crops, a feat that could only be accomplished through persistent and daily labor, the evidence of which could be seen in the form of ash. There was a layer of it mixing with the brown soil beneath.

The place looked like it should be a beehive of activity.

But there was no one in sight. No workers. No guards.

No Ella.

Were we spotted at the gas station? Kenyon wondered. *Did they evacuate? Are they hiding inside?*

He could tell Feesa wanted to leap the wall and find out for herself, but she didn't fully understand the strength of mankind. The men they'd attacked earlier were unsuspecting, caught out in the open. It had hardly been a fight. But here, with a wall separating them, if the occupants of Hellhole were ready for a fight, the Chunta could be mowed down in a hail of gunfire before reaching the shanty town. For all he knew, there was a minefield between them and the house.

He placed his hand on her hairy arm and felt the muscles beneath quivering with anticipation. Her mind was primitive, but she understood that this was the place they'd been told Peter Crane had been taken. "Patience."

Her hand squeezed and crushed the branch to which she clung. They were in the trees again, just high enough to spy inside the camp, but not close enough to leap over the wall. The trees had been cleared away, thirty feet back. The space between the tree line and the wall had been filled in by densely packed cauliflower plants. The bulbous white heads would provide firm enough footing, but each step would let out a rubbery crunch. They wouldn't be able to approach without announcing it. And leaping over would be impossible from this distance, even for Feesa. Whoever built this place had planned its defenses well.

They're in there, he thought. *Waiting. And with those biodomes, starving them out isn't an option. Damn.*

"We go," Feesa said, pointing at the farmhouse. "Revenge inside."

"We wait," Kenyon replied, then repeated the mantra that had carried the Chunta this far and helped them overcome a myriad of deadly encounters. "Watch. Listen. Think. Plan. Attack."

"Just attack," Feesa said.

"Then Chunta die."

Feesa looked about ready to tackle him out of the tree and rip out his throat. The female warrior had bonded with him in more ways than one, but the Chunta, like all ExoGenetic creatures, were guided by instinct first and intellect only on rare occasions. Luckily for Kenyon, Feesa was one of the most rare ExoGenetic creatures, capable of rational thought, and at times, restraint. She opened her mouth, sliding the long hooked teeth from their cheek pockets, and hissed at him. But she didn't attack.

Kenyon wasn't sure if Feesa had simply retained a portion of her human intelligence, or if she'd lost it and then evolved a new primitive intelligence. That she could still speak limited English suggested the former, but if she had any memory of her life before the Change, she never spoke of it, nor seemed disturbed by what she had become. *Smart enough to understand revenge,* Kenyon believed, *but not emotionally complex enough to experience regret.*

Kenyon on the other hand... Regret fueled his need for revenge. He'd put his trust—his love—in a woman who betrayed him. Who might have planned to betray him from the very start. He'd been a tool. Nothing more. And even after several weeks, his chest still burned with a newfound fury. Not because he'd never really had her, or lost her to another man, but because despite all of that, he still loved her. And he hated her all the more for it.

Sloshing water revealed the return of their scouts. They'd sent two of the females around the wall's perimeter, searching for weak points or signs of life. Feesa exchanged words in the Chunta's ape-like language, which was composed of grunts, a few actual words and a good number of hand gestures. The returning females scaled the trees as the conversation came to a close, joining the fifteen other warriors waiting to attack. Their steeds were positioned deeper in the swamp, tended to by a handful of smaller males, all waiting to be called to action.

"Wall all around," Feesa told Kenyon, tracing a circle in the air with her black, claw-tipped finger. "No people." She snarled, her embedded teeth stretching the skin of her face. It was a horrifying sight, but one he'd grown accustomed to. "No revenge."

"They're here," he assured her, pointing at the biodomes. "Inside. Hiding."

Had the residents of Hellhole fled, the two scouts would have picked up their scent.

"Think," Feesa said.

Kenyon nodded.

"Plan." Before Kenyon could agree, she added. "My plan." Then she turned to one of the females perched in a nearby tree and let out a deep huff, a few barks and a finger pointed at the house.

The female Chunta obeyed immediately, leaping down from the tree. She landed in the cauliflower with a crunch that was far from stealthy. Then she charged across the gap toward the wall, leaving a mangled path of vegetation in her wake that anyone would spot.

He wanted to chide Feesa, to tell her she didn't think hard enough, but he knew better. Not only did she have the patience of a ball-clamped bull at a rodeo, but he understood the Chunta. They weren't the disciplined surgical strike team Viper Squad had been. They were a brute force instrument of destruction that was made more effective when they were guided. Right now, Feesa was at the helm. If the female's fact-finding mission bore fruit, he had no doubt that Feesa would consult him before taking action. They'd built up that trust, though he was aware seeing Peter, her hated enemy, might send her into a primal rage. And that could undo his own plans for a protracted revenge, but he could live with that. As long as Peter Crane and his brood didn't.

He watched the female leap to the top of the wall. She clung to the carved spikes that had been hardened by fire. When she hoisted herself up into clear view of anyone on the other side, Kenyon expected a bullet to tear into her. But nothing happened. The female looked back to Feesa, who urged her onward with a bark and waved hand. The female jumped down and loped toward the house. When she reached several feet in without being blown to bits, Kenyon was convinced there was no mine field. When she strolled through the shanty town without incident, he felt positive the residents were holed up inside the house. But when she stepped onto the steps of the farmer's porch without being gunned down, he began to doubt every scenario he'd imagined so far.

The distant female took one step at a time, her body language shifting as she did. *What the hell?* Kenyon thought. The female normally stood hunched over, but by the time she reached the top step, she was standing tall again. Like a human. *Is she trying to trick the people inside?* Kenyon nearly laughed at the ridiculousness of it. And when the female rapped her knuckles against the door, all casual, like a neighbor just stopping by to say 'hello,' Kenyon did laugh.

Feesa grunted at him. Was this all part of her plan? Had all this been transmitted during the grunting exchange? If so, the Chunta might be more intelligent than he gave them credit for. That meant they'd been holding back, hiding their true selves from him all along.

Not trusting him.

And for the first time in weeks, Kenyon wondered if he should so fully trust these...monsters.

He shook his head, unable to consider the idea of being betrayed by another woman, especially one as devolved as Feesa. She might be able to come up with a plan that involved knocking on a door, like people used to, but she lacked the subtlety to string him along for weeks.

He glanced at her, watching her yellow eyes track the movement of her scout.

How smart are you? he wondered.

Her eyes shifted toward him, meeting his gaze. She squinted.

Too smart, he decided.

Then Feesa beat her chest twice and coughed a series of low chuffs. In response, the Chunta warriors shook branches, getting geared up like ancient soldiers about to charge the field of battle. "Go," Feesa commanded, and the horde descended from the trees as one, charging the wall.

Feesa reached a hand out for Kenyon, and he understood the unspoken request. At times like this, when the tribe was on the move, Feesa would carry him. It was degrading, but he couldn't move as fast as the Chunta, and he certainly couldn't scale a twenty-foot wall without help. He hesitated for just a moment and then moved toward her arms.

But before they could leap down together, a male Chunta sprang into the tree. His sudden arrival startled Feesa, and she nearly bit his face off. The male reeled back, but then barked a few words, one of which Kenyon recognized.

"Petah." The male pointed behind them, toward the dirt road approaching the camp's gate. "Petah."

Feesa gave a nod and chuffed a few commands. She then turned to Kenyon and said, "Peter." She pointed toward the road. Then she said, "Ella," and pointed at the farmhouse.

Before Kenyon could respond, the large leader of the Chunta sprang from the tree and headed for the road, leaping between trunks and calling out to the nearby males gathered with the steeds. Then Kenyon was scooped up in the male's arms. He was smaller than Kenyon, but far stronger. The male dropped down to the ground and followed the other warriors' path to the wall, which he scaled with ease, even while carrying Kenyon. Just seconds after Feesa's departure, Kenyon found himself deposited inside the compound. Ducking low, he brought his assault rifle around from his back and scanned the house, looking over the barrel. He'd taken the AR-15 from one of the dead men at the gas station. It wasn't a long range weapon, but in his practiced hands, it would do the trick. Seeing no immediate threat, and knowing this would be his one and only chance to breech Hellhole's defenses, he joined the charge.

TWENTY

The hurled potato missed its mark—Mason's nose—but struck his forehead and sent the Ascot hat fluttering away. The blow did daze him, though, and as he stumbled back wiping at his eyes, Ella realized some of the soil clinging to the root vegetable had sprayed into his eyes.

A growl escaped her lips as she got her feet underneath her and sprang toward the man. She drove her fist into his gut. He doubled over, clutching his stomach with one hand while still pawing at his eyes with the other.

"Bitch," he hissed.

Ella hooked her fingers and swiped at his face. She was aiming for his eyes, hoping to make his temporary vision problems permanent. Instead, she struck his cheek, digging three troughs through his skin. He screamed in pain, reeling back.

I've got him, she thought, eyeing the bulging jugular vein on his neck.

Her stomach churned. Survival in a post ExoGenetic world meant sometimes devolving into something like the beasts that now populated it. Occasionally, savagery was the only way to survive. And if it meant saving her family and ridding the world of one of its worst monsters, she would go down that path and deal with the ramifications to her soul another time.

Hooked fingers reached out, ready to latch on.

She opened her mouth, teeth bared. She lacked the sharp canines of a true predator, but the human jaw was strong enough to bite through raw human skin, muscles and veins. One bite. *One bite and he's done.*

Ella dove for his neck.

And missed.

Mason's heel slapped into a raised garden bed and he toppled backward. Ella sailed over his body, and when her shin struck the same bed, she sprawled onto the concrete floor, tumbling into a collection of hard metal gardening shovels, which collapsed atop her with a loud clanging.

Wounded, but not defeated, Ella shrugged off the shovels with an angry shout and leapt to her feet. She turned to continue her assault, but Mason was already up and facing her, standing in the garden bed. He had one eye squeezed shut, his left hand on his gut, and rivulets of blood running down his cheek, but his right hand clutched a handgun. He leveled the weapon at her chest. Then he moved it lower.

"How long will it take you to die, if I shoot you in the stomach?" he asked. "Hours, I imagine. Of course, shock will set in long before that.

You won't struggle much then, will you? No, you'll be as docile as a bunny." His face lit up with a grin. "Oh that's good. Bunny. That's going to be your name. I'll even get you ears and a little fluffy tail to wear." He frowned. "Or not. You won't be any fun when you're dead. My tastes aren't that aberrant."

"You need me alive," Ella said, trying hard to hide her anger. "ExoGen—"

"Will believe whatever I tell them. You tried to escape. I had no choice." He motioned to his bloody cheek. "I've got the wounds to prove it. And it's your daughter they really want."

He stepped out of the raised garden bed. "I wonder why that is. Why are they more interested in a little girl than in the great Ella Masse, architect of the apocalypse? Of course, maybe I'll say she escaped. Let them head off into the wilderness in search of your precious daughter. She could be my Bunny. She'd look precious in a set of ears."

Ella took a step toward him, fingers hooked once more.

He stepped back and raised the gun at her head. "Not another inch."

"They're going to kill you," she said. "You know that, right?"

"Words of a desperate woman."

"Hellhole is a direct threat to their plans."

"And what plans might that be?"

Ella wasn't entirely sure. She'd never been let in on that secret. But she had her suspicions, and she decided to share them with Mason. "They're rebooting the human race. On their terms. With the creation of RC-714, ExoGen stopped mucking with the genomes of plants and turned their attention toward other forms of life, including humanity. They're building better people. Better animals. And when the ExoGenetic world eats itself into oblivion, ExoGen would repopulate the world. Humanity as we know it is nearly extinct. It's ExoGen's creations that will inherit the Earth."

Mason stood silent for a moment, and then said, "Why would they doom themselves by creating a replacement species?"

"They're changing themselves, too," Ella said. "You've seen what RC-714 can do. Imagine if you could select the adaptations. What kind of person could you build? What kind of person could you become? And for their plan to work, humanity—all of it—needs to perish."

She motioned to the dome around them. "This place wasn't supposed to exist. You and everyone else here should be dead. The only reason you're not, is because of me. Because of the good people you locked up in a cage." She pointed at the vegetation growing all around them. "People who could have helped undo the damage ExoGen did...with my help. And now...you naïve, pitiful man, you're going to die."

Mason grinned. "Perhaps. But I still have something they want. I still have you. And Anne." He squinted. "She's one of them, isn't she? A new kind of person. What's different about her?"

Ella didn't move. Didn't talk.

"Tell me!" Mason stepped closer, leveling the gun at her head, finger on the trigger.

The decontamination chamber hissed and opened.

Mason didn't flinch. Didn't take his eyes off of her. He'd learned how dangerous she could be.

"If this is not a matter of life and death, I will cut out your tongue and have it cooked in a pot pie." Mason didn't know to whom he was speaking. Ella didn't think it mattered. But when a man replied, Mason looked thrown.

"Uh, sir. I'm sorry, but—"

Mason gave a quick glance toward the door. Too fast for Ella to attack, but she had no intention of attacking. While Mason felt afraid to take his eyes off of Ella, she was free to look at the newcomer. He looked like one of the good ol' boys from the swamps outside the compound, but she didn't recognize him. What she did recognize was the terrified expression on his face.

"What the fuck are you doing in here!" Mason shouted, and he squeezed off a round toward the door. The bullet ricocheted off the wall just below the glass dome and punched a hole into a raised garden. The man ducked back behind the door, but he didn't fully retreat. Just as fast as he'd taken the shot, Mason pointed the gun back at Ella.

"They're gone, sir!" the man shouted.

"Who is gone?"

"E-everyone."

The coiled muscles wrinkling Mason's face flattened a bit. "What do you mean, everyone?"

"The captives. The wall guards. The workers. Even your girls. They're not in the house."

"Shawna, Charlotte and *Sabine* are missing?"

"They're not here. I checked. They're all, just...gone."

"You're the *lookout*, Chad. You can see the whole compound from the third floor. How can they just be *gone* without *you* seeing?"

"I-I..."

Even Ella could guess that the man had fallen asleep on the job. Probably had many times before. Life in Hellhole had gotten too safe. Too comfortable.

Mason fired off two more shots toward the door, shouting in anger. Ella took a step toward him, but stopped when the gun swiveled back in her direction.

"There's just me and Dave left. He's watching the front door."

A hissing filled the air behind Chad. It was followed by a buzz and a flashing red light. The airlock had been overridden and the system was flashing a warning. Whoever was coming in might be contaminating all this food. And whoever it was likely knew that. Something was seriously wrong in Hellhole.

Chad ducked back inside the decontamination chamber and partly closed the door behind him. She could hear two men whispering in a rapid fire verbal sparring match that ended with, "Shit...shit!"

The door reopened and Chad's head poked out. "Sir...someone is at the door."

"One of the missing people?" Mason asked.

"Uh...no. A big, hairy lady. She's knocking on the door."

Ella snapped her head toward Chad and took a few steps in his direction.

"Hey!" Mason said, stepping in front of her, gun raised.

She looked around him. "Describe her face."

After a few hushed words with the second man, who could only be Dave, Chad leaned back out. "Long teeth coming out of her lower jaw, poking into her cheeks. Real gnarly looking."

"Do you have any weapons in the house?" Ella asked Mason. "Bigger than that?" She motioned to the gun in his hand.

His face twitched with confusion.

"You're going to need them," she said.

He said nothing. Just stared at her.

"If you stay here, you're fucked. We're all fucked."

"What's out there?" he asked. "Who is the hairy woman?"

"Friends of Peter's wife." She looked Mason in the eyes. "Who he killed five weeks ago...in front of them."

TWENTY-ONE

During his life, formerly as a Marine, and recently as a survivor of the ExoGenetic apocalypse, Peter had made a good number of tough calls. Sometimes people died as a result. Sometimes at his hands. Most often the dead were his enemies, occasionally an ally, and once...his wife. And now he was faced with another tough call.

Option one: he could keep driving and give the wheel a quick twist, flinging both Boone and the Rider from the back of the truck. It was the safest and fastest option. The Rider probably wouldn't be killed, but Boone certainly would be, by the impact, or the Rider.

Option two: he could stop the truck and join the fight, helping Boone defeat the Rider. Boone had a better chance of survival, but would risk the Woolies, or the gator catching up. And if that happened, they were all going to die.

Option three: he could try something reckless without stopping and maybe save Boone's life in the process, or maybe screw up and crash, which would bring the outcome back to option two.

The crux of this internal struggle was Boone.

Was the man an ally?

Was he an enemy?

They had fought side by side. Had saved each other's lives. That meant something among warriors. But was there a difference between trained soldiers and weekend warriors? Could he trust Boone, who had revealed himself to have a questionable moral compass? But maybe the man just needed redirection. If too much time under Mason's influence had brought out Boone's baser instincts, perhaps some solid redirection could bring out his best? Like Luke did with Vader, Peter sensed some good left in the man.

Convinced there was a chance, even if just a small one, that Boone could be redeemed, Peter's mind was made up for him.

It was time to get reckless.

With one hand on the wheel, his foot on the gas and his eyes on the road, Peter leaned forward and reached under the driver's side seat. He felt nothing at first, and he worried that Boone's men had already discovered the hidden weapon. Then his fingers grazed something solid. It had been jostled deeper under the seat. Had one of the kids been in the truck, they probably would have had an easier time retrieving it from the back.

He leaned a bit further and found himself stopped by the steering wheel. His shoulder felt about ready to pop from his socket as he stretched out. The bumpy rubber grip tickled his fingertips, but it clung to the carpeted floor, pressed down by the weapon's four and a half pounds. He needed a few more inches.

A shout of pain twisted him around. The Rider's long, hooked teeth had punctured Boone's neck. Without thought, Peter twitched the wheel to the left, kicking the truck's back end out just a bit. The sudden movement nearly toppled the two combatants in the truck bed, but the Rider adjusted its body and remained upright, slipping its teeth out of Boone's flesh.

With a shout of rage, Boone took advantage of the distraction and slipped his thumbs into the Rider's eyes. The creature howled in pain, but what might drop a man to the ground had the opposite effect on the Rider. Instead of reeling away from the thumbs about to burst its eyeballs, the Rider leaned into it, mouth open, ready to exchange its eyesight for blood.

Peter wasn't sure if the creature was just in a mindless rage, or if it understood that its body could evolve the ability to regrow eyes, or develop another sense to replace its eyes. It didn't really matter. Either way, Boone was outclassed. And soon, he'd be dead.

"Shit," Peter said, twisting the wheel hard to the left, doing his best to not throw his passengers, while keeping them on the road around a bend. Back on a straightaway that continued as far as he could see, Peter stretched for the weapon again and came up short. Knowing time was short, he toggled the adjustable tilt switch on the side of the wheel, which sprang up. It still wouldn't allow him to lean straight down, but that wasn't the plan.

Leaning to the side, Peter slipped down beneath the steering wheel. He kept one hand on the wheel with the hopes of maintaining a straight course, but when the back of his neck struck the leather wheel-grip, he was pretty sure they were careening toward the swamp at a slight angle.

Peter's hand slipped beneath the seat, easily reaching the hidden weapon. He gripped the handle, pulled it out and sat back up. The road came back into view. So did the swamp. Peter turned hard to the right, narrowly avoiding the drop-off into several feet of water and even more muck. The sudden move kept the truck on the road, but pulled Boone's feet out from underneath him. The man toppled backward and the Rider followed him down.

The Rider lifted its head up, howling in victory. Its prey was pinned and defenseless. The creature's eyes had been compressed. One of them was a mess of blood and viscous white fluid. But the injuries only fueled its mania.

Peter lifted the Smith & Wesson Model 500 revolver and aimed it over the back seat. He had discovered the weapon behind the counter of a convenience store they had pillaged for water and any food old enough to safely consume. They hadn't found much, but the gun was a rare gift. It was a .50 caliber hand cannon. Not quite as long barreled as Dirty Harry's, but equally as powerful. And that meant a few things. First, anything roughly the size of a human hit by a single round would find itself with a basketball-sized hole in the bullet's wake. Something like a Woolie might take two or three rounds, but a single shot in the right spot would still do the trick. As for the gator, Peter had no idea. But the Rider? One shot was all he needed, if he didn't miss...or hit Boone.

And one shot was all he might get. Firing a weapon like the Model 500 generally required two hands. The kickback would be substantial, and if the weapon didn't buck from his hand, it might very well break his wrist. On top of that, he was firing one of the world's most powerful handguns inside the enclosed truck cabin. The padded floor and ceiling would absorb some of the sound, but every hard surface inside the vehicle would reflect the cacophonous boom right back into Peter's ears.

This is going to hurt, he thought, leveling the sight through the back window. As soon as he drew a bead on the monster, its lower jaw opening wide enough to envelop Boone's head and whatever limb he tried to defend himself with, Peter pulled the trigger.

The explosion slammed into Peter's ears and forced his eyes shut.

He didn't see the weapon tear free from his hand, but he felt it leave his fingers and then strike his forehead. As though the impact of a spiraling four pound revolver wasn't bad enough, it was the scorching hot barrel that struck him, hissing briefly as it burned a red line above his brow.

When he opened his eyes again, the first thing he saw was a clean hole in the rear window. The bullet had punched through so suddenly that the rest of the glass remained intact. And beyond the window...nothing.

Did the Rider bite down?

Did he miss?

When the Rider hunched its back and rose into view, Peter knew he had failed and that Boone was dead.

Then the rest of the hairy body rose up, and he relaxed. Red blood chugged from a gaping wound where its head had been.

Boone sat up, hands on the headless Rider's chest. He pushed the creature up and then shoved it hard, sending the ragdoll body toppling into the road.

When the scent of smoke tickled his nose, Peter faced forward. He shouted, but could only feel the air bursting from his lungs. Aside from a buzzing, he heard nothing else. Peter turned hard, following a fresh bend in the road. When the big truck was back under control, he lowered the steering wheel and pulled the revolver off of his pants, which had begun to burn. He placed the cooling weapon in the passenger's seat and focused on the road.

A moment later, he jumped when something tapped his shoulder. He spun to find Boone leaning in through the back window, shouting something.

Peter tapped his ear. Shouted, "Can't hear! Gun was loud!"

Boone shouted something else. Peter still couldn't hear him, but the man's smile and obvious relief hinted that Boone was thanking him.

And then everything changed. Boone's face morphed back into fear. His eyes wide. His forehead a mountain range of wrinkles. Peter could even hear a little bit of Boone's screamed warning. All of that and Boone's pointed finger turned Peter's gaze forward. To the road. And what stood in its center.

A Rider.

Female.

She was large. Taller than Peter. In one hand she held a spear. Her free hand was pointed at the truck. *No*, Peter thought. *At me.*

On the surface, this Rider looked a lot like Kristen had. For a moment, he wondered if she had somehow survived their last encounter and was back to haunt him. But the eyes were wrong. Where he saw a hint of the wife he'd once had in Kristen's eyes, here he saw only a monster.

A monster out for revenge.

The idea that this creature might have followed him all this way simply because he killed the tribe's ExoGenetic leader surprised him. Then again, Ella and Anne had been pursued halfway across the country by the even less intelligent Stalker pack.

Peter eased up on the gas.

He heard Boone shout. His voice sounded like he was speaking through a tin can. "What are you doing? Run it down!"

Peter's instincts were the same as Boone's.

"Kill it and grill it!" Boone shouted, his voice clearer.

Well, not exactly the same, Peter thought, slowing even more.

At first he wasn't exactly sure why he was slowing down, rather than speeding up. But then he figured it out. The soldier's worst enemy.

Empathy.

For the enemy.

Peter stopped thirty feet short of the lone female. It wasn't until he opened the door and stepped out that he noticed she wasn't actually alone. Hidden just inside the swamp on either side of the road were seven

Woolies and four male Riders. *Where are the other females?* he wondered, scanning the area, but then he refocused on the living blockade hidden in the swamp. Had he sped through the female's position, he would have been met head on by a living wall.

And the confused and somewhat disappointed look on the female's face told him that might have been their plan. She and Boone were equally confused by his actions.

"Hey," Boone whispered, as Peter stepped down onto the dirt road. He was back inside the truck cab, leaning between the front seats. He handed the Model 500 handgun to Peter, keeping it below the window. "If yer fixin' on going out there, best take some protection. Also, you know, there's a good chance we might have trouble crawl'n up our backside any moment now."

Peter took the weapon and slipped it behind his back, tucking it into his pants. Then he stepped out from behind the door, hands raised. He walked toward the lone female, who was now even more confused, but had yet to take on an aggressive stance.

All that changed when Boone slipped back into the pickup's bed and swiveled the machine gun forward. The female raised the spear, cocking it back, ready to throw.

But she didn't.

Instead, she waited, and with every step Peter took, her arm lowered a little further. She might want vengeance on Peter for what he did—he couldn't think of any other reason she'd be here—but she was also smart enough to be curious about his strange response to her aggression.

She's still an ExoGen, Peter thought. If she moved to throw that spear, he wouldn't hesitate to draw the handgun and fire. He was no Billy the Kid, but he could draw a gun and fire accurately, faster than most, especially at such close range.

Twenty feet from the ExoGenetic woman, Peter stopped. They stood in silence for a good ten seconds, and then Peter spoke first, offering the only words he could think of that might carry his true feelings about what had happened to his wife. "I'm sorry."

TWENTY-TWO

Ella sat on the first floor staircase, hands linked behind her head as instructed. She kept the grip light, her head still recovering from the blow that knocked her unconscious. Mason stood at the bottom of the stairs, revolver leveled at Ella, but his eyes on the front door. The hairy woman standing on the far side of the door, visible through the side windows, was swaying back and forth impatiently, waiting to sell Girl Scout cookies, or Mormon Jesus, or Jehovah's Witness Jesus. She was a Rider. There was no doubt about that. The hooked teeth were impossible to mistake, and that adaptation, combined with the hair-covered body, was an unlikely combination to be repeated.

But why was it knocking on the door?

To call it strange behavior was an understatement. ExoGenetic creatures were driven by instinct. By *hunger*. They didn't knock on doors. Then again, they weren't supposed to talk, either, but Peter had communicated with Kristen before he shot her. Perhaps the other Riders could speak as well?

It didn't matter.

None of it.

What mattered was that the creature outside wasn't just her enemy, but the enemy of every living thing that wasn't also a Rider or a Woolie. It was a predator. They were its prey.

"You need to give me a weapon," Ella said.

Mason waved her off, keeping his attention on the door, but his weapon trained on her. Dave stood by the door, clutching an assault rifle that he didn't look very comfortable holding.

Ella guessed he'd never fired the weapon, at least not at anything living. The men outside the compound, the ones who had taken them captive, were the real fighters. Dave and Chad guarded the house, and manned the third floor lookout, but they weren't even good at that.

"Mason," Ella said. "The creatures outside are killers. Savages. And my kids are missing."

"They're not all your kids," he said, turning toward her. "Are they?"

"They are now."

"How noble of you."

"Let me save them. Let me help you fight."

"What good are hair and teeth and claws against bullets?" Mason asked.

Ella laughed. "When was the last time you stepped outside these gates?"

He said nothing, which was answer enough. He hadn't been in the wild since before the Change. He'd heard stories, but filtered through the bravado of his men.

"I should have known," Ella said. "Rape and subjugation are the tactics of a coward."

Mason's left eye twitched, but he said nothing. Just stared.

Then the Rider knocked again, louder this time, hard enough to rattle the thick wood.

"Shit," Dave said, taking a step back from the door.

Chad entered the foyer, arms clutching an array of weapons. Rifles and assault rifles. All of them presumably loaded, but there wasn't a spare magazine or even loose ammunition in sight. He stumbled, fell to his knees and let the weapons clatter on the hard wood floor. "Sorry, sorry."

The barrel of each and every weapon was pointed in Dave's direction, and when he saw them hit the floor, he reversed course, back toward the door. His fear of a misfire wasn't unfounded, but in that moment of confusion, he mistook the falling weapons as the greater danger.

Ella slowly backed up a step.

Dave's back pushed against the side window beside the door.

The solid glass panel was ten inches wide and four feet tall. It shattered inward as a large, hair-cloaked fist punched through. The thick fingers opened like a fisherman's net, wrapping around Dave's face. The man's muffled scream rose to a high pitch as he was lifted off the floor, and then was silenced as he was yanked through the window.

The ten inch wide space was far too narrow for Dave's body. As his chest shot through the space, the jagged edge peeled away his shirt, and his skin from both his chest and his back. His sudden motion came to a jarring halt as his buttocks and hips became jammed in the narrow space. Past the thudding of his twitching legs, there was a pop and a slurp.

Then the body, half inside, half outside, hung limp and still.

Even Ella was immobilized by shock.

She, Mason and Chad stood motionless, eyes on Dave's savaged remains. Five quiet seconds ticked by.

The spell was broken when Dave's head and torn-free spine arced back through the window like one of those 'The More You Know' stars. And there was a lesson here: never underestimate the ExoGens. It was a lesson Ella found herself learning over and over. Making any kind of assumption about any ExoGenetic life—in this case that the Riders lacked the intelligence, mental and emotional, to track down their slain leader's killer—was deadly.

Ella backed away another step, preparing to flee upstairs. The windows on the second floor were barred, but the third floor might not be. And if it wasn't, maybe she could hide?

She stopped when a wide-eyed Mason turned to her. His face was slick with sweat and his lips were quivering. His first real up close and personal experience with an ExoGen wasn't quite as glorious as his men had likely described it. "Okay."

"Okay, what?"

"A weapon. Take your pick."

"You aren't afraid I'll shoot you?"

He frowned but then said, "I'd rather be shot than end up like that." He waggled his revolver at Dave's *The More You Know* head and spine.

Ella moved down a step, not fully convinced. But a second look at Dave's head, torn free from his body, twisting coils of nerves still attached to the spine, helped cover up her animosity for Mason. She would fight beside her enemy, for now, and if they survived, she'd put a bullet in his dick. And then his head.

She stood and made it two steps down before a voice called through the broken window. "Hello, in there."

The voice wasn't just human. It was familiar. It was unmistakable. Eddie Kenyon had survived, and he'd tracked her down. She closed her eyes and shook her head. They should have killed him. Instead, they'd allowed this very dangerous man to befriend and join forces with inhuman savages, all of whom wanted her and Peter dead.

"Don't answer him," Ella warned, but Mason's body language had already shifted. While the old man was no good in a fight against monsters, he could verbally spar with the best of them.

Mason swiveled his handgun back around toward Ella's chest. "Sit."

Ella sneered, but obeyed. She wasn't far from the weapons, but couldn't risk diving for one until Mason's eyes shifted away from her.

"I said hello in there," Kenyon repeated, louder. Closer.

From her perch on the stairs Ella saw more hairy bodies climb up onto the porch. They spread out to either side. Waiting. Strategizing. When the time came, they could each plunge through a window and bring the fight inside. Mason and Chad might get off a few shots, but the brute force and speed of the Riders would quickly overwhelm them.

"Sorry for the messy introduction," Kenyon said, "but these ladies aren't really known for their subtlety. Let's call it a show of force. A taste of things to come, if you do not reply right this *God-damned second.*"

"We're here," Mason said. "We're listening."

"Excellent," Kenyon said. "So let's get right to it. We have come a long way and my patience is like paper."

"Yes, sir," Mason said. "What can we do for you?"

Ella enjoyed hearing the terror in Mason's voice, but would have preferred it be in response to her, not Kenyon and a bunch of female Riders.

"We are looking for a group of people and have reason to believe you are sheltering them here."

Mason's gaze became incredulous. Ella could nearly hear his thoughts, 'You brought this upon us?' If bending his index finger didn't cause him so much pain after cracking against her skull, he might have even pulled the trigger, but he refrained and said, "Anybody that's here, that you want, you can have."

"Appreciate that," Kenyon said. "Let's start with Crane. Peter Crane."

Incredulity turned to anger. "He's not here."

"Don't fuck with me." Kenyon's voice shifted into rage so fast that Ella wondered if he'd resorted to eating ExoGenetic food.

Maybe he's not fully human anymore, Ella thought. *Maybe he's one of them.*

"He left 'bout two hours ago. But he'll be back. We have his kids."

"They inside the house?" Kenyon asked. "Because there's nobody out here."

"That wasn't you?" Mason asked.

"What wasn't me?"

"The missing people."

"You are the first person I've spoken to since I had a sit down chat with your men at the gas station. What's your name?"

"M-Mason."

"Mason. My name is Edward Kenyon. You can call me Eddie. You sound like a reasonable man. Like a real Southern gentleman. How about we stop talking through a closed door and you tell me where everyone is. If this is an ambush, I—"

"Ella is here," Mason blurted out. "I don't know about the kids, I swear. But Ella is here. Right behind me. You want her, too, right?"

After a beat of silence, Kenyon spoke. "You have no idea."

"I'll bring her out." Mason shoved the gun at Ella's face and motioned for her to stand up. "Just...Just get down from the porch, okay? Give us some breathing room."

Heavy feet stomped over the front porch as the shadows hovering by the windows faded back.

"Come on out," Kenyon called.

Mason hissed at Chad and then motioned to the door with his chin. "Open it."

Chad looked horrified, but part of him was still equally afraid of Mason. He flitted to the door like a nervous mouse, starting and stopping, until his hand wrapped around the knob and twisted. The door swung open, smooth on its hinges. He pushed open the storm door next, cringing as the glass pushed up against Dave's headless and gored body. Dave's wet flesh squeaked against the glass, leaving deep red smears.

Kenyon stood ten feet back with a group of female Riders. He stood partly behind two of them.

Living shields, Ella thought, wondering if the two creatures understood why he had positioned them that way. They might not fully understand the danger posed by the weapons Mason and Chad carried, but Kenyon certainly did. And he was armed with an assault rifle of his own, though he kept the barrel low and unthreatening.

Mason waved Ella out and she complied. As she passed Mason she met his eyes and offered him a fiendish grin. "Your funeral."

A flash of doubt and horror flickered over his face, doubly so when he noticed she'd ripped her shirt, revealing the bra he'd supplied her. Then she was outside, on the porch, limping, crying and holding one hand to her head. "Eddie, thank God."

Kenyon's face was a frozen mask. He didn't look angry or confused, but Ella knew that it was his poker face. Just because he wasn't showing emotion didn't mean he wasn't feeling it. The question was, what was he feeling. Anger? Hate? Concern? The emotion she was hoping for, the one that would get her the result she sought, was love. If he loved her still, despite her betrayal, he wouldn't be able to ignore what she said next.

Stumbling toward the steps, she said, "He sent Peter away to be killed. He's probably already dead." That didn't get a reaction, but it wasn't really supposed to. That information was only offered to lend credence to what came next. "He kept me here. Dressed me like this." She motioned to her Southern belle outfit and let her hand stop over her chest, pulling Kenyon's attention to the lacy bra he knew she would have never worn by choice. "Eddie..." She fell to her knees, eyes on the ground and the large hairy feet at the bottom of the steps. "He *raped* me."

TWENTY-THREE

Peter gauged the distance between him and the Rider, then took a step closer. If the creature attacked, it would be close, but he thought he could manage it. They'd have to then survive the horde of male Riders and Woolies positioned on either side of the road, and whatever might still be following them, but facing problems one at a time was the only way to ensure things got done right. It had been drilled into his head during Marine training, and it made a lot of real world, logical sense. In the same way as finishing folding laundry before starting the dishes, you didn't aim at a new target until the first was down. Getting ahead of yourself was a good way to get dead, he'd been taught. Just one of many lessons learned during his time as a CSO that kept him alive.

So he ignored the future problems presented by the monsters closing in from all directions, and focused on the one standing right in front of him, spear aimed to kill, but still in hand.

The creature was showing restraint.

And the look in its eyes—confusion—suggested it had understood his apology.

"I'm sorry," he said again.

No reply.

"For Kristen."

No reply. No reaction.

"For killing your leader."

The female snarled. That resonated.

"Family," she said, her voice deeper than his. "Kill family."

The words stung. Peter hadn't just killed his wife and his son's mother, but this Rider's surrogate family member as well. *No wonder they tracked us down.* But what was Kristen to this Rider? A sister? A mother figure? Something more...intimate? Kristen was as heterosexual as someone could be, but she'd changed in nearly every other way, so it wasn't impossible.

"Leader," Peter said, and then patted his chest with both hands. "She was my wife. *My* family."

The female growled again, and then stabbed her spear into the dirt road. She let go of the weapon that she really wouldn't need if she decided to kill him, and pointed at his chest. "You killed family."

"*Protected* family," Peter said. "Kristen—your leader—tried to eat my son. Her son. She tried to *eat* him."

The female showed no reaction, including anger, which Peter took as a good sign.

"Do you understand?" Peter asked.

A nod.

"Do you have a son? A child?"

The Rider's face contorted. "Not...anymore."

Peter didn't have to ask. He knew the child's likely fate. But the Rider seemed to be in a sharing mood.

"Daughter." The female linked her arms like she was holding a baby. She rocked them back and forth, looking at the memory of a bundle. For a moment, her eyes looked nearly human. Then her natural ferocity returned. "Killed by...monsters." She opened her arms, looking at the gnarly hair dangling from them. "Like me."

"You would kill to protect your daughter," Peter said. It wasn't a question. With parents, it never was.

"I did kill," came the quiet answer.

"I did the same," Peter said. "I killed my wife, your leader. I killed her to protect my son. I am sorry for that, but...I would do it again."

The female grunted, and Peter had trouble hiding his shock. Was he getting through to her? Could this creature reason? He'd been surprised when Kristen was able to recognize him and Jakob, and to think clearly enough to demand her son back. But this...this was a step beyond. The Riders were evolving, becoming more intelligent. And with intelligence, they were gaining understanding. And empathy.

But all the empathy in the world couldn't change the fact that he and Boone had killed even more Riders, though most of the dead could be chalked up to the ExoGator. Then again, the Rider caste system seemed to value the much larger and stronger females. So far, he'd only killed males.

He needed a way to remove himself from the hit list, and the only way he could think to do that was nearly as disturbing as ending this confrontation in battle.

Peter put a hand on his chest. "My name is—"

"Peter," the female said. "Peter Crane, enemy of the Chunta—" She opened her arms to indicate the Riders and Woolies. "—of Feesa—" She placed a hand on her hair-cloaked breast. "—and of Eddie Kenyon."

Peter tensed at Kenyon's name. He'd suspected the man's involvement, but hadn't yet confirmed it. If Kenyon was working with the Riders...the *Chunta*...then working through whatever lies, or truths, he'd told them could prove impossible. Just because they'd found some common ground didn't mean the Rider was planning to let him walk away. But this creature valued family, and understood the pain of losing it so deeply that she had pursued him across a large portion of the country. He wasn't sure if Feesa's bond with Kristen had really been that deep, or if his wife's death had picked free the scab sealing in the pain wrought from her daughter's death. But there might be a way to make things right, or at least salve the wound.

He risked a step closer, hands outstretched. "Kristen. Your leader. She was like a mother to you?"

"Sister," Feesa said. "She was sister."

"She was my wife." Peter took a few steps closer. They were just ten feet apart. He looked for signs of aggression, but saw none. So he stepped even closer. Within arm's reach, he stopped. He pointed at Feesa. "Your sister." Pointed at himself. "My wife."

A nod and grunt were confirmation that she heard him, but it was the sudden blink and widening of her eyes that told him she understood. He waited for her to say it. She looked up, eyes meeting his. "Brother."

In-law, he thought, *but close enough.* He smiled, reached out slowly and placed a hand on her hairy arm. "Sister."

And then he sweetened the deal. "My son. My daughter."

Feesa inhaled loudly, a smile on her lips. Her shifting teeth tugged at the skin of her face where the tips were hidden. "Nephew," she said. "Niece!"

Peter nodded. In a screwed up, post-Change world, none of this was far from reality. There were no laws to govern such things, and family could be determined however anyone chose, especially if that someone was strong enough to tear a man in half.

Peter stayed silent. Feesa's twitching eyebrows reminded him of the Golden Retriever he'd had growing up. Named Mr. Miggins, the dog's eyebrows spoke a language of their own. Young Peter had tried to find meaning in the dancing brows, but came to the conclusion that Mr. Miggins's eyebrows revealed he was pondering something—usually food or tennis balls. But Feesa had a bit more going on upstairs than Mr. Miggins.

Her deep thinking about new familial connections ended with a look of grave concern. One that Peter shared.

"Kenyon?" he asked.

"Will kill family," she said, and then added the magic words that gave Peter an inkling of hope. "Our family."

"We can stop him," Peter said. "Together."

Feesa grunted with something that sounded like agreement, but then she cocked her head to the side and looked beyond Peter. "But first, that."

She said it so casually, that Peter thought she must be referring to *Beastmaster* or Boone, who was still manning the gun. But then Peter felt a rumbling underfoot. As he turned to look, he knew what he was going to see, but still felt a measure of shock upon seeing it.

The ExoGenetic alligator, bits of flesh and clumpy brown hair dangling from its jaws, galloped toward them. A cloud of dust billowed in its wake, giving it the appearance of some kind of hellish beast. But this was no denizen of a supernatural underworld. It was a flesh and blood creature, modified by science gone awry, but still mortal.

Still killable.

"Boone!" Peter shouted, pointing at the gator. He turned back to Feesa. "Let it pass. Then attack from behind."

When Feesa began barking at the surrounding Riders in a language that was far from the English language, Peter assumed she understood, and he ran for the truck. He leapt into the driver's seat and shouted out through the open rear window. "Hang on and aim for the eyes!"

"Just go, man!" Boone shouted, and then he yelped in surprise as the whole truck rocked to the side.

Peter glanced back. Feesa had leaped into the truck bed beside Boone, spear in hand. She crouched and looked through the window. "Go!"

Well, all right then, Peter thought, and crushed his foot against the gas pedal. *Beastmaster* surged through the first twenty miles per hour of acceleration and then started to crawl slowly faster. Peter looked in the rearview. The gator was going to reach them long before they matched its top speed. If his new friends didn't help balance the scales, they were all dead. Given the ease with which the gator had dispatched both Riders and Woolies during the earlier pursuit, he didn't have high hopes.

TWENTY-FOUR

Starting an insurrection was far easier than Jakob imagined it would be. Granted, he didn't have a lot of experience in such things, but he thought there would be some pushback. A fight. Maybe even a few dead people as a result. But Mason was a hated man. The guards patrolling the wall, the two guys who had been manning the gate—Marcus and Stevie—and every other hard working person inside the compound, were all but giddy about the idea.

Word spread fast, and people gathered inside the unfinished shell of the biodome still under construction. Most of it was complete, except for the glass, which had to be collected from a warehouse hundreds of miles away. The walls and the distance from the house were enough to hide them from view, though Marcus had assured him that the lookouts were notorious nappers. Still, Jakob, Anne, Alia, Carrie and Willie had snaked through the compound using water tanks, solar panel arrays, storage sheds and shanty villages for cover, spreading the word as they went. "Meet in the unfinished dome. We're taking Hellhole."

Jakob felt a little like Paul Revere, riding through towns, warning of the Red Coats. It was a fun fantasy, and helped him cope with the reality of what was going to happen. Blood would be spilled. People would die. Maybe even him. Or Anne. Or Alia.

And now, here they were, a small army of nearly seventy-five people. It was more people than Jakob had expected to ever see in one place again—including three babies, all of them Mason's.

Despite the large number of people gathered, clumped into nervous, whispering groups, the majority of them weren't in any condition to fight. Mason kept them hungry. They were just strong enough to do their work, and desperate enough to follow his commands. Of the seventy-five souls happy to see their oppressor overthrown, only nineteen of them were in any shape to fight. And of them, only fifteen had weapons, and that included Carrie, Willie, Anne and Alia. The guards had access to spare weapons and ammo, but not nearly enough to arm everyone. Hell, half the people weren't strong enough to hold up a rifle for more than a few seconds anyway, let alone aim and fire, and deal with the recoil.

After hiding the weak, hungry, young and old behind the wall of the dome, the small group of fighters gathered in a tight circle. Jakob waited for someone to speak, half expecting the aged, but feisty Willie to lead the charge. But when he looked around the circle, he noticed all these people had one thing in common: they were looking at him.

Jakob's pulse quickened. Apex ExoGenetic monsters he could deal with. Public speaking, not to mention leading men and women into battle... His stomach clenched and he nearly vomited in front of them all. He focused on his father. Imagined him in this same situation. How would he handle it? How would he speak to these people?

Jakob met Anne's eyes first, her gaze so intense and confident that it bolstered him. Alia smiled at him and gave a nod. Her belief in him helped, too. But it was the desperate hunger in the eyes of the rest of them that gave him the strength to push past his anxiety. Empathy became anger, which he used to fuel his bravery. He met the eyes of the men and women around him one by one. Willie and Carrie. Marcus, Stevie and Isabel, who'd greeted them at the gate. Three women in maid uniforms, who'd fled the house of their own accord after noticing the gathering throng headed for the unfinished dome. Out of all the people ready to fight, those three seemed the most eager. Clutching hunting and semi-automatic rifles, they looked like something out of a Grindhouse movie.

"Thanks for coming," Jakob said to the group, and he closed his eyes at how dumb it sounded.

"Ain't an AA meeting, kid," Willie said.

The joke got a nervous chuckle from everyone but the maids.

Funny or not, it helped Jakob relax. "What kind of fight can we expect?"

"Right now?" the maid named Sabine said, "Not much."

"Two guards in the lookout," said a second maid, Charlotte, "but Chad's a pushover. He'll avoid a fight if he can. Probably will root for us, though he's probably not brave enough to turn on Mason, or Dave, who *is* loyal."

The third maid, Shawna, spoke next. "The trouble is that they have a house full of weapons and a defensive position."

"If they hold out until Boone and the boys get back..." This came from Isabel, who Boone had seemed interested in, even if he showed it in an inappropriate way.

"They're the real problem," Stevie said. "If we can't take the house before they get back, we're fucked."

"Is Boone that bad?" Jakob asked.

For a moment, no one answered. They seemed to be considering the answer. It was Isabel, the object of his rude affection, who replied. "He's a Southern prick and occasional testosterone-fueled asshole...but he also sneaks the pregnant women food. Helps maintain things when others are too tired or hungry. When Mason tells him what to do, he falls in line without complaint, but on his own... He's not all that bad. And as much as he is loyal to the old man, the boys are loyal to him. They're like frat brothers or something. With guns."

"So if Mason is dead," Jakob said. "Is he going to be set free like the rest of us, or is he going to seek revenge?"

Isabel just shrugged. "I'll try to talk him down. He might listen to me. And if that doesn't work—"

"We'll kill him," Sabine said. "All of them."

"If we don't have to—"

Sabine cut Jakob short with a pointed finger. "You don't know what it's like inside that house. Not all of the 'boys' are like Boone. Some are worse than Mason."

Half the people in the circle were nodding in agreement. This wasn't just about freedom for them, it was about vengeance. And he couldn't blame them. They had freed Lyn Askew from her Questionable cage, and had given her what meager food and water the group had, but she was severely malnourished. And she sported scars and bruises from numerous beatings, some at the hands of Mason, some from Boone's men.

Knowing there was nothing he could say to undo years of abuse, Jakob nodded. "Do what you have to."

Anne's small hand gripped his wrist. She mouthed the word 'Mom' at him.

Jakob flinched back from the word. With all of the excitement of mounting an insurrection, he'd forgotten about Ella. He turned to the maids. "There is a woman inside. A prisoner."

"He'll have her in one of these," Charlotte said, motioning to her uniform, "before the day is out. Probably trying to have his way with her right now. It's the same initiation we all got."

Jakob's mind froze up a bit, his thoughts stuttering as he tried to comprehend and deny the horrible words he'd just heard. "You mean...like..."

"He's going to rape her," Shawna said. "If he hasn't already. And if we don't take this place from him today, he'll keep on raping her, right along with the rest of us."

"Fuck this shit." It was Anne. Despite being the youngest and smallest member of the group, she was armed with a handgun. Three of the unarmed people were adults, but Anne had far more experience with weapons than anyone else, including Jakob. She racked the slide, chambering the first round in the 9mm handgun, and stormed toward the exit.

"Anne," Jakob said, chasing after her. "We need to do this right."

She wheeled around on him. "We need to do this *now*."

"We won't be much use to anyone if we're shot before reaching the house."

"Mom is in there. She's...she's..." Anne bared her teeth and slapped Jakob's cheek. "You just pretend to care about her. To care about both of us. But you've never really seen us as family, have you?"

"Anne," Jakob reached for her.

She swatted his hand away. "Go have your little scrum." Her forehead scrunched up, confused for a moment, like she'd said something strange. Then she refocused her glare on Jakob. "I'm going to save my mother."

Anne ran.

Despite being younger and smaller than Jakob, Anne could match his fastest sprint. He had no hope of catching her, but he wasn't about to let her charge into a fight alone. She was wrong, and stupid, and impulsive, but she *was* his sister, and he loved her, even if she didn't believe it.

"We're doing this," he said to the others as he ran backward after Anne. "Now!"

There was just a moment of hesitation, but then Alia followed. Then the maids. And then the rest of them. They had no real plan, but at least surprise would be on their side.

Anne followed the biodome walls toward the house, staying close and low, so anyone looking out from the third floor wouldn't see her. *Stupid,* Jakob thought, *but not dumb.* Jakob followed her lead and motioned for the rest to do the same. They moved in a single file line, snaking toward an uncertain fate.

Anne slowed when she reached the back of the house. She peeked into one of the quarter-sized basement windows and then scooted past. Jakob caught up with her when she stopped at the second. He put his hand on her shoulder, turning her around. "We're with you," he whispered, motioning to the line of people paused behind him. "*I'm* with you. Always will be. But you can't go out there first."

"Why not?"

"You know why," he said. Of all of them, Anne was the least expendable. She had the secrets to ending the Change locked away in her head. She needed to survive. More than him. More than Ella. More than any of the rest of them, and she knew it.

"Fine." She leaned against the wall and let him step past, but snagged his belt as he moved toward the front of the house. "Check the window, dumbass."

Jakob sighed and peeked through the basement window. Nobody home. She let go of his belt and he crept toward the front corner of the house, stopping a foot short. He turned around, eyes wide, and tapped his ear. "Listen," he mouthed to the others.

There were voices. More than one. He couldn't make out what they were saying, but he recognized Ella's voice. And then a second voice. His body tensed. The AK-47 in his hands grew slick from his sweating hands.

Eddie Kenyon...

How is he here? How is he alive?

Jakob held an open palm to the group leaning against the side of the house. Then he pointed at Willie and waved him forward. The old man hobble-jogged to the front of the line. Jakob leaned in close to the man's ear and whispered. "Keep Anne hidden and quiet."

He knew his sister might hate him for it, but if Kenyon was here, she was in more danger than ever.

"Ain't going to be easy," Willie replied. "I've seen what kind of fuss she can kick up."

"Do what you have to do," Jakob said, glancing at Anne who looked irate at being left out of the hushed conversation.

"Aight," Willie said, leaning back. Then he thrust the butt of his rifle into Anne's head. She dropped, but Willie caught her in one arm.

Jakob was enraged. If Kenyon wasn't around the corner, he would have attacked the man. Then Willie hoisted Anne up over his shoulder and mouthed, "Safe and quiet."

Despite his anger at Willie's method, Jakob couldn't deny its effectiveness. Anne would survive, and she wouldn't be around to get herself in trouble. He gave Willie a nod and watched him head back toward the biodomes. Then he heard Ella's voice loud and clear.

"He raped me."

Had Anne been conscious a few seconds longer, and heard that, she would have charged out firing. Jakob was tempted to do the same, but restrained himself. Instead, he slid up to the corner, peeked one eye around the edge and snapped back. He'd seen just a snapshot of what awaited them, but it was enough.

We are so screwed, he thought, and he turned to face the group of insurgents. Killing Mason and a few men might be possible, even for this untrained group of half-starved people. But taking down Riders? His mind flashed back to his previous encounters with the savage creatures. They were stronger, faster, and far more brutal than a human being could be without consuming ExoGenetic food. But they weren't impervious to bullets. His father proved that when he put a round in his mother.

What would Dad do? he asked himself. *Would he wait? Would he fight?* Jakob's thoughts turned to Ella, the only person around the corner who was not his enemy. She was important, and had become a mother-figure in his life. He wasn't sure if he loved her like he did Anne, but he cared about her. And she cared about Anne. Would die for her. Would want to be left to this fate to protect the girl. But this wasn't her call. It was his. And he knew what his father would do. Aside from Jakob, and maybe Anne, Ella was the most important person in the world to his father. And had been for far longer. He loved her. Had loved her even while he loved Jakob's mother. He might have chosen to stay with Kristen over Ella, but Jakob thought that was more for him, than his mother.

Dad would fight for her, he thought. *He would risk everything for her. Everything except for me.*

But Peter wasn't there. Jakob knew his father might sacrifice Ella to save him—he had done as much when Kenyon caught up to them at Alia's house—but that wasn't a decision Jakob could make for him. Dad loved her, and would risk his life to save her. Jakob wanted to do the same. But unlike Anne, or even his father, he wasn't going to rush into a fight he didn't think he could win. Hoping he was making the right call, he turned to face the group and motioned for them to retreat.

TWENTY-FIVE

"What?" Mason said. "I-I did no such thing!"

Kenyon stood his ground, eyes moving from Ella to Mason and then back again.

"We are civilized here," Mason said. "Good people. Surviving. She and her upstart family have been trying to undo all that since they arrived."

"This morning," Ella added. "We've been here just a few hours. How could we disrupt civilization that quickly?"

"The same way you ended it for the rest of the world." It wasn't a logical argument. Mason was trying to appeal to Kenyon's sense of justice. She was the woman who ended the world, after all. Or, at least, that's what the few people surviving outside of ExoGen's San Francisco facility believed. The truth was much more complex. It involved a cabal of people working with her, and then when she had tried to warn people, working against her. Since then, she'd been forced into their employ once more, against her will. Much of it was inexcusable, and in simpler times, worthy of a death sentence. But Eddie Kenyon didn't give a shit. He drank ExoGen's Kool-Aid long ago. He might not know the finer details of their long term plan—even Ella didn't know that—but whatever it was, he was on board.

Or was he?

He wasn't here with helicopters and guns a-blazin'. Instead, he kept the company of monsters. Of Riders. He looked comfortable with them, and they had apparently fully accepted him as one of the pack. This wasn't the ExoGen pickup summoned by Mason, which meant more trouble was on the way.

"Look at me." Ella pointed at her forehead. She didn't know what it looked like, but you didn't take a punch to the forehead without something to show for it. She placed her fingers against her head. It was hot and swollen and conjured a very honest hiss of pain. "I didn't do this to myself, Eddie."

From his position behind the living wall of Riders, Kenyon said, "You'll say anything to survive, Ella."

"That's right," Mason said. "She's a liar. She's—"

"Shut. Your. Mouth." Kenyon pushed his way through the two females, showing no revulsion at the coils of dirty hair rubbing up against him. Even across the twenty foot distance, Ella could smell their stench. Kenyon seemed not to notice.

He's gone native, Ella thought, looking him over from head to toe. Kenyon was still human as far as she could see, which meant that he'd avoided eating ExoGenetic food for the past five weeks. It also meant she had a slim chance of reasoning with him. Or at the very least, manipulating his still very human emotions and desires. Betrayal or not, Kenyon was obsessed with her. He might make her life a living hell, but he'd also keep her alive, and if she was alive, there was hope. Of escape. Of survival. Of fixing the world.

Kenyon stopped ten feet away and crouched. "Tell me the truth."

There was no threat tacked on. Didn't need to be. Ella understood the situation. If Kenyon even suspected she wasn't being forthright, this would end the way he had probably been imagining it for the past five weeks. Part of it anyway. She had no idea what had befallen Peter or the children.

"Fine," Ella said, sitting up a bit straighter, letting an angry fire burn behind her eyes. Kenyon knew the look. He liked the look. Had said so on a number of occasions. "He *tried* to rape me. Was *still* trying when your hairy friend knocked on the door. It wasn't going so well for him until he drew that gun." She motioned to the revolver, which shifted toward her head. "He calls this place civilized, but—"

"Enough!" Mason lunged forward, caught a handful of Ella's shirt, hauled her up and placed the revolver's barrel against her head.

Ella let out a yelp of surprise, despite Mason's actions being exactly what she'd been hoping for. While she was still in mortal danger, Mason had simultaneously made himself Kenyon's enemy and rekindled her ex-boyfriend's protective feelings for her. The pair had been potential allies, but now...now one would kill the other. And given the number of Riders now spreading out, poised to attack, it was pretty clear that the remainder of Mason's time on Earth could be counted down in minutes, if not seconds.

Ella tried not to smile as Mason's arm wrapped around her throat. He dragged her back toward the front door. "One move from you or your ugly bitches, and I'll put a bullet in her head."

"They can understand you." Kenyon looked at the Rider beside him. "Can't you, ugly bitches?"

"Understand," the nearest Rider said. "Kill old man now?"

Mason doubled his pace, but Ella let her body become a dead weight. He could just shoot her, but she was the only thing keeping him alive at the moment. She didn't think the house would help his situation much, but walls were walls. They provided a sense of security, even if it was unjustified.

"Chad!" Mason barked. "The door!"

But Chad had begun backing away, moving down the farmer's porch. He held one hand up and the other out to his side, clutching the assault weapon by the handle in as non-threatening a posture as possible. "If it's all the same to you…" He was speaking to Kenyon, not Mason. "I'll just walk away."

"You traitorous son-of-a-bitch! I knew I shouldn't have trusted a Yankee like you!"

"I'm from Idaho," Chad said, still backing off.

Ella could feel Mason's hand shaking, drilling the revolver's barrel into the side of her head. He wanted to shoot Chad, to vent his anger into the man's skull, but he'd leave himself wide open to attack, and not just from Kenyon or the Riders. The moment that barrel came away from her head, she would strike.

Kenyon watched Chad take a few more steps. "Wait."

Chad stopped, petrified. "Sir?"

Kenyon pointed his assault rifle at Ella. "Was she telling the truth?"

Ella understood the situation instantly. If Chad denied her story of attempted rape, Kenyon would likely shoot her and Mason. But if he confirmed it…the stalemate would continue.

Luckily for her, she had told the truth, and Chad had seen enough to at least confirm a part of it. Even better, confirming the story would keep his attention on Mason. The moment she and Mason died, all attention would shift to Chad.

"Uh, yes, sir. He had her locked up in the dome. When I found them, he had her on the ground, pistol aimed at her head. Looked like she had put up a fight, though."

"She would," Kenyon said.

"And she wasn't the first one. He dresses them up. Watches them bathe. Has a two way mirror in the bathroom. Sometimes he—"

That was all Mason could take. He shifted the barrel of his gun away from her head and toward Chad. Ella tilted her head forward the moment the barrel cleared her skull, and then with all of her strength, threw her head back.

The gun went off.

Chad screamed and dropped to the porch.

Ella's head struck the weapon, and then Mason's face, which she felt fold inward under the force of her strike. His grip loosened. She tore herself away and ducked, knowing what would happen next.

But it didn't play out exactly the way she pictured. Instead of a bullet shot by Kenyon, Mason's end came at the tip of a spear. The weapon was thrown with such force that the blade punched through his face, exited his skull, shattered the storm door's window and embedded in the solid wood door beyond. The storm door shook from the impact, its screws tearing loose from rotted wood. The door came loose, slipped over Mason's twitching form, and toppled to the porch. Mason hung like a puppet in storage, waiting for someone to bring him to life. Then he went suddenly still. His bowels let loose, drizzling stench onto the porch.

Ella moved away from the widening puddle and caught sight of Chad, lying on the porch. He was clutching his arm, still very much alive. She gave him a glare that said, 'stay down,' and turned to face Kenyon, who seemed amused by what had just taken place.

He turned to the Rider beside him. "What was that?"

The furry female shrugged. "He said ugly."

"And not very bright," Kenyon said, eliciting a sneer from the creature, but nothing more. "He had information I could have used."

The female motioned to Mason's lifeless body. "Ask him questions now."

Kenyon's confusion shifted toward annoyance when the female barked a laugh and the others joined in, hooting and slapping themselves.

Kenyon focused on Ella. "I keep on trying to tell them they have poor senses of humor—the punchline usually involves a corpse—but they seem to think they're ready for prime time."

Ella forced herself to stand up straight, despite the fresh pain pulsing through her head. She felt dazed, near passing out again, but through strength of will alone, she managed to stay upright, and step toward Eddie.

Each step down the farmer's porch threatened to send her sprawling, but she didn't use the railing. Didn't want to appear weak. She needed Eddie's affection, but also his respect. Without both, he wouldn't be malleable.

But her body had other plans.

Upon reaching the bottom step, a wave of nausea swept through her. The world spun. She reached for the railing and missed. Knees buckled. She toppled forward, but instead of landing on the ash-covered, scorched earth, she was cradled in a pair of strong arms.

When she opened her eyes again, she saw blue sky and the outline of the farmhouse cutting into it. Kenyon's face slid into view. He looked concerned.

"That's good," she said.

"What's good?" he asked.

She blinked, trying to think clearly, but felt drugged. "The view."

Kenyon looked up at the farmhouse. The sky. The cumulus clouds, promising an afternoon rain.

"This isn't impossible, you know," Kenyon said.

"I don't know."

He looked at her again, amusement mingling with concern. "Once this business with you and your biodomes is wrapped up, we're going to start again. First in San Francisco. Then in other locations around the world. Anywhere you want, Ella. Where do you want to go?"

Kenyon's face blurred, and his words drifted in and out of focus.

Where do I want to go?

"Boston," she said, then cringed as she realized the word had been spoken aloud.

"Boston?" Kenyon sounded surprised. "You know it snows there like six months out of the year, right?"

Ella's pulse quickened. Adrenaline spiked. She'd nearly ruined everything. Her thoughts began to focus. "Kidding," she said. "San Diego. Better yet. Baja. There aren't any borders anymore, right?"

"Right," he said. "And I can make that happen. I can."

As Ella's mind cleared, she began to recall some of what he'd said. None of it made sense to her, but Kenyon clearly knew more than she did about what ExoGen was planning. "How? When?"

"How about this?" he said. "I'll tell you. And I mean everything. No secrets. But first you tell me what's in Boston." While she tried to come up with something believable, he shook his head. "Is that where you've been headed all this time? Kind of a roundabout route, don't you think?"

"You're not with ExoGen," Ella said, looking at one of the Riders. "They left you to die. You don't need to—"

"I've never not been with ExoGen." The words came out like a growl. Kenyon rolled his neck, tempering his anger. "You can either be with them, or dead. Eventually, anyway. And I'm a survivor. Like you. I might have been left for dead by that asshole, Mackenzie, but that wasn't a corporate move. You and your boy toy might have made things personal for me, and believe me, I have dreamed up scenarios for all your deaths that would make you sick, but my loyalty is unflappable."

Ella knew that was true. It was why she was still breathing and not slain in one of the horrible manners he had dreamed up.

"So, you, me and the girls here can pay a visit to Boston, see the sights and head back to San Fran before the first leaves of Fall start to change color. I hear it's beautiful, but I'd rather be on the West Coast when the snow starts falling, wouldn't you? And with the Chunta—" He leaned in close to whisper. "That's what these nasty ladies call themselves." He reverted back to his natural speaking voice. "—we won't have to worry about surviving the journey. Not as much anyway. Though I think our relationship needs to stay platonic. Feesa, their leader since Peter offed his wife, has kind of a thing for me."

Ella couldn't hide her revulsion.

"We're survivors," he said. "We do what we have to. And honestly, it wasn't that bad. Mostly I just pictured you."

Ella wanted to vomit, slit his throat and laugh all at the same time. She'd traded a loveless pervert for a lovesick psychopath. But at least she understood this psychopath. The problem was that he also knew her, and now he knew that Boston was her ultimate destination. Boston wasn't a small city, though, and George's Island was just one of many dotting the coast. *He'll never find it,* she told herself, but the thought lacked conviction. Kenyon was a smart man. And determined. That he'd survived the wild on his own, and befriended a tribe of ExoGens revealed as much.

But as long as Peter and the kids were free, there was a chance they could reach the island first. Once they plugged Anne in, Ella's presence shouldn't be needed. She wasn't certain about that. Anne's...design had never been tested. Any number of things could go wrong. But there was still a chance.

Ella closed her eyes and pushed her will toward the children. *Run. Wherever you are. Run.*

It was the closest she'd come to praying in a long time, and apparently just as useless.

"Put up your hands and step back!" The voice was angry and full of faux authority. It was also young and very familiar. Ella opened her eyes to see Jakob, standing in the farmhouse's doorway, an AK-47 raised at Kenyon's head. "Get away from her. Now."

TWENTY-SIX

Jakob had looked death in the eyes more times in the last few weeks than he thought anyone should throughout their lifetime. Nearly every living thing in the world wanted to kill and eat him, and not necessarily in that order. But in all of those instances, he hadn't tried to hide his fear. Wouldn't have been able to, even if he had tried.

But now, Ella's life was on the line.

The woman his father loved.

His sister's mother.

So when he aimed the AK-47 at Eddie Kenyon, half his mind was focused on the target. The other half was trying to hide his shaking, keep the contents of his stomach locked down and keep the wetness in his eyes from spilling over. If Kenyon saw any of these signs of weakness, he might act. And if he did that, Jakob was dead.

Kenyon would outshoot him. And not because Jakob was a bad shot, or even afraid of taking a human life. What he was afraid of, aside from his own painful demise, was that his bullet would take the wrong human life. In the time it took him to pull the trigger, Kenyon could slip behind Ella.

Jakob was there to save Ella, not kill her.

What made it all worse was that Kenyon showed no fear at all.

"I don't recall the prodigal son returning with an AK-47," Kenyon said.

Jakob said nothing. He'd put everything he had into his first words. Speaking now would reveal the quiver in his voice. Instead he adjusted his aim slightly, putting the crosshairs between Kenyon's eyes.

"I can wait," Kenyon said. "Kid like you can't hold that weapon up forever. Better off just taking the shot now."

Jakob blinked.

He was right.

But the moment he pulled the trigger, several things would happen at once. Ella might be shot, either by Jakob or Kenyon, though he doubted Kenyon would kill her. After what he'd seen and heard, he was pretty sure that Ella's ex still clung to the idea that they had some kind of future. Then there were the Riders. As dangerous as Kenyon was, they were worse. And Jakob's rag-tag militia, who were taking up positions throughout the house, wouldn't be much safer behind walls and bars that the ExoGenetic women could tear through like paper.

It would be a blood bath. For both sides. But Kenyon had the advantage. He had Ella, and he was right; he could wait. The assault rifle already felt heavy in Jakob's arms. He'd gained a good amount of strength and stamina on the road, not to mention survival skills. But five weeks of toughening couldn't really compensate for years of sitting behind a computer screen, shooting up digital bad guys and taunting human opponents with variations of 'noob,' 'newbie,' and his personal favorite, 'umad bro?'

In the multiplayer gaming realm, his style had been bold, reckless and effective. He'd charge into a room, praying and spraying, draining his rapid fire weapon of choice, and more often than not, it worked. But only because there was no fear associated with what was essentially a suicidal tactic. His life was expendable because if he died, he would respawn a few seconds later and be right back at it. He understood that. But most players still reacted with fear, as if their digital life still meant something, and that's why it worked.

In games.

This was real life. If he died here, there would be no second chance. And praying and spraying...that would get Ella killed for sure.

He lacked his father's skill, strength and patience. He couldn't take a masterful shot and know, without a doubt, that he could hit Kenyon and not Ella. He couldn't come up with a plan that would then deal with the primitive Rider rage that would follow and still likely lead to his and Ella's demise.

Umad bro? he thought at himself. As much as he liked using the obnoxious taunt, he hated being on the receiving end of it even more. He squinted, adjusting his aim once more, as a new kind of rage tamped down his fear and he considered, really considered, trying something crazy.

But he couldn't do it alone.

Luckily, he didn't have to.

Glass shattered behind him. Windows belched glass from the first and second floors of the house. It clattered against the porch floor and slid down the porch roof like rain water. A dozen weapons slid through the gaping holes, aiming at Kenyon and the Riders, who were growing agitated.

Kenyon smiled. "Well, now. Looks like a genuine stand-off."

"A stand-off is when both sides are evenly matched," Jakob said, surprising even himself. His rising anger had soothed his churning stomach, bolstered the strength in his arms and removed the fear from his voice. "This isn't a case of mutually assured destruction."

Kenyon scanned the area, looking at the weapons pointed in his direction. "But I have her." Faster than Jakob could react, Kenyon slipped fully behind Ella. To put a bullet in Kenyon would mean putting it through Ella first.

Jakob's aim wavered for a moment, but then zeroed in on Ella. If Kenyon attacked, he'd have no choice. *Please God,* Jakob thought, *don't make me have to kill her.*

Ella's eyes met Jakob's. Once she had his attention, she gave a subtle nod. Permission to shoot. Then she glanced at her shoulder, and followed it with a wide eyed glare. She wasn't just giving him permission to shoot her, she was telling him to. If he put the bullet through her arm, it would hit Kenyon's as well. If they were lucky, it would make him drop his weapon, or at least give Ella the chance to break free or attack. If they were unlucky, and his aim was off by a few inches, Ella could die.

Do something suicidal, Jakob thought. *He'll never see it coming.* But this wasn't his life he was putting at risk.

"I can see it in your eyes, kid," Kenyon said. "You have the look of a man about to do something stupid."

Jakob felt a measure of despair return. Kenyon saw it coming, saw it broadcast on Jakob's face.

"Aww, don't look so sad." Kenyon chuckled. "You're not your dad. Probably never will be. Some people are born strong. Some people go through the forge and come out strong on the other side. Like Ella. But most people...most people just melt. You're melting, kid."

"Umad bro?" Jakob said.

"What?"

"You mad?"

Kenyon's voice took on the familiar tone Jakob had heard in many a team deathmatch game. "*What?*"

"You think you've got the win. You think you're walking out of here alive? That any of you are? Ella would rather die than go with you. I know that, because she told us all about you. About your whiny voice. About how you fawn over her like a little school boy. About how she played you. A bat of the eyelashes, and you did exactly what she wanted. Even now, even after knowing the truth about what you mean to her, you're still willing to risk everything just to get her back? One of us never left high school, and it isn't me."

Kenyon said nothing, but looked furious.

Jakob finished with the coup de grâce that lowered the IQ of most guys. "She also told about your little dick."

Kenyon's eyes twitched, but he didn't move. Didn't talk, either, which meant he was getting angry. Really angry.

The real icing on his rage cake was when the dick comment elicited chuckling from the Rider females.

"So, bro," Jakob said. "Umad?"

"Little shit!" Kenyon shouted, stepping back from Ella and raising his weapon.

Jakob cringed at the realization that Kenyon was reversing the tactic Ella had requested. He was going to put a bullet through her—maybe a bunch of them. The resulting spray of shattered lead would burst out the front of her body and strike Jakob.

But Kenyon never got the chance.

A single round was fired from the second floor window, striking Kenyon's shoulder. He spun, dropped his weapon and fell to the ground. Someone from the second floor had saved Ella's life.

Momentarily.

The Riders twisted to watch Kenyon fall, and then coiled to spring. Ella would die first. Then Jakob. Then the people holed up in the house, and maybe even the rest of Hellhole's residents hiding in the unfinished biodome, including Anne.

But the next sound to cut through the air wasn't a gunshot, a scream or an ExoGen battle cry. It was the thunderous *whup, whup, whup,* of a helicopter.

TWENTY-SEVEN

"You're late. Get up."

Anne opened her eyes. The sprawl of her bedroom surrounded her. Clothes covered the floor, posters hung on the walls, and her dog, Jasper, stood bedside, wagging his tail.

"C'mon, now" her mother said, rapping the locked door with her knuckles.

"I'm up," Anne said, but something about her voice sounded off. When she sat up, Jasper couldn't hold himself back anymore. He jumped onto the bed, stepped into her personal space and started licking. Anne fended him off, shaking his cheeks and ears. Then she squished up his loose fur, transforming his Labrador face into something closer to a pug. "Who's a squishy boy? You are."

There was that voice again. *I need a drink,* she thought, but instead of heading for the bathroom, she climbed out of bed and moved to her desk. While the rest of the room looked like it had survived a nuclear war, the desk was a gleaming bastion of organization. It wasn't empty. Not even close. But the text books, note pads, pens and pencils all had their place.

She pulled a sketchbook out from beneath the stack of biology books and gently sifted through the pages, finding the most recent entry. There were notes scrawled in pencil, sketches of wildflowers and a folded up piece of paper towel. She opened the towel to find a pressed flower. "Hello, little daisy."

It looked perfect. Better than the last one, which had lost petals on one side, and looked like a balding man with a bushy beard.

Three knocks filled the room, and she nearly shouted at her mother. But then she realized where the knocks had come from and clamped her mouth shut. Anne moved to the window, tugged the shade down and let it snap up. The boy on the other side nearly fell away in surprise, but he managed to cling to the overhang.

Jasper leapt up, front paws on the sill, and barked.

"He needs to go out," her mother shouted from somewhere in the house.

"I know!" Anne replied and opened the window.

Jasper assaulted the boy with licks. The boy laughed, pushed the dog aside and slid into the room. It wasn't a graceful entrance, but it was silent.

He'd had practice.

Had been visiting her for years.

But...who is he? Anne wondered, and then she realized there was a third person in the room. A girl with brown hair, like hers, but straighter and longer. A lot longer.

The girl petted Jasper and said, "I'll let you out in a minute." Then to the boy, "You're early."

"You're late." He smiled and Anne saw something familiar about him. "Overslept again? You know, just because you get 'A's on all your tests doesn't mean that Mrs. Heintz won't dock you for missing classes."

"Won't miss any if you leave and let me change." The girl gave the boy a playful shove.

"I'll just turn around." The boy faced the window. "Won't peek, I swear."

"Pete!" The girl said, kicking the boy.

Pete? Anne tried to speak, but she couldn't. This was *her* room. *She* was late for school. Who were these kids, and what were they doing in her room?

It's a dream, she thought. But that wasn't right. It was more than that. *It's a memory. Mom's memory. And the boy. He's...dad.*

"If my parents find you up here, you're a dead man."

He nodded and smiled. "Even deader if you're changing. But it'd be worth it."

The girl...Ella...smiled. "Thought you weren't going to look?"

God, Anne thought, *they flirted like that when they were kids, too. How old are they anyway?* She looked at the pair. Fourteen at least. Maybe fifteen. Teenagers in full bloom.

Peter shrugged, and headed back to the window.

"Perv," Ella said, but she didn't look at all upset.

"Meet me out front?" Peter said.

"You should go ahead. My grades aren't really a concern, but yours..."

Peter shook his head. "Not going to leave you."

"My hero."

Peter hung outside the window, poised to climb back down the pipe he had used to scale the wall hundreds of times during their childhood. Anne remembered it all. Remembered what happened next, too. "Heroes get rewarded, you know."

Without thinking it through, Ella lifted her shirt and flashed Peter. She'd done it twice before, but never after having just woken up...braless.

Peter was so stunned that he lost his grip and fell.

Anne felt herself slip into her father's perspective. She saw the blue sky above, and then coughed in pain as she struck the ground. Peter had sprained his ankle that day. Hopped to the front stairs, threw himself on them and pretended he'd tripped. Instead of school, he and Ella spent the morning at the hospital. No one found out about the pipe. Her father was a crafty man, in more ways than one, and he really did love her mother. And she loved him. She'd understood this on the surface level, but had never really felt that kind of romantic love, or even affection for a member of the opposite sex. And now, she'd lived her mother's feelings for her father, which was eye-opening, and kind of gross.

But it helped her understand them.

The vision turned hazy and speckled as a tingling sensation rolled from her fingers and toes to her torso.

Then darkness, followed by a face.

When she saw Willie standing over her, looking concerned, she knew the dream-like memory had come to an end. "Sheeit, kid, you had me scared."

"Says the old asshole who knocked me unconscious."

"Did what had to be done."

Anne sat up and found herself back in the unfinished biodome. She was lying on the concrete foundation, surrounded by the feeble and hungry residents of Hellhole Bay. She winced and held the back of her head. "You throw me down like a sack of rocks? Geez."

"You had a seizure or something," Willie said. "Bucked yourself free."

"Maybe that's what happens when you clock a twelve year old girl with the butt of a rifle?"

"Like I said—"

"Did what you had to do. I heard. How long was I out?"

"Just got back." Willie shrugged. "Not much more than a minute."

"What's happening?"

"Don't know. Your brother got spooked by something. Said to bring you here. Seemed like he thought you were in a specific kind of danger."

ExoGen, Anne thought. *Has to be.*

Anne looked back and forth, scanning the group of people hiding along the back wall. Not one of them had a weapon. But Willie did.

The old man noted her attention and took a step back. "You got some sass to you, but ain't no way you're disarming me."

She considered the idea, but quickly dismissed it. Willie was old, but he had already proven himself tough. He'd probably knock her unconscious again.

"You're Ella's girl?" a tired voice asked. It was the woman they'd come here to find, Lyn Askew. "You look a lot like her. Like your father, too."

"You knew my father?" Anne asked. She'd woken with a large chunk of her mother's childhood memories dumped into her mind, like they were her own, but this woman wasn't in any of them.

"Knew of him. She kept a photo of him in her office. Spoke highly of him when I asked. I think losing him was one of the toughest experiences of her life."

"Probably harder for the wife he was cheating on."

Lyn smiled. Her dry lips cracked. Beads of blood formed and smeared like lipstick. The woman didn't notice. "Imagine so. But it was good to see them together. Is she happy?"

Happy? "Lady, the world has gone to hell, largely because of my mother's work. She's one of the most hated people on the planet, by the few people who are still alive and capable of feeling anything beyond abject fear."

"But not him," Lyn pointed out.

Anne sighed, her thoughts drifting back through the past few weeks. Her memory recalling window visits made by young Peter. She felt the joy he brought her. "Yeah," she finally said. "She's happy."

"And you?"

"Me? What about me?"

"I noticed you're a little more...fleshed out than your family. You've been enjoying the fruits of our labor, haven't you?"

"What's she talking about?" Willie asked.

"Nothing."

Lyn waived her off. "I helped work on you, you know. Tell me, how does it taste? As good as I've imagined? Better, I'm guessing. I put some of that same work into the food here." She motioned to the completed domes behind her. "Made it safe to eat, but it lost some of the flavor. Not all of it, mind you. Still the best vegetables I've ever had...when I was allowed to eat them...but not the same as the good stuff. Not what you've been eating."

"Shut-up, lady," Anne growled, but it was too late.

"Now, hold on a minute." Willie gripped her shoulder. "You've been eating the ExoGenetic crops? On the outside?"

A few of the people around them heard his question and perked up. A few more looked terrified and shuffled away.

"It's okay." Lyn dismissed Willie with her hand, but could only keep it up for a second before her strength wavered. She'd been fed and given water, but it would take days of the same before she really started to recover from the mistreatment she'd suffered as one of Mason's Questionables. "The girl is immune to the effects of RC-714."

"Bullshit," Willie said. "How?"

"She was made that way. Designed. And when you're building a person, it's not impossible to remove all those genes that RC-714 wakes up. Through millennia of evolution, all living things adapt to new environments and evolve, sometimes becoming something stunningly different from where it started. When this happens, the old, now useless adaptations are locked away as junk DNA, never to be accessed again. It's like partitioning a hard drive and separating old data into an encrypted file. RC-714 removed the encryption. But with Anne..."

"You wiped the hard drive clean," Anne said. "But not completely."

Lyn looked confused. "How do you mean?"

"I mean I've got my mother's memories. Some of them anyway. And I know things she knows, but I shouldn't. And, you all put a thumb drive in the *Back. Of. My. Head.*" Anne tapped her head with each of the last four words.

Lyn looked mortified. "I—I had no idea. It doesn't sound possible."

Anne turned the back of her head toward the woman. Pointed to the mole that covered the USB port. Her mother had cut it open five weeks ago, to show Peter, but when it healed, it didn't heal shut. It was more like a tab of skin that could be opened and closed. So she dug a nail in and lifted the skin flap.

Willie leaned back, repulsed. "Who does this to their kid?"

Lyn leaned closer. "But...why?"

"All of her research is in there," Anne said. "But I think it's more than that. I think she made a digital copy of herself. Of her knowledge. Even her memories. And some of them are leaking out."

Willie turned away, rubbing his hands through his hair, clearly disturbed by what he'd seen and heard. Lyn turned her eyes down, deep in thought, no doubt pondering the thumb drive's purpose. While the pair were lost in thought, Anne stood. Without making a sound, she weaved her way past the people now staring at her. She gave them fake smiles and kept on going, heading for the one way out of the dome where Willie couldn't follow.

The door connecting the unfinished dome to the finished one led to a functional airlock and decontamination chamber. It was no doubt locked from the inside, the outer access panel turned off, but Anne knew her way around the system as well as anyone. She knelt at the controls and pushed against what looked like a solid metal wall. It shifted in with a clunk.

Anne glanced back. Lyn was still on another planet. Willie had started to look for her, but was searching in the wrong direction.

She pulled the panel away, revealing coils of wires and circuitry.

Where did Mason get all of this? He might have been able to put it all together, but he certainly couldn't duplicate this technology. There were supposed to be ten biodomes up and down the East Coast. Her mother had marked them on a map at Peter's request. But Anne guessed at least six of those, maybe more, never got built. Mason had stolen these domes, from the people they'd been intended for. People who could have helped her mother. Without knowing it, he had helped ExoGen's cause.

"Hey!" Willie had spotted her and was charging toward her. The old man's scowl said he meant business.

Anne flipped a switch that activated the outer door. She left the panel off and punched in a five digit sequence into the keypad.

"The hell are you doing?" Willie said. And when the door whooshed open, he broke into a jog. "Hey! Kid! I told your brother I'd—"

Willie's voice was silenced by the closing door. He thumped his fists against the outer glass, shouting something, but his voice was muffled beyond the point of discernment. And without the five digit override code, he wouldn't be following her.

Standing in the first chamber, Anne began shedding clothes. She'd been in the wild far too long for the system to reliably suck up every bit of ExoGenetic material from all the folds of her clothes. She discarded her shoes, pants and shirt, until all she had on was matching white underwear and a tank top. "I look like Ripley," she muttered, wondered who Ripley was, and then she recalled a movie her mother had seen as a child. The film had terrified young Ella, but didn't seem all that dissimilar from the world her mother had helped create.

Anne stepped into the decontamination room, closed the door behind her, and stood still as the turbines did their thing, whipping her body with a tornado of wind, stripping every loose fiber and seed from her body, clothes and hair. When it was done, she stepped inside the familiar confines of a biodome. It smelled lush and delicious. Her mouth watered. But she didn't linger or even take a snack for the road. She ran barefoot, across the greenhouse, where it attached to the next biodome via a second decontamination chamber.

Mason hadn't taken any chances. Even if one dome became contaminated, the others wouldn't be. Had he been a good man, Hellhole compound would have been an oasis. She repeated the process, over and over until she reached the final decontamination chamber leading to the farmhouse. She entered the chamber, waiting somewhat impatiently for it to run its course, and then stepped out into the farmhouse. To her right was a laundry room, stacked with folded clothing. She ducked into the room and tore through the clothing until she found a pair of blue sweatpants that weren't obscenely too large. She cinched the drawstring tight and slipped back into the hall. She could hear people moving around on the first and second floors. Hushed voices. *The house was supposed to be mostly empty,* she thought, glancing into the kitchen for a knife or a frying pan. Then Charlotte walked across the hall, ducking low, a rifle in her hands. *They already took the house?*

Commands were hissed across the first floor and repeated upstairs. A moment later, several windows shattered. It sounded like every window at the front of the house. She stepped into the hallway and froze. The front door was open. Jakob was framed by it, standing on the porch, aiming an AK-47 at her mother. No, not at her mother...at the man hiding behind her like a coward.

Eddie.

She couldn't hear what was being said, but she understood the situation. She ducked into the kitchen, found a knife and then tip-toed to the staircase. There were eight people on the first floor, all aiming their weapons outside. *That's a lot of firepower for one man,* she thought, then she sprang up the stairs. An unarmed woman standing at the top of the stairs, no doubt positioned to help coordinate, looked surprised by her arrival, but said nothing. Anne had been knocked out and carried away, but they were still on the same team. That, and Anne gave the woman her best, 'get the fuck out of my way,' glare, while doing nothing to hide the blade in her hands.

"How many are out there?" Anne asked.

The woman shrugged. "Not sure it matters. They're huge. Starting to think this was a bad idea."

Anne ignored the woman's fear and headed for the bedroom at the front of the house. She stepped inside the room and found Carrie and

Shawna, each armed with a rifle, pointed out the window. Both women turned when she entered, but said nothing. Anne quickly assessed the pair, moved to Carrie and whispered. "You even shot a rifle before?"

"Not really."

"Not really? That's pretty much a yes or no question." Anne wrapped her small hand around the weapon's barrel. Carrie resisted. Wanted to be part of the fight. Good for her, but bad for the people she was supposed to be covering, which included her brother and mother. "You can give it to me, or I can give you this knife."

Carrie glanced at the menacing steak knife. Anne hadn't directly threatened her, but Carrie read between the lines and lifted her hands away. Anne hefted the big rifle up, leaned her shoulder into it and looked out the window.

She nearly gasped, but held it in. Kenyon's companions were just about the last thing Anne expected to see. Riders. Each of them as ugly as Jakob's mother had become before Peter killed her. And they seemed to be following Kenyon's lead, waiting for a command.

She focused on what was being said and nearly laughed when she heard Jakob say, "She also told us about your little dick."

Kenyon didn't like that, but he stayed hidden behind Ella. *Hidden from Jakob*, she thought, adjusting her aim. *But not from me.*

When the hairy beasts beside him revealed they had a sense of humor, laughing at Jakob's jab, laughing at Kenyon, the man's face turned red.

"So, bro," Jakob said. "Umad?"

"Little shit!" Kenyon took a step back and raised his weapon toward her mother's back.

Anne exhaled.

Slipped her finger around the trigger.

Prayed that Carrie had chambered a round.

And squeezed.

The rifle bucked hard, punching her shoulder back with the same force Willie had used to knock her unconscious. The boom echoed and faded, giving way to Kenyon's scream of pain, and then the thunderous roar of modern killing machines. Anne adjusted her rifle's aim, as the first Apache attack helicopter swung past overhead. It made a tight circle over the compound and then hovered. Then a familiar, blue Black Hawk helicopter flew into view and descended. A soldier clad in black stood in the open side door, manning a machine gun.

Kenyon leapt to his feet waving his good arm.

The soldier leaned forward a little, looked surprised, then offered a wave. After speaking to the pilot for a moment, the chopper began to descend, its rotor wash blasting the house, kicking up a cloud of ash and flattening the weaker buildings in the nearby shanty town.

It took all of Anne's willpower to not shoot Eddie in the head. But if she did that, then these choppers might open fire, killing everyone in the house and the family she hoped to save.

Then she realized it wasn't her family she should be worried about.

They're here for me, she thought. And while she wasn't a coward, and would happily face these odds in a fight, she was beginning to understand that the fate of the human race might just reside in her head. If ExoGen found her...the human race would be replaced by whatever ExoGen was cooking up.

She ducked back out of the window and turned to the two women. "I need to hide. Now."

TWENTY-EIGHT

Eddie Kenyon felt like he'd been dipped in the Jordan River by John the Baptist himself, remade and reborn. But this transformative moment wouldn't be followed by miracles, parables or his martyrdom. His remaining time on Earth *would* change mankind's outcome for the next two thousand years, though. Probably longer. Time would be measured in three epochs: B.C., A.D. and A.C.—*After Change.*

Ella refused to see it, covering her vision with moral scruples. And people like the now dead Mason were incapable of seeing it.

But he could see it, just as clearly as he could see the familiar Apache helicopter swinging into position. The war machine had enough firepower to wipe out every living soul in the Hellhole compound, human or otherwise. And it wasn't alone. He could hear the second Apache, not far away, and the Black Hawk, which roared into view above the farmhouse. The side door was open. His man, Hutchins, stood behind the machine gun.

The open door and prepped weapon told him they hadn't just stumbled on Hellhole. They came here knowing they would find people, and if they came here at all, it meant they knew exactly who they would find. Hutchins was here for Ella and Anne, still trying to complete their mission, so they could return to the safety of ExoGen's San Francisco facility.

Kenyon glanced at the limp form of Mason, hanging from the open front door. He offered the dead man his silent thanks for summoning ExoGen to the site, and then waved at the chopper. He smiled when Hutchins responded with a smile and wave. Despite being left for dead, these were still his men.

And that meant the brazen little shit Peter had spawned would soon meet his maker, along with everyone else in hiding in the farmhouse, including the asshole who put a bullet through his arm. As the chopper descended, sending a whirlwind of ash and debris into the air, Kenyon looked at the wound. It was more than a graze, but the bullet had punched clean through. He'd had worse. Much worse. But the bullet had hit a nerve or tendon, limiting the functionality of his right hand.

He knelt to pick up his weapon, hoping that no one in the house was stupid enough risk a confrontation with the Apache. When no one fired on him, he grasped the weapon with his left hand. He'd still be able to fire it, but his speed and aim would be diminished until his right arm healed. With two Apaches and a Black Hawk, though, not to mention the hardened men inside them, he could order the deaths of everyone here without pulling a trigger.

And he wasn't the only one who knew it.

"Eddie," Ella said. "You can let these people live."

"I could," he said, and let that linger.

"I'll come with you."

"We already played that game once," he said, recalling the last time they had captured Ella and flown away, only to be sent back after her daughter. Eddie's priority had been Ella, and he'd allowed himself to be duped by her affections, which part of him still believed were genuine. But ExoGen had different priorities. They wanted Anne, and he wouldn't be allowed to return home without her. "Where's Anne?"

"I don't know," Ella said, and he actually believed her. If Mason had her locked up inside the house, then she might not really know where the girl was. But the kid would know.

He turned to Jakob. "Back to square one, Jake."

"Go fuck a duck," Jakob said, but he kept his weapon aimed at the ground.

"You've been around Anne too long," Kenyon said. "Picked up some of her potty mouth."

"You've been screwing ExoGens too long," the kid replied, but he was only pretending to have a set of balls. Kenyon saw right through his bravado. But he did raise a valid point.

Kenyon observed the Chunta for a moment. They were nervous and confused by the arrival of the choppers. They probably viewed them as ExoGenetic predators, but they might also remember seeing them before.

With the arrival of his men, and their modern weapons, the creatures became a liability, and he'd have no problem leaving them, or worse. But for now, he needed their unpredictable nature contained.

"Chunta," he said, addressing them all. The hairy females gave him their attention. He pointed at the helicopters. "Friends." He patted his chest, wincing as he moved his right arm. "My friends. *Your* friends."

They didn't look convinced, but they didn't attempt to argue, either.

"Trust Eddie," he said, and he nearly backhanded Ella when she laughed. But he controlled himself and gave the nearest female a pat on the arm. She looked him in the eyes, her true thoughts unreadable, or perhaps non-existent. "Trust Eddie."

When the female grunted her agreement, he said. "Stay here." He pointed at the farmhouse, indicating the people hiding within. "Watch them. If they move, kill them."

A louder grunt meant she understood. Killing was second nature to the monsters he'd lived among for more than a month. But that dark time in his life would soon be a memory he could let go.

The chopper landed a safe distance away. Hutchins stepped out from the side door, a second man now manning the gun. But Hutchins didn't approach. Wasn't about to put himself at risk. He could see the weapons still sticking out of the windows. Could see the Chunta bobbing and anxious, and was probably confounded by the fact that the monsters weren't simply tearing into every human being around.

Kenyon pointed his rifle at Ella and motioned toward the Black Hawk with it. "Let's go have a chat with our old friends, eh?" He smiled at Jakob. "And you, enjoy the last few minutes of your life. Too bad, dad's not here to share in the fun."

"Eddie," Ella said. "Don't be a dick."

Eddie chuckled. He missed Ella's straight forward nature. And even if she didn't love him, she was going to be with him. They would ring in the A.C. together. And if they could find Anne, who was undoubtedly nearby, Ella would do whatever he asked. No one was more precious to her than her daughter.

"Hey, I'm just having a good time. If I were being a dick, the kid would be dead already." And he really did want to kill the kid. The problem was that if Ella didn't know where Anne was, and Peter was M.I.A., or perhaps already dead in the swamps, then Jakob might be the only person who knew where Anne was hiding. And if they didn't find her soon, the girl was bold enough, and probably skilled enough, to head out into the wild on her own, never to be found. "Now move it."

He followed Ella toward the chopper, appreciating the sway of her hips in the flowing white skirt. She'd cleaned up well under Mason's brief care. Eddie still didn't appreciate the shaved head look, but it would grow out. And really, any look Ella tried would be better than the Chunta punta he'd experienced.

Granted, not all of it had been bad. He'd gotten to know a more primal side of himself, but it was comparable to finding the virtues in a fruitcake. A starving man might be able to find them palatable, but if an apple pie came along, well, the fruitcake is seen for what it is: an ugly, nasty-tasting brick that people were willing to buy once a year, but not eat.

With Ella back, he was done with metaphorical fruitcakes.

Hutchins looked slimmer than Kenyon remembered. Had kind of a haunted look in his pale eyes, too. Viper Squad had seen some tough times without his leadership. But they were still alive. Still fighting. And very present.

When he and Ella got within fifty feet of the chopper, Hutchins came forward to meet them. The rotor was still slowing, but talking over the engine's whine would be tough. He moved with caution at first, but broke into a faster walk when Kenyon stepped out from behind Ella and smiled. When the two met, Kenyon shook the other man's hand and winced from the pain. Hutchins drew back. "Shit. Sorry, sir. Didn't see that you were wounded."

Kenyon looked at the bloodied arm. "The least of our concerns."

Hutchins looked past him at the gathered forces of people and Chunta. "We didn't think you were alive. Some guy radioed from this location. Said he had Ella and the girl."

Kenyon nodded, but said nothing. He had a lot of questions, and a good number of requests, but there was one pressing issue that needed to be resolved. "Where's Mackenzie?"

"We went back for you," Hutchins said. "But by the time we got there, your body... You, were gone."

"Where is he?"

"Dead," Hutchins flexed his hands. "Should be, by now. We were going to shoot him. For what he did. But he got away. Pretty sure he had a bullet in him, though. Even if he didn't, there's no way he'd make it alone."

"*I* did," Kenyon said, looking back at the Chunta. "Though I wasn't exactly alone."

"Mackenzie isn't you, sir."

That was true. Mackenzie was a soldier. A good soldier. But he played by the rules, and Peter being a Marine—and a CSO to boot—had shifted the man's allegiance. Despite there being no U.S. government, and no more Marine Corps, the man couldn't betray a fellow jarhead. And that kind of straight forward thinking didn't work in the new world. If you weren't willing to break any and every rule or notion of right and wrong, and didn't have men and helicopters to back you up, you were as good as dead.

"Good enough," Kenyon said, though he regretted not being able to crush Mackenzie's head beneath his boot. He'd thought of nothing but revenge for the past month, and so far, the objects of his wrath were all still alive. Someone had to die today, but first he would reclaim his future.

"How many are left?"

It was a vague question, but Hutchins understood it. "Manke, Kissock and Drummond...obviously."

They were the pilots. Kenyon had already deduced as much. But he didn't need pilots now, he needed boots on the ground.

"Then there's Mendez and Crawford."

Kenyon had already seen Mendez take Hutchins's position behind the machine gun, where he should stay. But Crawford was a good fighter. Loyal, too. "Who else?"

"Uhh, that's it, sir."

"What the hell happened?"

"We were on the ground. Refueling. Thought we were safe, but this... I think it might have been a spider. It-it..."

"I get it," Kenyon said. He was disappointed in Viper Squad, but a team is only as good as its leadership, and while Hutchins was a solid warrior, he wasn't exactly Alexander the Great when it came to strategy. "I want Crawford with us. Tell the choppers to kill anything that moves..." He pointed to the Chunta. "Except for them. For now."

"What about her?" Hutchins motioned to Ella.

"She's going to call Anne for us."

"I'll do no such—ahh!"

Ella's voice was cut short by a shout of pain, as Eddie snatched her pinky finger and snapped it quickly back. He didn't want to hurt her, but he knew how to draw pain without permanently disfiguring. And when Anne heard her mother crying out, the girl would come running.

TWENTY-NINE

Hiding was for cowards. Anne believed it with all her heart, but she also *knew* better. Hiding meant surviving, and survival was the name of the game. Sometimes an enemy could be defeated simply by staying alive long enough for something else to kill it for you. In this case, hiding meant the human race as it had evolved over millions of years, still had a chance to reclaim the planet from what ExoGen had done to it.

She believed that even more than she believed hiding equaled cowardice. But was that really how she felt, or were those her mother's emotions leaching into her, along with her memories and knowledge? Or maybe she was having a similar emotional response to those memories? She was her mother's daughter, after all, even more than the average daughter.

Shawna the maid, who wasn't really a maid, but had been dressed up like one, led her to a large bedroom at the back of the house. It had a king size bed, perfectly made with the fluffiest, most inviting comforter set that Anne had ever seen. As she walked past the bed, part of her longed to climb into it, fall asleep and forget the world and her part in it. Then she smelled the room. It was distinctly masculine. Like something she'd smelled as a child. Her father's scent.

That's mom's memory, Anne thought, identifying the scent as Old Spice, and recalling the cologne's beige bottle with a sailboat. Her mother had liked the smell. But it was tinged with something else Anne couldn't identify. Something that made her wince. Shawna too, though she suspected the woman knew what she was smelling, and it twisted her face up with discomfort. Bad things happened in this room.

Shawna rounded an old dresser that looked hand-carved, like some kind of ancient antique. Above it was a fancy gilded mirror, like something out of a fairy tale. *Probably taken from a museum,* Anne thought, and she paid the furniture and décor no more attention. Shawna opened a door, revealing a walk-in closet stocked with the clothes of a Southern gentleman.

"We're going to hide in a closet?" she protested. "Isn't that like a cliché or something? Won't this be the first place someone will look?"

Shawn ignored her and began separating the shirts hanging on the left side of the closet. "I found this by accident. I didn't go inside, but I think I know what it is."

"I don't see anything," Anne said. "It's just—"

Shawna pressed on the wall. The small amount of pressure revealed a thin rectangular seam. When she removed her hands, a door popped open. It was just three feet tall and two feet wide, but big enough to fit through. Big enough for an adult to fit through. "I don't think this was part of the original house. But Mason was a contractor. I think he added this space, or at least converted a large closet into two separate spaces."

"Why would he need a secret room inside a house he controlled?" Anne asked. "Is it like a safe room?"

Shawn frowned. "I don't think so. Let me go in first.'"

"Whatever is in there, I can handle it." Anne pushed the woman aside. "I have seen things that would make you puke. Hell, I've done things that would make you puke. Nothing in here could be worse. And we don't really have a choice."

"Suit yourself," Shawna said. As kind as the woman was being by hiding her, Anne sensed that the woman had paper-thin patience. And who could blame her? She'd been a prisoner and slave for how long? And now a kid she didn't know was bossing her around.

But Anne didn't think there was time for being nice. Not now. Not until Kenyon was dead or gone. Because if he found her... She didn't want to think about it, but images of ExoGen came unbidden to her thoughts. Her earliest memories were just a few years old. At first, they weren't that bad. People were kind. In retrospect, they were too kind—the sort of nice that people put on like a mask to hide what they were really thinking. Then came the tests: mental, physical and emotional. Her mother took part in some, at first, but was later pulled from the project. The project of her. These memories had been vague up until now. Or perhaps repressed. But her mother's leaching memories were bringing out details.

While her mother grew more fond of Anne, treating her like an actual daughter, rather than a creation, Anne began to feel more and more like a lab rat. She didn't know what they were looking for, or testing for, but they were relentless, until one day, they weren't. She had, apparently, failed their tests. It was then that she had been allowed to live with her mother full time.

A memory slipped into her mind. Her mother's. And unlike most, it was more recent.

She was in an office. Someplace fancy. The air was pure. Smelled like a thunderstorm. A bald man sat behind a desk, back to her. He was looking out a window, large enough to squeeze an elephant through. It looked out upon an empty city with a massive red bridge and a fog shrouded ocean beyond. The view was both disconcerting, and inspiring.

"Lawrence," Ella said. "You don't need to terminate this one."

"I heard you grew attached," the man said, his voice echoing off the sharp angles in the sparsely decorated space. "You know better."

"None of them need to be terminated," Ella countered.

"You know we don't have the resources to feed them yet." The man's fingers tapped on the armrest. Bored. "Nor do we have the time or personnel to raise them. Teach them. If bleeding hearts ran this place, rather than logical minds, we would have hundreds of malnourished, under-educated, potentially rebellious people to look after, all of whom would keep us from continuing our work on schedule and without distraction. But you've known that all along. It's why you haven't raised this issue before, despite your resistance to our—"

"You murdered humanity," Ella said. She was trying hard to stay cordial, to not ruffle the feathers of the man whose word was law.

"And you gave us the knife," the man said, "which is why you are still alive. Your skills and knowledge will help what's left of the world, something you have at least attempted to make peace with. Your work *is* progressing. But this...obsession with the girl? It needs to stop."

"I won't continue my work without her."

The man's fingers stopped tapping. "An ultimatum? You've made them before. We both know you prefer life over death. You have never done well with pain."

"People change," Ella said. "You of all people know that better than most."

"The question is why?" Lawrence said. "We changed the world. Not quite overnight, but in evolutionary terms, RC-714 did what took billions of years for evolution to achieve, in the blink of an eye. But what could change a woman like you, who even while she is repulsed by her own work, and toils against it in vain—we know about your biodomes, by the way—always returns to it? Drawn by insatiable curiosity. Pushed by threats of violence. Of starvation. Of being set loose in the wilds of the new. You always return to work."

Lawrence swiveled around in his chair, facing Ella for the first time. He had a kind face and a genuine smile. His head sparkled in the sunlight filtering in through the window. His eyes matched the water in the bay behind him. And his loose clothing looked like something out of a kung-fu movie. This was a man who should be stretching on a yoga mat, not overseeing the end of life on Earth. "So what about this girl, subject 229—"

"Anne."

"—would spur you to make such a threat? And why do you think that after all your failed attempts at resistance, things will be different this time?" He leaned forward, elbows on the desk, his smile unwavering.

"Because this time I mean—"

"Why?"

Ella froze up, not wanting to answer.

"Let me help loosen your lips," Lawrence said. "ExoGen specializes in genetics. It's right there in the name. Half of the people working in this facility, and thus half the people alive on this planet, are, like you, geneticists. Now, you might be one of our more gifted minds, but even some of the people in the sanitation department know how to run basic DNA tests."

When Ella said nothing, Lawrence laughed. "So strong willed, and yet so easy to disarm." He leaned back in the chair. "I had the girl tested the moment you allowed her to share your quarters. I knew what the results would be when I learned that you had named the girl, but was still surprised when my suspicions were confirmed. But you have always been one to try the unconventional. It's what makes your genius so potent. So valuable. And it's why I would rather not have to threaten you, or even worse, follow through on those threats. But I still need to hear it from your lips. Tell me, who is the girl to you?"

"My daughter," Ella said. "And if you let her live...if you let me have her...you never need threaten me again."

"And if I don't?"

"I will be all out of reasons to live."

Lawrence squinted at her. "You didn't make her for the experiment, did you?" His smile slowly returned. "You made her...for yourself. Like a pet." The smile became a laugh. "Ella, you would never admit it, but your mind is as twisted as you claim mine to be. And when you see that for yourself, I will let you into the fold. But for now...I will let you keep the girl."

Anne stumbled out of the memory and into the small room hidden inside the walk-in closet. When she looked up and saw the room's contents, she wished she could retreat back into that horrible memory.

THIRTY

Ella looked Jakob in the eyes as she was led past him. She said nothing, but tried to communicate a simple message with her facial expression alone: *I'm sorry.*

He just glared back at her. Angry at Mason. At Kenyon. At the Riders. Probably at her, too. He'd risked his freedom, his life, in an attempt to rescue her, but had really just delivered himself as a second bargaining chip. Kenyon hadn't even disarmed the boy, or the rest of the people in the house. Didn't have to. No one wanted to commit suicide by Apache helicopter.

Though as suicide went, it would be one of the faster ways to die. The attack helicopter's rockets and chain gun didn't just kill people, they erased them. Turned them to sludge. They were brutal weapons. Overkill, really. But they were also merciful in their swiftness. Death would come faster than the nervous system could register it.

Despite the graveness of their situation, she wasn't without hope. First, she trusted that once Jakob knew Kenyon was involved, he would have hidden Anne away before revealing himself. If he'd done a good job, Anne was far from here, maybe not even in the compound anymore. Maybe even with Peter. And that was her second hope. Had been for most of her life. Peter was alive. Of that, she had no doubt. But was he fighting for his life somewhere else? Against Boone and his boys? Was he lost in the swamps? Or had he already returned, maybe even waiting inside the house? Whatever the case, if he showed up, she'd be ready. And if he didn't...she'd do what she did best—survive.

But what she wouldn't do is let these men have Anne. She'd die before letting that happen.

So as she took the steps onto the farmer's porch, she steeled herself for the pain to come, and determined that she would not scream.

She paused in the doorway where Mason's corpse still hung. Blood tapped out a rhythm on the hard wood floor. She heard movement in the house as people scurried about, hiding, retreating or simply trying to get a better view. She ignored them and turned her attention to Mason. His death had been too sudden. Too merciful. But that didn't mean she couldn't vent her rage on him. She punched his torso three times, twice with her freshly broken finger. Then she grasped his arms and drove her knee into his groin, again and again. On the fourth strike, the spear tip slipped free of the door. His body crumpled at her feet.

She kicked the body twice and then stopped. Sweat coated her forehead. Her muscles twitched. The man's violent sexual advances had affected her more than she thought.

"He really did what you said," Kenyon said. He actually looked concerned.

"Tried to," she replied, and hoped he might learn a lesson from her brutalization of a dead man. She stepped over the corpse and into the house. There were two women and one man in the living room to the right of the foyer in which she stood. One of them was Alia. The girl looked at her with a newfound fear. Ella regretted it, but Alia needed to grow a thicker skin. The days of Millennial coddling came to an end right along with the rest of civilization. She wanted to tell her as much, but didn't even let her eyes linger on the girl. If they were lucky, Kenyon wouldn't recognize her. When Kenyon stepped into the foyer behind her, the girl wisely looked away, letting her hair cover her face. Hutchins and Crawford stepped in after them, scanning the hallway and the surrounding rooms with their weapons.

"Ella," Kenyon said, glancing at the armed residents of Hellhole Bay positioned in the living and dining rooms on either side of them. He didn't even show a flicker of concern. "I'd rather not do this. You've been through enough."

"Much of it at your hands," she said. "And we both know how this is going to go, so why don't we get to it?"

"You've changed," he said.

"We're all evolving." Ella held out her left hand, offering him another finger. "Some of us slower than others."

"I came here to kill you, you know." He sniffed, feigning sincerity. "I dreamed of it. Your death. And Peter's. Even the kids'. That's what kept me alive. Tracking you. Hunting you. You made it hard. I couldn't have done it without the Chunta. But even with their help, the only reason I'm here at all is because I hated you so much.

"And now that we're here, and your life is in my hands... I know that what I thought was hate, was jealousy. Because I love you. And I want what's best for you. That's not a life on the run. Or in a shithole like this. You and Anne can live long, safe lives."

"While ExoGen remakes the world?"

"That can't be stopped. It's far too late for that."

Ella didn't like the sound of that. "What have they done?"

"You'll find out when you come back with me," he said. "You can enjoy the fruits of your labor. You can live out your life...again and again. With Anne. With me. Regain ExoGen's trust and they might even let you help shape the future. Your morality is questionable, but your abilities will always be valuable to them.

"Tell you what. I'll even throw in the kid. Peter is a no-go, for obvious reasons. Just saying his name makes me want to slit my own throat for being kind to you. But I will spare his son. I'll take him to San Francisco with us, and I will let him live out his life. Just once, though."

That was the second time Kenyon alluded to being able to live more than once. Had ExoGen discovered some sort of immortality gene, buried in the junk DNA that she had helped unlock?

It was a tempting offer. Being human came with a mystery expiration date. Erasing that fateful moment...if really possible...would be seductive to most anyone on the planet. But giving up her daughter, not to mention the human race she'd already done enough to destroy, wasn't worth a thousand lifetimes.

In response to his offer, she reached up, took hold of her own finger, and with a quick jerk, snapped the digit. A roar of pain built in her chest, but abject defiance kept it in. "You won't make me scream. I will die first."

"Mmm," Kenyon said. "What about you?"

The question confused Ella until she saw where he was looking: in the living room, at Alia. She was glad Jakob was still outside. If he saw this, she had no doubt he'd try something stupid.

Kenyon snapped his fingers. "What's your name? Alex? Anna? Starts with an A, right?"

Alia peeked at him through her overhanging hair.

"Yes, you," Kenyon said. "Come over here, now, or I'll order my men to shoot your boyfriend outside. And please do leave your weapon on the floor."

Alia lowered her rifle. Placed it on the floor. Her hands quivered, electrified. She stood slowly, on wobbly legs, and stepped toward the foyer. The man and woman she left behind just watched, despite the weapons in their hands. They might have been brave enough to make a stand against Mason. But against Kenyon, a gaggle of Riders and three military helicopters? Whatever strength they had mustered had faltered. Though at least one of them had the gumption to take a shot at Kenyon. Whoever it was, she hoped he'd never find out.

When Alia stopped in front of him, he put his fingers under her chin and lifted it. She was covered in grime, but her quivering lower lip and tear-filled innocent eyes betrayed her weakness. Jakob was still adapting to the world, and would one day be able to fill his father's shoes. But Alia...her days were numbered. This might even be her last.

"Where is she?" Kenyon asked.

"W-who?"

"The only 'she' in your group not currently present."

"I d-don't know."

"You're a very bad liar."

Alia said nothing, but looked close to breaking down.

Kenyon turned to Crawford. The man had a block-shaped face and a square nose, like a pugilist who had taken too many hits to the face. "Knife."

Crawford drew a long blade from the sheath on his hip, spun it around in his hand and handed it, hilt first, to Kenyon. The blade came up under Alia's throat so fast that the girl yelped.

"That's good," Kenyon said. "But try it a little louder for me."

The girl's resistance broke at the same moment her skin did. She screamed like only a teenage girl can, as piercing as a siren.

"Alia?" It was Jakob from outside.

"Stay outside, Jakob," Ella called. "She's okay."

"If he—"

"Stay outside!" Ella shouted.

Something on the second floor thumped. All eyes turned upward.

"Sweep the first floor," Kenyon told Crawford. Then he gave Alia a shove. "Up."

Alia started up the stairs, clutching the railing as she went. When Ella moved to follow, Kenyon pointed the knife at her. "You stay here." He looked to Hutchins. "If she tries anything stupid...shoot her legs."

Kenyon headed to the second floor, prodding Alia with the barrel of his rifle. When they reached the second floor, Hutchins adjusted his aim toward Ella's thigh.

"I used to think you were a nice guy, Paul," Ella said, using Hutchins's first name.

"Never really liked you much," he replied.

"Don't let Eddie hear you say—"

The scream that tore from the second floor was full of genuine pain. As hardened as Ella was, the sound worked its way through a chink in her emotional armor and brought a tear to her eye. Whatever innocence the girl had managed to cling on to was being ripped straight out of her heart. And everyone who heard it reacted in a different way, but all at once.

THIRTY-ONE

Beastmaster was a heavy truck with an amazing suspension that absorbed bumps and potholes with ease. Most of the cross-country trek, on road and off, was fairly smooth. But now, the truck bucked like a sugar-high kid in a bounce house. Peter struggled to maintain a straight course down the middle of the dirt road, which was smooth as far as dirt roads went. There was the occasional string of divots carved out by the rain, and large rocks spread out like road pimples, but none of that accounted for the rough ride. That came from the monster charging up behind them, its massive weight sending shockwaves through the earth with each heaving step.

The machine gun roared to life in spurts. In between the gunfire, Peter heard Feesa hooting loudly. He wasn't sure if the she-beast was frightened by the gun, pumped for battle or communicating with the Riders. But she hadn't attacked Boone, so he figured it was one of the latter two options.

Behind them, the ExoGator gained. It could out-pace them with ease. The only hope they had of outrunning it were the Riders, who surged out of the swamp in pursuit of the beast as it passed. The gator, locked on target, paid them no attention.

Woolies bounded onto the road, their shaggy hair undulating as they quickly matched the gator's speed.

Peter punched the steering wheel. "C'mon you slow son-of-a-bitch!"

Hundreds of tons of ExoGenetic horrors were careening toward them and *Beastmaster*, whose name Peter might have to rethink, was accelerating like a pot-smoking quadriplegic turtle.

"Faster!" Boone shouted from the back.

For the first time in his life, Peter felt Scotty's pain, and he nearly added the Star Trek engineer's Scottish brogue when he replied, "Going as fast as I can!"

When Boone squeezed off another fusillade of bullets, Peter watched in the rearview. If any of the rounds struck the gator, it showed no sign. But Peter did notice one of the Riders twitch and fall back off its steed. He held his breath, waiting for Feesa to exact her revenge on Boone, but she had either not noticed her brethren go down, or didn't understand that Boone's bad aim was the culprit.

Peter tore around a bend in the road, focusing all his attention on not driving the truck into the swamp. After turning hard in one direction, and then the other, the road straightened out again.

The gator didn't bother taking the turns. It plowed straight ahead, shattering trees and displacing thousands of gallons of water. Its crazed efforts pulled it ahead of the tribal ExoGens and closer to the truck.

Before Boone could open fire again, wasting even more ammunition, Peter called out. "Boone!"

The man ducked down and looked through the open window.

"Get in here and take the wheel," Peter shouted.

Boone gave a quick nod and slipped through the window. After falling into the back seat, he popped up behind Peter. "Can't shoot that thing for shit." Then he vaulted into the front passenger's seat beside Peter.

"Take the wheel," Peter said, and when Boone took hold with one hand, he added, "Foot on the gas. Ready?"

Boone slid into position, his foot hovering over Peter's.

"Now!" Peter yanked his foot away and Boone shoved his down. There was a brief jolt of deceleration—something *Beastmaster* had no trouble with—but then they were hauling forward again. Peter pushed up out of his seat and then slipped over Boone's head to the back seat.

"How much further to the gate?" Peter asked.

"We're only 'bout a mile out as the crow flies, but it's a winding road, so roughly two miles, give or take."

Which translated to just over two minutes at their current speed. Not a lot of time, but more than enough for the gator to make a meal of them. "Just keep us on the road," Peter said and started pushing himself through the tight back window. His ribs scraped against the frame, popping through one at a time, but he fell into the truck bed beside Feesa's large, hairy and odorous feet.

Before standing, Peter scooped up the two large rubber bands attached to either side of the bed. He looped the carabiners at the ends to his belt and then stood up. The truck tore around a bend a moment later and he had no trouble staying upright. He clutched the machine gun, leaned his shoulder into the stock and looked down the metal sights. His finger looped around the trigger, but he didn't squeeze.

In the time it took him to clip himself in, stand and aim the weapon, the Riders had made their move. Two of the Woolies now flanked the gator on either side, their Riders coiled and ready to leap.

What the hell are they trying to do?

Before he could surmise the plan, Feesa raised her arms and bellowed a call, like some kind of Neanderthal orchestral composer. The Woolies reacted as one, turning in and thrusting their splayed horns. They struck with enormous force, bending and then punching through the gator's thick hide. Upon impact, the Riders, each a foot shorter than Peter, sprang into the air, spears in hand.

The two Riders arced through the air and landed atop the gator's back, just as it started reacting to the pain in its sides. The faster of the two males thrust his spear into the gator's back. He had something to hold on to when the monster bucked. The slower of the two was launched away, catapulted into the swamps, where he struck a tree, his body impaled on a branch, hanging limp.

The gator reared up its head and thrashed from side to side, losing momentum as it tore free from the horns. Rainbows of blood sprayed from the many puncture wounds, but it didn't look like enough to make a creature that size bleed out. The wounds would coagulate long before that happened.

But if the man on top can—

Peter's thoughts were cut short when the gator leaped into the air, performing what could only be described as an airborne death roll. The self-propelled ExoGator's spiral failed to fling free the strong male Rider, but it didn't have to. The man-thing was smeared beneath the massive reptilian body as it came back down to the dirt road, sliding as it continued to roll.

And then as suddenly as it leaped up, it sprang back to its feet, stopped on a dime and wheeled around. It caught one of the two closest

Woolies in its jaws, crushing it with untold PSI of force. The second Woolie was struck by the massive tail, which snapped out and slapped the Woolie into the swamp. Its body careened through trees and water with equal ease, coming to a stop far out of sight.

What followed was a crunching, slurping mess as the remaining Riders and Woolies slammed into the gator's side. The massive reptile let out a low, guttural growl that sent pressure waves pulsing through the air, but Peter suspected it was more an expression of frustration than pain. It reacted by thrashing back and forth, its massive jaws opening wide and snapping back down, over and over.

Riders screamed in pain.

Woolies groaned pitifully.

After a few bites, the gator's snout came up red. Blood and flesh sprayed with each bite. It was a gory fireworks display. And with each pop of flesh, each muffled scream and each flung and severed corpse, Feesa deflated a little more. Her bravado melted away.

Peter watched her, and to his surprise, he felt pity for her. She had been a woman once. Fully human with a life of her own. With a daughter, and maybe a husband. She hadn't asked to have that life stripped away. She still mourned the loss of her daughter. And now, this tribe of ExoGen monsters turned family, who he had wounded by killing Kristen, was being torn apart.

Feesa had suffered a lot.

They all had.

He leaned up from the weapon, which, as they increased the distance between them and the gator, became useless. "Feesa." When she didn't respond, he put his hand on her hairy arm. "Feesa."

She reeled around on him and roared. The stench of her breath made him wince, just as much as the four inch fangs about to bite off his face. But she didn't bite. Instead, she sank back down into a hunched position, eyes on the truck bed.

Peter paused for a moment. The gator wasn't entirely finished mauling and consuming the Riders, but it had heard Feesa's cry. And like most ExoGens did, it responded by turning its attention to whatever living thing remained. He lost sight of it as they rounded a bend, but had no doubt it would resume the chase. And when that happened, he needed Feesa to be more than a hairy mass of mourning.

He nearly told her that it would be all right. That she would get through it. But that was the kind of comfort people liked to hear. Then he remembered who he was speaking to. Despite the loss of her people and the very real anguish she was experiencing, she was still an ExoGen. At heart, she was guided by hunger, but for the Riders—the 'Chunta,' Feesa had called them—that unquenchable desire to hunt, kill and consume had been replaced by something else: revenge.

"Feesa!" he shouted. She started and looked about ready to attack, but the display was short-lived. Peter didn't want it to be, so he shouted again. "You are Chunta! You are strong!" He pointed behind them, where he expected the gator to emerge at any moment. "Alligator killed Chunta. We—" He thumped his chest, "—will kill alligator." Then he pointed over the roof off the truck. "We will kill Kenyon. We will protect our family."

That perked her up a little.

"Chunta sacrificed themselves to save our family." He was laying it on a little thick, but he didn't think her emotional states were very complex. She understood the big bold strokes of his stilted proclamations. She understood what family was. And for now, through some primitive familial loyalty, Peter and his own, were part of her brood. He thumped his chest, bringing the message home. "My family is your family. Your family is Chunta. *I* am Chunta, and we can still save them."

Feesa stood up so suddenly that Peter flinched back. Had he not been strapped in, he might have toppled over the side. But he sprang back into place as Feesa lowered her face to his. Her baritone voice rumbled out from between her long bottom teeth. "I...trust you."

He didn't hear a question mark, but took it as such. "Yes. Family... family is everything. And ours is still alive."

The truck skidded to a stop. Peter looked forward and saw the closed gates of Hellhole Bay just ahead. "Gates are closed!" Boone shouted. "And ain't no one manning the post." Peter scanned the top of the gate. There had been a lookout position just to the side, before. Now, it was empty. They were locked outside.

He pointed to the gate and spoke to Feesa. "Family is inside."

"Kenyon too," she said.

"Can you open the gate?"

She responded by bounding onto the truck's cab and then launching off of it. Her weight shook the vehicle and dented the roof, but Peter barely noticed. She landed near the top of the gate and started scaling it to the top.

But Peter didn't see her reach the top or drop down to the far side. All of his attention snapped back to the road behind them, as an explosion of trees, blood and water gave way to the gator, a quarter mile behind them. It skidded across the road, dug down with its long claws and then pounded toward the back of the truck. It was bringing all its millions of years of evolution, coupled with a few years of rapid-fire adaptations, to bear on a lone man, standing his ground. Not because Peter was brave, but because there was no other choice.

And then, something in his mind clicked. Beyond the pounding of primeval feet, the chug of *Beastmaster*'s engine and the rushing of his own blood, Peter heard something familiar, and close. Behind him. Inside the compound.

Helicopters.

They found us, he thought, and he removed his finger from the trigger. As much as he wanted to drill a hole through the ExoGator's eye socket, he didn't want the people on the far side of the wall to know he was coming, though once the gate opened, it would be impossible to hide.

THIRTY-TWO

"What has been seen, can never be unseen." Those words had been spoken by Jakob two weeks previous, when he'd stepped around a tree against which Anne was leaning, pants down, going to the bathroom. She'd thrown a turnip at him and chased him back to their parents, but the embarrassing—for both of them—event became a funny story. And 'What has been seen, can never be unseen,' became a catchphrase for a few days. When they saw an ugly creature. When mom delivered a meal. When Dad woke up in the morning. The phrase went through her mind now as she looked up at the small room into which she'd fallen, but the phrase lacked all trace of its former humor.

"Shh," Shawna said, crawling in after her. "Are you trying to announce where we're hi—oly shit." The woman paused half way through the door, her eyes angled up toward the walls.

For a moment, the two of them stared in silence, frozen by revulsion. Then Shawna seemed to remember that she was an adult, and as such, the moral guardian of anyone whose age still began with the prefix, 'pre.' "Don't look at it. Just stare at the floor."

Anne heard her, but didn't listen. As much as she wanted to, she couldn't look away.

Shawna crawled the rest of the way into the room and then leaned back out, pulling the separated clothing back together. Then she pulled the door shut, yanking on the small handle, until the seam disappeared once more.

"Seriously," Shawna said. "This stuff isn't good for your brain." She then began plucking the 8x10 photos off of the wall.

Despite the woman's verbal concern for Anne's psychological wellbeing, Anne knew better. Shawna was embarrassed. She might eventually take all the photos off the wall, but she was starting with the photos of herself. In some, she was alone. Changing. Bathing. Standing in front of a mirror. But in others, she had company. The man Anne assumed was Mason. His old raisin-like body was a stark contrast to Shawna's plump, grape-like curves. But what was he doing, pressing his gross self, up against her, his face warped with what? Pleasure? And her face... She didn't look happy. Or sad. Or angry. She looked dead. She looked...

Unconscious.

Then Anne saw it. *Really* saw it. What his body was doing to hers. To the other maids—Charlotte and Sabine. To women she didn't recognize. And a few she did, including Carrie.

Anne nearly threw up, but contained her revolting stomach.

She looked away from the walls and found herself looking through a window that revealed the bedroom. She ducked down, afraid of being seen. "Get down!"

Shawna ducked with her, clutching the lewd photos of herself. "What is it?"

"A window," Anne said, keeping her voice quiet. She pointed up at the window, but even now she was starting to realize the truth. She'd walked right past the gilded mirror and hadn't thought anything of it. But it wasn't just a simple mirror. You couldn't see in, but you could see out.

"I should have guessed." Shawna stood back up and resumed pulling down photos. "I don't care if there really are just a hundred people left in the world. Mason didn't deserve to be one of them."

"He's not the only one," Anne said, but didn't elaborate. Instead she inspected the rest of the room's contents, careful to avoid looking at the walls. There was a video camera mounted on a tripod. It was positioned off to the side, but it could be set up in front of the two way mirror. The cord dangling from the camera led to a computer sitting atop a desk in the corner of the room. There were two flat-screen monitors, speakers and a very nice, high-end printer. Stacks of photo paper and ink cartridges lined the floor of one wall.

What looked like a thick notebook sat next to the computer keyboard and mouse. Anne opened it to find page after page of DVDs, carefully labeled with names and dates, and slotted into protective sleeves. Anne noted that the dates on the first ten pages went back to well before the Change. She turned dozens of pages at a time, counting more than thirty different names. Then she reached a page with just three DVDs, and stopped, not because it was the last page—though it was—but because she recognized the name on the final DVD: Ella Masse.

Anne's eyes flicked to the printer. A single page lay face down in the tray.

She reached out for it slowly. Her fingers fumbled with the page edge until she lost her patience and crushed the whole page in her hand. She nearly fell over when she turned the image around and saw her mother's naked form. She had seen her mother with no clothes on several times. And she was expecting to see a candid shot of her. But the look on her mother's face... It was seductive.

"Your mother was a smart lady," Shawna said.

"She doesn't look very smart," Anne replied, wondering for a moment if this is how her mother seemed to get her way with men. "She looks like a slut."

"A smart slut, then." Shawna shrugged. "She was giving him the show he wanted. Disarming him. Distracting him. Men like Mason think with their...never mind."

Anne was about to say that she wasn't as young as she looked, but the truth, she was beginning to realize, was that she was far younger than she had been led to believe. She might look twelve, and act twelve, but her formative years had been rushed past. "I don't need to know."

Shawna looked relieved. "The point is, this photo of her doesn't reveal a weakness. It reveals a strength. Probably why she's still alive and Mason is a piñata."

Anne nodded. She knew it was true. *Mom would do just about anything to stay alive. For me,* Anne thought. *She stayed alive for me.*

No, that's not right. She stayed alive for everyone.

As much as Anne liked to think Ella's dedication to her was all about the bond between mother and daughter, she knew a large portion of it had more to do with what Anne meant to all of humanity. Lawrence might have thought to check Anne's DNA, but it had never occurred to him to search for a USB device hidden in her head. Why would he? It was ludicrous.

And Ella had clearly used these same...skills to enamor Eddie. Did she ever care about him? Or was he always a pawn? Would she be able to reignite his feelings for her? It seemed likely, since he didn't kill her on sight. Or was he now playing her to find Anne? Adults were confusing.

But what really befuddled Anne now was the sneaking suspicion, and concern, that Ella was also using Peter. Her father.

What if he's not my father? What if we look alike only because he and mom look alike?

The memories Anne had of young mom and dad didn't support this theory. She'd felt what her mother felt for him. But she also had a large chunk of her mother's memories missing, including the time period when Peter chose another woman over her mother.

That couldn't have gone over well.

But would she betray him? Would she manipulate him?

Yes, Anne decided. If it meant keeping Anne safe and undoing the wrong she had inflicted on the world. Ella would do anything.

Any-thing.

So the question was, in the case of Peter, did Ella need to lie, or was the truth enough?

"What are you going to do with those?" Anne pointed at the growing stack of photos.

"Burn them."

Anne handed the photo of her mother to Shawna. "The computer and DVDs, too."

The woman sneered at the disc collection. Confirmation enough. When Shawna looked back up, her eyes went wide with surprise and fear. She was looking at the two-way mirror.

Anne turned around and looked into Mason's bedroom. What she saw made her whole body go rigid.

Eddie stood in the bedroom, looking right at them.

He can see us! Anne thought, and then she realized the truth. Eddie was looking at his reflection, and forcing Alia to look at hers. The girl, who annoyed Anne most of the time, but had started growing on her, was wet with tears. Her whole face trembled. Kenyon had a long knife, the tip of it pressed against Alia's cheek.

He shouted something at her, making a demand.

Despite her fear, Alia shook her head, denying the man's request and gaining a boatload of respect from Anne. Alia might be a burden in the wild, but she was braver than Anne would have guessed. Defying a man with a knife to your face took a lot of guts. But in the case of Eddie Kenyon, it was also stupid.

Eddie relaxed a little. Let out a sigh.

"No," Anne said. "Stop."

Eddie showed no sign of hearing her.

Shawna wrapped a hand around Anne's mouth. "Shut-up!"

Eddie loosened his grip, but kept the knife in place. He spoke to her again. Anne imagined his soothing voice, reassuring her that everything was going to be okay, if she just did what he was asking.

Right when Alia started to buy into it, relaxing her body, staring right into Anne's eyes without knowing it, Eddie shoved the knife blade through her cheek and yanked it out just as quickly. There was a wide-eyed beat as Alia tried to comprehend was had just happened, then blood began to gush over her face, and from her mouth.

Alia screamed. It had to have been loud, but Mason's secret room had apparently been soundproofed. Anne couldn't hear a thing, but her tough heart broke for the girl on the other side of the mirror.

Alia was suffering for Anne.

"What the hell is he doing?" Shawna asked. "Why is he torturing her?"

"To get to me," Anne said. "To get me to come out."

Anne started rummaging through drawers, disgusted as more photos, DVDs, and other more tangible evidence of Mason's perversions spilled onto the floor.

"What are you doing?" Shawna asked.

Anne pulled a sharpened pencil from the drawer. It wasn't much, but it was better than nothing. "He's good at his job."

Shawna said nothing, but had a distinct, 'what's that supposed to mean?' look on her face.

"You're welcome to help me," Anne said. "But don't get in my way." Then she stepped to the small hidden door and yanked it open.

THIRTY-THREE

Kenyon winced. The girl's scream was far louder than he'd anticipated. It blasted into his left ear with the kind of high pitched decibels that went out of musical style when the 1980s came to a neon-clad closure. Despite the horrendous sound, and the pain it brought, Kenyon was pleased. Anne was a tough girl, but Kenyon knew part of her bravado was to hide her bleeding heart. She cared about people. All people. Even ones she didn't like. He didn't know if Anne and Alia were close, but he did know they'd been together for the past five weeks. That meant, if Anne was hiding in the house, she'd probably expose herself to save the girl. And if she wasn't, Alia would scream until she died.

Kenyon yanked the girl by the back of her shirt, positioning her between him and the open door. From here, Anne would be able to hear the screaming from anywhere in the house and out the front door. And if Ella or Jakob got any suicidal ideas, she'd make a good human shield.

When Alia began to cry, Kenyon leaned down next to her bleeding face. "You're going to scream for me now, aren't you?"

Tears mingled with blood as she nodded.

"If you make me ask again, I'm going to carve holes in your cheeks. Understand?"

She nodded once more and tried to groan an 'Mmm hmm,' but an uncontrolled sob bubbled up from her chest. She tried to hold it in, but the sound popped from the side of her ruined cheek, spraying blood onto Kenyon's face.

His smile gleamed white. He didn't mind the blood. And the girl was already screaming again, even louder than before.

Over the shrill anguish ripping through the air, Kenyon heard something new and disconcerting: the Apache's chain gun.

It's the kid, he thought. Ella wasn't foolish enough to risk her life, and everyone else's because of a scream. But Jakob, he'd also spent the past five weeks with Alia, and she was a looker. Probably head over heels. How could he not be? She might be the only teenage girl left alive on the planet.

Eddie chastised himself for not realizing it sooner, but it didn't matter. If the Apache was shooting at him, the kid was stew.

His smile returned.

Jakob's demise would definitely bring Anne running. Her friends were dying, and that was something he knew she couldn't abide. He'd seen her face every time they lost a member of their original party. Ella was cold and indifferent, the way a survivor had to be. Like Eddie. But Anne? Every life lost chewed her up inside. She eventually got good at hiding it, cloaking herself in a shell of indifference, but that didn't mean she was invulnerable to loss.

When the string of chain gun rounds echoed to a stop, Eddie prodded Alia in the back and said, "Again!"

As the scream bubbled up the girl's throat, something about the light in the room changed. A shadow. Moving fast. Kenyon's first thought was that one of the helicopters had flown past, blocking the sun for a moment, but he hadn't heard a change in the rotors' pitch. *Someone's in the room,* he thought, but he dismissed the idea. He'd checked under the bed and in the closet. The room was empty.

But his neck prickled when he detected just a hint of a pulsing vibration in the floor boards beneath his feet.

Someone's running.

Charging.

Move!

Kenyon shifted to the side, while twisting to face his stealthy attacker. The movement saved his life. Instead of puncturing his jugular, the pencil punched a hole in his already wounded arm. It hurt like hell, but wouldn't make him less capable than the bullet already had.

But the attacker wasn't done. The pencil came out with a slurp, reeled back and stabbed again before Eddie could counter. This time, the writing utensil struck a nerve in his elbow, sending an electric shock up his brutalized arm. He stumbled back, thrown by the pain.

Sensing she was free, Alia scrambled from the room, clutching her cheek, lost in terror. But as Kenyon turned to face his attacker, knife in hand, he forgot all about Alia. She'd fulfilled her role.

Anne had come out of hiding.

The girl stood before him, pencil wielded like a blade. She looked mostly how he remembered her, but with a shaved head. There was something different about her eyes though. He recognized the ferocity, but there was something else in the mix.

Confidence, he realized.

Anne charged, targeting his wounded arm. It wasn't a bad attack. The more holes she put in him, the more he'd bleed. And with loss of blood came loss of energy, and eventually death. And she nearly tagged him with the pencil again, but the rest of him was still operating at 100%, and eager for a fight. He sidestepped and kicked out his left leg, slamming his shin into hers.

A shout of pain burst from Anne's throat. She tumbled forward and nearly drove her face into the corner of a nightstand, which would have been unfortunate. She reached out and caught herself before colliding, dropping the pencil.

"You don't need to fight me," Kenyon said. "You and your mother can come back to ExoGen. You can live long, happy lives."

Anne grunted, pushing herself up, favoring her right leg. "We were happy."

"Out here? In this miserable world?"

Anne's eyes flicked around the room, no doubt searching for a weapon, but other than the pencil that had rolled through the open door and into the hallway, there was nothing. Kenyon held his knife out, letting her see the long blade. He also had the assault rifle on his back, but it would be impossible to quickly retrieve with one arm. She'd be out the door or trying to gouge his eyes out before his hand found the grip. "There are a hundred ways I can make you hurt, without killing you."

"And there's a hundred ways that I don't give a shit."

Kenyon remembered he was arguing with a twelve year old. Logic and threats weren't going to get him anywhere, especially with Anne.

"And what about your mother?" he asked.

"She's taking care of herself," the girl said.

Kenyon was about to reply when Anne's words sank in. She hadn't said Ella could take care of herself. She said Ella *was* taking care of herself. Present tense. It was then that Kenyon heard the sounds of a struggle rumbling up from the first floor. Hutchins and Crawford had been engaged, and so far, not a single shot had been fired.

Then a voice rolled up the staircase. "Alia!" The kid. Not dead. So who had the Apache shot?

Anne charged with a scream, fingers hooked like claws, something she'd learned from her mother. Kenyon aimed for her arm and swung the knife. The cut would be deep, and take the fight out of her, but it wouldn't kill her. The blade slid through the air, and struck nothing. Anne dove beneath it, rolling onto her back and then kicking up hard.

Kenyon felt his balls compress. The sensation was followed by pain and nausea that threatened to drop him to the floor. But that wasn't what happened. There were few things more painful, but most men struck in the nuts fell to the ground, not out of pain, but for attention. He did pitch forward though, and that's when Anne drove the same foot up into his chin.

He staggered back, but caught hold of Anne's extended leg. With a surge of anger, he lifted the light girl and flung her across the room. She bounced off the bed, struck the far wall and fell over the side.

Kenyon stumbled back into the wall, shattering a framed painting of a farm, the kind the world used to subsidize. He fought against the urge to puke, and kept his eyes on the bed, waiting for Anne to reappear. And when she did, the gloves would be off. He would try not to kill her still. She was his golden ticket, though he didn't really understand what made her so valuable. But he had every intention of beating her to within an inch of her life. No more kid gloves.

Anne vaulted around the back of the bed, charging him head on. "Asshole!"

He swung with the knife and realized too late that Anne was also armed and swinging. At first glance, he thought it was a baseball bat. When it struck his knife hand, lancing pain up his arm, he recognized the weapon as an oversized rubber phallus, which she wielded like a cudgel. The knife clattered to the floor, but Kenyon wasn't holding back now. She might have caught him off guard—again—but she couldn't stop him. Not with a dildo.

With his hand free of the knife, he grasped onto her wrist and squeezed hard enough to elicit a scream of pain. Then he flung her like a trebuchet. She slammed into a dresser, above which was an ugly gold mirror.

Anne groaned and started pushing herself up.

"Stay down, Anne," Kenyon said, stalking toward her.

"You can stick that big—"

Kenyon kicked her in the gut. She buckled forward, gasping for air. Didn't even fight back when he leaned down and wrapped his fingers around her throat. She kicked when her feet came off the ground, but she lacked the energy to hurt him. She raked her nails over his arm, drawing blood, but as the oxygen to her brain dwindled, so did her efforts.

Not too hard, he told himself. He wanted her unconscious, not dead.

"Just go to sleep," Kenyon cooed. "Close your eyes. That's a good girl."

Despite the pain she'd caused him, he really did like Anne. When they'd trekked through the wild after first leaving ExoGen, he'd even let himself see her as something like family. A God-daughter. Maybe even a step-child someday. It was a fantasy, and one that would likely never be realized now, but things like anger and hate can fade over time, especially when you're safe and well fed.

Anne's eyelids flickered as consciousness drifted. *Just another second.*

Kenyon blinked. His view of the room shifted. Made no sense.

What the hell?

Instead of looking at Anne, and his own reflection in the mirror behind her, he saw a sideways view of the floor. Anne was still there, no longer in his grasp, but the world had gone from horizontal to vertical.

How did I end up on the floor?

Pain was his answer, throbbing at the back of his head along with a spreading liquid warmth.

A foot stepped into view, barefoot and feminine. A decorative butter churn dropped to the floor beside it. A woman dressed as a maid crouched down between him and Anne. She shook the girl gently, whispering before turning to the door and yelling, "Help! Someone help!"

Eddie could hear movement in the house.

People shouting. People screaming.

Gunshots rang out, inside and outside. Something bigger than his bedroom scuffle was going on.

Get up, he told himself. *Get up and get out.*

While the maid was focused on Anne, he slid across the floor, reached beneath the bed and took hold of the dropped knife. His body ached with every movement, but he fought against the pain. *Save it for later, Eddie. Just fucking move!*

Eddie swung the knife.

Metal slipped through skin, muscle and tendon. The maid shrieked and dropped like Achilles, but without the legendary build up. He wanted to kill her, but he sensed there wasn't time. While the woman writhed in agony, Kenyon got his feet beneath him and stood.

Footsteps approached the doorway, rapid fire, coming to help.

He threw the knife.

A woman walked into it, taking the blade in her chest. She toppled over beside the maid, still alive, but not even close to putting up a fight. Kenyon pulled the assault rifle over his head and laid it on the bed. He then hoisted Anne off the floor and slung her over his shoulder, balancing her limp form. Next he retrieved the weapon and turned to the window, prepared to kick it out. But there were bars on the far side of the glass.

Mason had turned the place into a prison.

Kenyon stepped over the women on the floor and into the hallway.

Ahead of him was the staircase to the first floor, which sounded like a battle zone, and the staircase to the third floor. Would the windows up there be barred as well? Kenyon replayed his memory of the home's outside. The windows were barred, but he had also seen a small deck with a door. People fleeing Mason's prison might not be able to get past the door, and if they did, they probably wouldn't throw themselves from a third floor balcony. But Kenyon had a keychain made of bullets, and he wouldn't have to jump.

He took a step toward the stairs and stopped when his name tore through the air. "Eddie!"

He glanced down toward the first floor. Ella was there, covered in blood, rifle in hand.

"You'll come with me now," he said. "You have no choice."

"There's always a choice, Eddie," she said, and she raised the weapon to fire.

Eyes wide, Eddie dodged to the side as a fusillade of bullets chewed up the banister. He ran up the stairs for the third floor, propelled by the sound of Ella Masse, charging up after him, out for blood.

THIRTY-FOUR

Jakob acted without thinking. He realized it two steps into his sprint, but there was no going back. And he was pretty sure that meant he was toast.

The Riders stood close enough to pounce on him, though they seemed a bit overwhelmed by the number of people, the three helicopters and Kenyon's disappearance inside the house.

Then there were the choppers. One had stayed a safe distance back, slowly circling the house, high above. They'd no doubt spotted Hellhole Bay's residents hiding in the unfinished dome, but hadn't opened fire on them. The Black Hawk was on the ground, its rotors churning slowly, ready to speed back up, but it wasn't defenseless. A man stood behind the large machine gun, moving it back and forth at the house, looking for targets, of which there were many. And then there was the Apache. Its ominous insect-like cockpit was turned directly toward him. He wasn't an expert on attack helicopters, but he knew this one had a machine gun, or two, and a crap-ton of rockets hidden inside the tubes mounted on either side.

He heard the whine of a chain gun spinning up. He recognized it from video games, though the real thing was far more metallic and grating. His eyes crushed shut while his legs kept pumping.

A Rider roared.

He heard it charging.

Bullets scorched the air.

Hot wetness splashed against him. He was struck hard, all at once, the pain everywhere, just as he'd imagined.

Except, he kept on feeling the pain.

He'd been struck, but not by chain gun bullets.

He tried to move, but found himself locked in place.

Couldn't see anything.

Am I paralyzed?

Am I dead?

He decided he wasn't. Because despite the darkness and immobility, he could hear. Everything was muffled, but he could hear the thrumming machine gun beating out a steady rhythm. He could hear shouts, and screams and small arms fire. All of it mixed with the hooting of angry Riders.

He could also smell. Noxious and visceral. Meat and blood. Then he tasted it, slipping through his lips and along the side of his tongue.

His thoughts returned to death. The scent of his own gore. The fading audio. The darkness.

But through it all, the pain continued. If his soul was slipping into the hereafter, wouldn't the pain fade, too? Or was that hell?

I'm alive, he told himself, focusing on his limbs. *Now get up and deal.*

Jakob pushed with his arms. His body shifted upward, but only moved an inch off the ground before falling back down beneath a massive weight that stole his breath away and sent stars dancing in his vision. He might not be dead yet, but he soon would be.

During that second of momentum, a sliver of light illuminated the fleshy prison pinning him to the ground. Marbleized gore and bones wrapped around him. A corpse. He could feel the hot organs slipping over the back of his legs. He kicked and found his feet free to move.

Fighting back his emotional percolation, Jakob bent his knees and shimmied them up toward his chest, creating a gap. Fresh air billowed in, but it served only to coil more of the stench deeper into his nose. His stomach lurched and dry heaved. He used the motion to slide out of the slick weight. His progress slowed as something sharp, like a set of claws, raked his back, lifting his shirt. The fabric peeled off over his head as he spilled back into the light of day and saw three Riders, or what used to be Riders, piled up where he'd been lying. Then he saw what had been clawing at his back and dry heaved once more. They weren't claws. They were jagged, exposed ribs. His shirt, removed from his body, hung from the longest of them.

The creatures had launched an attack only to be mowed down by the Apache, who had also been firing at him. Their bodies were shredded and turned inside out, inadvertently protecting him from the bullets.

Rider's weren't stupid, but they weren't exactly smart. Or lucky.

Jakob's intelligence was debatable. Anne reminded him of that every day. But his luck...his luck was undeniable.

The Apache peeled off around the side of the house as gunfire from the second floor pinged off its body. The helicopter could tear the home apart, but with three men inside, they were holding their fire.

The Black Hawk was spinning up again, prepping to leave the ground and its dangers behind.

The Riders that hadn't been cut down had thrown themselves into action. Two were chasing after the Apache. One was headed for the Black Hawk, and three were assaulting the second floor of the farmhouse, shaking the bars mounted over the windows and trying to reach the people inside, peppering them with bullets and screams.

The path to the first floor was open, right up to the door. That's where the last of the Riders was, pounding its fists into the porch and shrieking like a deranged chimpanzee.

Jakob took only his third step toward what was supposed to be an impulsive rescue attempt, but was stopped again, this time by the realization that he was now unarmed. He looked at the leaking mass of ExoGenetic flesh and saw the butt of his AK-47 sticking out. He crouched down and grasped the wood stock, eyes up, hoping no one would spot him.

If not for the massive amount of blood lubing the bodies, he wouldn't have been able to move the weapon, but it slowly came free until the rifle was birthed, covered in blood, mucus and who knew what else. Jakob quickly tried wiping the weapon clean, but he realized his entire body was equally covered in gore.

That didn't mean the weapon wouldn't work. His father had taught him about common weapons over the past few weeks, and one of the best things about AK-47s was that they were virtually weather proof, functioning despite sand, and dust and water. So the rifle might still fire.

Might.

He found out a moment later when a battle cry turned his eyes up. One of the Riders had spotted him, covered in the blood of its tribe, standing over their bodies. It flung itself off the farmer's porch roof and dropped down toward him, fists raised.

Jakob raised the rifle, tripped back over a Rider's severed limb, and pulled the trigger. The weapon barked like a faithful dog, cutting a line of red splotches up the Rider's body. The creature looked undeterred until the line reached its head. All of its coiled rage disappeared, and the beast fell at his feet.

Pushing himself up, Jakob ran for the door this time, his legs shaky, but his determination surging. "Hey!" he yelled at the Rider blocking the door. It spun around and lunged, claws reaching. The thing had been waiting for a target and found one in Jakob, but he had already fired. Four rounds struck the diving monster head on. It fell to the porch and tumbled down the stairs next to Mason's corpse, as Jakob vaulted up them.

He raised the weapon, clutching hard against the slippery film coating it. But he didn't fire.

Couldn't fire.

Like the Rider before him, there was too much going on to attack one side or the other without killing friend and foe alike. The man named Hutchins had Ella around the waist, his back against the hallway wall, his face red with the effort of trying to control her.

"Ella," the man shouted. "It doesn't need to go down like this."

But Ella had other ideas. She had one leg extended up against Crawford's throat, pressing him back against the opposite hallway wall. With her free arm, she swatted at his hand, which held a pistol he was attempting to point in her direction. Beyond the brawl, he could see people rushing about, some keeping track of the choppers, some fleeing, but no one helping Ella.

They don't know who to help, he realized. Ella was as much a stranger to most of them as Hutchins and Crawford.

But Jakob knew who was who, and what he had to do.

He shifted the AK-47's dripping barrel toward Crawford, who was close to turning that gun on Ella, and who posed the greatest threat to Jakob as well.

When he heard a fight further up in the house, and what he thought was Anne's voice, he nearly pulled the trigger. Not wanting to shoot Ella's foot off, he shouted, "Drop it!"

Three sets of eyes turned toward him and simultaneously widened. Even Ella looked horrified by his appearance. Then she snapped back to the struggle and used the distraction to her advantage, slamming Crawford's gun hand against the far wall, pinning it in place.

"Jake," Ella said. "You don't need to—"

"They need us," Jakob said, and Ella knew exactly who 'they' were: Alia and Anne.

Ella looked confused for a moment, but then Anne's voice filtered down from the second floor. "Asshole!"

"Do it!" Ella shouted, all of her concern for what taking a human life might do to Jakob evaporated by a single word from her daughter.

Anne was upstairs.

Alia was upstairs.

And so was Eddie Kenyon.

Jakob pulled the trigger, firing a single round that punched through Crawford's head and into the wall behind him. His head left a red streak as his body slid to the floor.

Covered in the remains of things that once were human and having borne witness to countless horrible deaths, including his own mother's, Jakob felt very little over taking the man's life. *It was justified*, he thought, when doubt started creeping into his thoughts.

Ella wasted no time debating right and wrong. No longer contending with Crawford, she twisted and drove an elbow into the side of Hutchins's head. Once, twice, three times. The third strike hit his temple and his grip wavered. Ella tore free and raised an open hand to Jakob. "Weapon!"

Without thinking, Jakob tossed her the AK-47. She caught it and turned toward the stairs, just as Eddie Kenyon stepped into view. Anne hung limp over his shoulder.

"Eddie!" Ella shouted, and aimed up at the man.

He stopped and looked down at her, something like a smile on his face. "You'll come with me now. You have no choice."

"There's always a choice, Eddie." Ella raised the weapon and fired as Eddie ducked to the side. When Ella took her finger off the trigger, Eddie's footfalls could be heard pounding up a flight of steps. Ella raced after him, taking the steps two at a time.

Before Jakob could follow, he was struck in the leg. Off balance, he had no defense against Hutchins, who got back to his feet and flung Jakob into the staircase. The man shouted, "You crazy bitch!" after Ella and then he retreated out the front door.

Jakob groaned and rolled back to his hands and knees. Moving slowly at first, he started up the stairs after Ella.

At the second floor landing, he turned to head up the next flight when he heard crying. He turned toward a closed bedroom door. "Alia?"

He pushed the door open. Alia was on the floor, clutching her face, covered in blood. She shrieked and winced back.

"Alia!" He rushed in and fell by her side. She yelped in fright, but fell into his arms.

"I'm sorry." She quivered against him, broken. "I'm sorry."

"It's okay," he told her. "You're okay."

She wasn't, not really. She'd been injured, maybe not mortally, but it wasn't something that would heal fast, or that she'd ever forget. And they were nowhere near out of danger yet. But he couldn't think of anything else to say. So while she continued to repeat, "I'm sorry," again and again, he countered each apology with, "It's okay."

As they fell into the tennis match chant, Jakob heard a familiar deep and rumbling machine gun, coupled with a roaring engine.

Beastmaster! Jakob thought, a trace of hope returning.

But then there was something else.

Something bigger.

Its arrival shook the house.

Something *much* bigger.

THIRTY-FIVE

In every conflict, there was a point of no return. When a soldier had to take action, damn the consequences, or things would get FUBAR faster than could be corrected. That moment was rapidly approaching Peter, about fifty feet per second, as the galloping horror closed in on the immobile truck.

But what could he do, really? Shooting the creature wouldn't have that much effect, unless his aim was impeccable. And that would be nearly impossible. Despite the long legs, the gator's long body and snout made it run in a kind of awkward vertical slither, like a reptilian ferret.

He could run, but there was no way that would extend his life beyond a second or two, and it would mean abandoning Boone. They could attempt to scale the gate, like Feesa had, but that would likely end with them being plucked off the wall and gobbled up.

If we survive this, I'm picking up some grenades, Peter thought. He'd passed on the explosive devices before, because unlike most projectile weapons, they couldn't be sound suppressed. The best way to kill ExoGenetic creatures was to not invite more to the party. The machine gun mounted in the back of *Beastmaster* was the one exception to that rule. It was a weapon of last resort, and was generally used on the move.

Peter looked down the machine gun's sights, shifting his aim up and down, attempting to match the rhythm of the gator's gait. But its head moved in jerky circular motions, so he held his aim steady. He timed his trigger finger with the moment his small target slipped back into the kill zone, or in this case, the wound zone. He had no illusions about killing the beast. He just wanted to slow it down.

Fire, he thought as the gator's black eyes slipped in and out of view.

Fire.

Fire.

He let his finger twitch with each pass.

Fire.

Fire.

He pulled the trigger, letting loose a burst of bullets that started low and traced a line upward. He saw the gator's skin bend and ripple as the large rounds punched against it. The eye snapped shut for a moment, but it was just a flinch. The thing didn't even slow down.

As he looked down the sights again, Peter's ears perked up. He could hear the gate's locks sliding away, one by one. Feesa was doing her job, but maybe not fast enough. Then, over the din of helicopter blades, he heard gunshots. And shouting. He felt a moment of confusion, as his mind backtracked. The battle inside the compound had begun, while he was aiming at the gator, but he'd filtered it out.

The hell is going on in there? he wondered, but he already knew. Choppers meant ExoGen, and if they were here, and Kenyon was here, Anne and Ella were in grave danger. They might not be killed, but they would certainly be taken. For Peter and the rest of humanity eking a living outside San Francisco, that was a very bad thing.

He pushed all his worries aside and focused once more on the gator.

He had just seconds before its arrival.

Fire.

Fire.

He pulled the trigger again, this time holding it down and following the gator's circular motion, peppering its face and snout with three rounds every second. Four seconds in, and just four more from being bitten in half, the gator convulsed.

Mid gallop, the monster pawed at its face. With the limb raised up, the body crashed down to the road, grinding to a stop just forty feet away from Peter. It scratched at its face, trying to dislodge what had caused it such sudden pain. But the bullet was too deep and too small to retrieve. The gator just ended up smearing the gooey remains of its ruptured eyeball.

The creature opened its jaws wide and let loose a guttural growl of frustration, plastering Peter with a wave of fleshy breath. Tufts of Woolie fur dangled from its traffic cone-sized teeth. The mouth snapped closed, the sound clapping against Peter's ears. Then the beast death-rolled with nothing in its mouth. It flailed across the road, churning into the swamp, where loosely rooted trees toppled beneath its girth.

Then it stopped.

The waters settled.

The creature's belly heaved with each breath, but it seemed to be calming, regaining its monstrous composure.

C'mon, Peter thought, but he dared not say anything. The gator's simple reptilian mind had forgotten them for the moment.

And that was when Boone revved *Beastmaster*'s engine. The rumbling exhaust sounded angry and alive.

The gator twitched its head to the side, looking directly at Peter with its one good eye.

Damnit, Boone, he thought, and then he noticed the truck was moving. He glanced forward and saw the gates opening. They were through, but too late. The ExoGator exploded from the swamp, slipping in the muck for a few steps before launching back onto the road.

The truck heaved forward in time with the creature. Peter fired at the healthy eye, but missed as the truck shook from an impact. Feesa had leaped onto the cab's roof. She was crouched and ready to leap, spear in hand. But she wasn't looking at the gator. She stared straight ahead.

Peter risked a quick look and saw the farmhouse, the familiar blue Black Hawk on the ground, an Apache in the air with its back to *Beastmaster,* a collection of Chunta on the ground and—

"Jakob!"

The boy broke into a run.

Several Chunta dove for him, hackles raised.

The Apache opened fire.

Blood and carnage ruptured like a fireworks display, fanning red in all directions, much of which splattered across the farmhouse's white exterior.

Peter screamed in time with Feesa, as their families were mowed down.

Small arms fire responded from the home's windows.

Peter tried to swivel the machine gun around to blow the Apache from the sky, but he was still locked in place by the rubber bands. And that was a good thing. Had he not been, the truck's rapid acceleration would have thrown him into the gator's open maw, just twenty feet back.

Filled with anguish and desperation, Peter screamed and held the trigger down, punching bullets into the Apex predator's throat. The massive tongue twitched and flailed, rising up over the throat like a meaty shield. But Peter kept on firing, digging a crater into its flesh.

The truck bucked as they rocketed over the bound logs bridging the wide stream. Peter's aim went high and he stopped firing.

The gator stepped down on the logs, shattering them. Its leg dropped into the stream, slamming its chin into the scorched earth. Ash billowed up around it, and in *Beastmaster*'s wake, but it was quickly swept away by the Apache's rotor wash. As the creature scrabbled in the stream bed, trying to pull itself up, the truck pulled away.

Peter unclipped himself from the rubber bands and ducked to the window. "Stay on that chopper!"

"But the gator!" Boone protested.

"Do it!" Peter said, burning with rage that dwarfed the gator's.

Boone didn't look happy about it, but as the Apache canted to the side and fled the gunfire coming from the house, the truck turned hard to follow it.

Peter clung to the machine gun as the truck's motion threatened to spill him over the side. When the truck straightened course again, Peter had the weapon turned forward, ready to fire over the cab and take down the Apache. The attack helicopter was tough. Built for war. They weren't easy to take down without a missile, but the M249 could do the job, especially if you knew where to aim. But the view between Peter and the chopper was brown and hairy.

He nearly fired through Feesa to take out the Apache. If the chopper hadn't killed his son, the Chunta clearly would have. And the females still left alive were assaulting the house, and the people within it. Feesa might have made peace with Peter, but her sisters hadn't. They were still aligned with Eddie.

"Get out of the way," he shouted at Feesa's back.

She reared around and roared at him, her face twisted with a fury that matched his own. She'd seen most of her tribe get decimated today, most recently by the chopper, but what could she do against a killing machine like that?

The Apache stopped and turned, its body now ninety degrees to the truck, its weapons aimed at the house, but not firing. *They have people on the inside,* Peter thought.

The pilot must have seen them coming, because the chopper suddenly swiveled in their direction. But the angle was wrong. It wasn't aiming at the truck, it was aiming behind it. Peter glanced over his shoulder. The gator had not only freed itself from the stream, but had also closed the distance.

Vengeance or survival? He had just a second to debate the matter. But it was Feesa who made the call.

Vengeance.

The warrior tribeswoman leapt off the truck's roof, denting it inward and soaring thirty feet in the air, bringing her face to face with the Apache and the shocked pilot behind the windshield.

Machine guns whirled, prepping to fire.

Feesa cocked the spear back.

Peter opened fire, punching a string of holes through the empty passenger's seat, distracting the pilot long enough for Feesa to lob the spear.

The idea of a spear taking down an Apache was ludicrous. But when it was thrown by a hulk of a woman, with a force greater than Peter could get out of his compound bow, it wasn't impossible. That was the lesson learned by the pilot when the spear punched through the windshield, and then his chest, just inside his left shoulder. Pinned back against his seat, and in mind numbing pain, the pilot lost control.

As Feesa landed on barren earth, the chopper twisted, tilted and descended straight for the truck.

Boone turned a hard left, plowing in the shanty village, sending sheets of metal flying like giant throwing stars. Peter ducked as a corrugated metal square spun over his head and struck the gator's side, digging in deep. But Peter barely noticed the fresh wound as he saw the gator's attention had shifted from truck to chopper, which plunged on a collision course with the massive reptile.

The gator lunged into the air, its jaws open wide.

The Apache spun in tight circles as it descended.

As the cockpit turned to face the attacking super-predator, the behemoth bit down. There was a crunch as the armored vehicle momentarily repulsed the immense crushing power. The spinning rotor blades struck the snout, cutting deep, but shearing away, one at a time. Angered by the fresh wounds, the gator bit down hard, and the cockpit began to fold inward as the locked pair dropped back down to the ground, but never made it.

Peter could only guess what went through the pilot's mind. He had been speared and then locked in the crushing embrace of an alligator as large as the Apache he thought would keep him safe. But the man's response, whether it be a calculated risk, or sheer panic, was deadly—to both man and gator.

The Apache's rocket pods flared to life, spewing a cascade of explosives that struck the predator head on and burst. Flesh and metal rained down in a tangled mess of monster and modern marvel. As the two killing machines burst into flames, Peter looked over the truck's cab and saw the farmhouse dead ahead. A moment later, the man named Hutchins barreled out of the front door and sprinted for the Black Hawk, which was spinning up for takeoff.

Peter was tempted to engage the second chopper, but there was still a second Apache around. He was also almost out of ammo, and he couldn't stop thinking about his son's fate.

As they neared the house, where a pitched battle between man and beast was taking place, Peter slapped the roof and shouted. "Stop here!"

The truck skidded to a stop. Kicked-up ash flowed over Peter as he jumped from the truck bed, and he ran toward where he saw his son fall.

One of the Chunta charged him, beating its chest, mouth open, teeth primed to sever meat and bones. Peter drew his revolver and leveled it at the monster's head, but didn't fire. "Feesa, friend!"

The creature slowed, but didn't stop. Peter pointed toward Feesa, who had just cleared the shanty town. "Feesa, family!"

He lowered the weapon and the Chunta turned and saw Feesa, who was now calling out in a booming voice. The fight went out of the Rider and she rushed toward her incoming leader.

Peter dove down by the heaped up dead Chunta, looking for his son's body, but all he found was an empty shirt hanging from exposed ribs. He yanked the shirt free, opening it wide. He didn't see a single hole.

He's not here. He's alive!

And then he heard his son's voice from inside the house, quickly followed by Ella's and a series of gunshots. Peter vaulted over the dead, took note of Mason's mauled corpse, and sprinted for the open front door. The inside of the house was a mass of confusion, but no one in the rag-tag group looked like a threat. He heard loud feminine crying from the second floor and took the steps three at a time. At the top of the stairs, he turned toward the sound and nearly collapsed with relief when he saw Jakob clutching a sobbing Alia in his arms. They were both covered in blood, but sitting upright, the way people do when they're not about to die.

Jakob whirled toward him, afraid at first and then desperate. "Dad! Upstairs! He has Anne!"

The sounds of a scuffle from the third floor, along with Jakob's declaration, propelled Peter around the banister and up the next flight of steps, where he suspected he would find Ella, Anne and the man he should have killed with his own hands. It was a mistake he intended to correct.

THIRTY-SIX

Ella's scientific mind sat in the backseat, buckled up and watched with familiar trepidation as her feral side took over.

Gunshots pounded her ears in the tight hallway. Wood splinted. A door was kicked in. Eddie had reached the third floor. And she wasn't too far behind him, rounding the stairway's corner. The door, its ruined knob and lock hanging limply, swung slowly closed. On the other side was Eddie, with her daughter, about to escape via the balcony.

And she wasn't going to let that happen. As valuable as Anne was to the world, as much as she loved the girl, she would be damned before letting ExoGen have her. Even if it meant risking her daughter's life.

The AK-47 in her hands was slick with the red sludge, and would be hard to aim reliably for more than a single round, but as long as she could see a quarter of Eddie's body, she thought she could make the shot. *Aim for the legs,* she thought. *Take him down and then finish him off.*

She struck the door with her shoulder, slamming it open.

The AK-47 came up, her finger started squeezing, but never finished.

The hallway was empty.

And then, the door pushed back.

The hard wood smashed into Ella's side. Coupled with her speed, the impact sent her sprawling. She struck the frame of the open door, spun from the second blow and fell to the floor, losing her grip on the assault rifle. As the weapon slid across the unfinished wooden floor and struck the leg of a folding table covered in someone's solitaire game, Ella spun around to the sound of footsteps.

Anne lay on the floor across the hall, unmoving, unconscious and maybe worse. Ella watched for a moment until she saw the girl's chest rise and fall. It was a moment too long. Eddie descended on her.

He jabbed the rifle butt toward her forehead, going for the knockout blow. Ella rolled her head to the side. Rifle struck wood, and she struck back. Ella kicked up hard with her left leg, aiming for Kenyon's crotch. He flinched back more than she was expecting, but the diversion still worked. While he was protecting his boys, Ella grasped hold of the assault rifle, slipped her finger around the trigger and pulled.

A spray of bullets buzzed past Kenyon's face, chewing up the ceiling and knocking free a cloud of dust. She tried to angle the barrel toward him as the weapon continued to fire, and she nearly succeeded as he held it at bay with just one hand. She mashed the trigger down until the magazine went empty. Kenyon looked aghast for a moment—she'd nearly shot his head off—and then he just looked pissed.

Really pissed.

Ella tried to roll out of the way of his foot, but her body was too big a target. He caught her in the side, slamming the air from her lungs. She tried to kick back, but she wasn't fast enough. His body dropped atop hers, straddling her.

She punched his wounded arm, eliciting a shout of pain, but he struck back, twice as hard, directly in the sternum. The blow compressed her chest, expelling the air from her lungs and flexing her ribs inward. There were two sharp cracks as ribs gave way, followed by a silent scream that had no air to give it voice.

All of Ella's fight faded away in the wake of that one punch, perfectly placed with devastating force.

"You know I love you, right?" he asked, a hand around her neck.

Ella wheezed in a breath that was cut short by a sharp pain in her fractured chest.

"Always have. Well, not always, but since we met. Do you remember that day? It was Lawrence who introduced us. Me, the head of security. You, the prized geneticist who didn't really want to be there, despite your role in fucking over the human race. Not that I mind, of course. I'm on board. My job was to watch you. To make sure you played nice. So I got you in bed. Gave me a reason to see you so much. Of course, it wasn't just a ruse. Lawrence thought so. Commended me on it. But it was real, for me. Just like it was for you."

Ella tried to speak, but she could only manage something that sounded like a whale call, as she attempted to suck in another breath. The pain in her chest kept her from breathing deeply enough to counteract the lack of oxygen in her lungs. She saw flecks of red and white, twisting in her vision. They'd have been pretty if not for the ominous message they brought: if she didn't get enough oxygen soon, she was going to pass out. And then she *and* Anne would be at Kenyon's mercy.

"Don't worry about speaking. I know you'd deny it. You can pretend all you want. You can tell Peter that you never cared, that all the sex was fake, that you were thinking of him the whole time. But you and I will always know the truth, and it can be our truth again."

He smiled and then punched her head. "You just need to sleep on it."

Despite the pain, Ella couldn't groan. Still couldn't breathe. The weight of his body and the pain in her chest kept her from even considering taking action, even blocking his second punch, which he delivered to her forehead.

Her vision faded in and out, teetering on the fringe of unconsciousness.

She watched through blurry vision as his fist raised up again, then dropped like a hammer. But when it came down, something was attached to it.

"Get off her!"

Anne.

Awake and on the attack.

The weight on Ella's body lifted away. Kenyon screamed in pain. She heard bodies tumbling. A moment later, Anne spit something on the floor. Kenyon stood above her, clutching his ear. Blood flowed between his fingers.

Beaten and breathless, Ella managed a chuckle.

The sound distracted Kenyon for just a second, but Anne took advantage of it, throwing herself at the man. But she wasn't fast enough or strong enough. Eddie hopped out of the way and shoved, using Anne's momentum against her. She slammed into the wall and fell to the floor. Not quite unconscious, but definitely out of the fight once more.

"You two are a real pair," Kenyon growled. "You know what? Fuck it, Ella. I'm done trying to save you. If you want to live? And I mean really live? With your daughter? You know where to find us."

He took hold of Anne's shirt, lifted her off the floor and dragged her to the door. Her little feet thumped over the cracks in the floor, each bump taking her daughter further away. And as the girl's limp feet bounced down the hall in time with the chop of the helicopter above, she knew she'd never see the girl again.

Ella wept as she dragged herself toward the hall. She lacked the strength to stand, and all the willpower in the world couldn't overcome her injuries. She sagged to the floor when she reached the doorway, head turned toward the far end, where Eddie stood with Anne. He dropped her by the door at the end of the hallway and started working the lock. There was a deadbolt, two sliding locks and a padlock.

When he reached the padlock and failed to yank it free, Eddie started back down the hall. When something large outside exploded, he stepped over Ella without a second look or a taunt. He returned to the hallway with the AK-47 in hand. Then he walked to the end, shot the padlock off and discarded the weapon.

Eddie opened the door, grabbed hold of Anne once more and stepped out into the light of day. He looked back at Ella, shaking his head as she raked her fingers against the wall, pulling herself up in a last, desperate attempt to save Anne. "You know where we'll be. And you'll always be welcome."

He looked up and started waving.

Ella took one slow step after another, moving down the hallway, toward Eddie. Toward the rifle. She tried to speak, to delay him, but she still had no voice. That she was mobile at all was miraculous.

The pounding pulse of a helicopter rotor roared down the hall. A tornado of air struck Ella head on, and it took all she had just to remain upright. If she went down again, she wouldn't get back up.

Eddie reached up and caught a metal wire with a carabiner and a harness at the end. He looped the harness around his waist and legs, wincing as he used both arms. Locked in place, he picked up Anne again, holding her to his waist with one arm. Ella wanted to scream at him. To tell him to lock Anne in, too. But Anne's safety wasn't his primary concern. He was just trying to escape. To survive. Just like everyone else, but in his own screwed up way.

Ella reached out a hand as she took one step after another, resisting the rotor wash, fighting against her pain and closing the distance. Anne's name squeaked out of her throat, but nothing could be heard over the thunderous chopper.

Eddie turned his back on her, eyes on the chopper above.

I'm going to lose her, Ella thought.

And then the view changed. At first she thought her vision had gone screwy again, but then she focused and saw the body of a man charging down the hallway.

And not just any man—Peter.

"Kenyon!" Peter shouted, his voice cutting through the din.

Eddie spun around and dropped Anne, his reflexes guiding him to defend himself. But there was nothing he could do to stop the two hundred pounds of solid Marine barreling toward him. Peter struck Kenyon head on. The pair crashed through the wooden railing, sailed off the balcony and struck the greenhouse's glass dome.

The impact knocked both men unconscious, and while Peter slid down the glass and out of view, Kenyon was lifted skyward like bait on the end of a fishing line. Ella bumbled to the end of the hall. Tried to pick up the AK-47, but lacked the strength to lift its slick body. When Anne groaned, she fell by the girl's side and checked her over. Aside from a number of superficial wounds, she found nothing life-threatening.

"Was that Dad?" Anne asked, wincing as she sat up.

Ella crawled to the edge of the balcony and looked over the side. She expected to see Peter's twisted body three stories down, but she found him lying just ten feet below, sprawled on top of the decontamination unit linking the house to the biodome.

He blinked and opened his eyes.

When he saw her looking down at him, he smiled. "You have terrible taste in men."

"No shit," she said.

Gunfire from around the farmhouse filled the air. It was joined by the rumbling thud of *Beastmaster*'s machine gun. The second Apache cruised past overhead, following the Black Hawk, as Eddie was reeled up by a winch. Bullets pinged off the fuselage until it was out of range. The two choppers rumbled away, headed north, and slowly faded from view.

"Do you think they'll come back?" Anne asked, pushing herself up.

"No." It was Jakob, standing in the doorway, covered in coagulation. Alia stood beside him, a blood soaked towel held against her cheek. "They don't need to."

"Why not?" Ella asked.

"Because," Jakob said. "They know where we're going."

THIRTY-SEVEN

Kenyon woke to the familiar white noise and vibration of a helicopter. Over the past year, he'd woken up under similar circumstances, and for a moment, his memories of the more recent past remained distant. But they returned with the pain. His body ached, just about everywhere. His left arm burned at a constant rate. It was the scorch of an open wound. And then it flared white hot.

He saw the Black Hawk's ceiling above. Then Hutchins leaning over him, concerned and annoyed. "Stop moving, God damnit."

The man had a hooked needle pinched between his fingers, a taut thread leading back down to Kenyon's arm. Kenyon relaxed. The pain was a good thing. If Hutchins was sewing him back together, it meant he would survive.

"Where is she?" Kenyon asked. As far as he could see, they were the only two in the chopper.

"Who?"

"Anne."

Hutchins slipped the hook through two folds of skin, pulled them tight and then said, "You don't remember?"

Kenyon closed his eyes. His memory was splotchy, still trying to catch up to the here and now. But he couldn't get past the pounding in his head, the nausea and the ringing in his ears. He recognized the symptoms. Had suffered from them, and others, on multiple occasions during the past year, and during his former life as a high school and college football running back. "I have a concussion."

"Makes sense," Hutchins said.

"Why?"

"You got tackled off a third floor balcony, fell nearly a story and crashed into a wall of solid glass strong enough to stand up to four hundred pounds of falling man meat."

"I was tackled?"

"Hard," Hutchins said. "After that, it was limp city. Honestly, I thought you were dead when I pulled you in."

A memory of falling flickered through his thoughts. Of pain. And disappointment. "I lost her."

"Yeah, you dropped Anne before—"

"Not Anne."

Hutchins frowned. "Right. Ella. I didn't see her."

Kenyon turned his face away from Hutchins, who might mistake his sadness for weakness. He remembered the fight with Ella. Remembered her nearly killing him, and what that felt like, to know she didn't love him. To consider the possibility that she never really had. Who had duped who? But after that...after opening the balcony door, Anne in hand, his memory was reduced to a twisting coil of emotions.

Desperation. Surprise. Rage.

The deep welling anger filled in one of the blanks. "It was Peter."

"Hit you like a missile," Hutchins confirmed. "For what it's worth, while you were pulled up, he fell. He's either dead or very broken. No way he could fall three stories without getting fucked up."

Kenyon turned back to Hutchins, his despair replaced by a growing anger. "You didn't stop to check?"

"We were under fire," Hutchins said. "You were completely exposed."

Kenyon grumbled his understanding, but he still wasn't happy about it.

"I can send the Apache back," Hutchins said. "Level the place."

"Apache?"

"We lost Drummond to an ExoGen. An alligator I think. Used to be, anyway."

None of this was acceptable, but he wasn't surprised. Viper Squad, without its leader, had lost its venom. And though their numbers had been drastically reduced, they still had firepower enough to kill their enemies and capture Anne *and* Ella. She might not love him now. Maybe hadn't before. But she would learn to. And if she didn't, maybe Mason had the right idea.

"Should I send Manke back?" Hutchins asked.

Kenyon shook his head. "He might kill our targets."

Hutchins nodded. He already knew that, but wanted Kenyon to make the call, and Kenyon respected him for it. He might not be a good leader, but he was loyal, and nowadays, that counted for something. Counted for a lot.

"We don't need to go back." Kenyon hissed in pain as Hutchins tugged on the stitch, cinching it tight and tying it off. "I know where they're going."

Not only that, but he was in no condition to fight. Not against Ella, or even Anne, and certainly not Peter—*if* he survived. But there was time to heal. Time to prepare. Instead of chasing their prey across the country, they could lay in wait. He always did appreciate ambush predators. The shock and panic of prey caught off guard was comical. And he longed to see that look on Peter's face.

Hutchins placed a bandage over the sealed wound. "Couple weeks and you'll be good to go."

Kenyon disagreed with the prognosis. As tough as Hutchins remembered him to be, Kenyon knew he was stronger than that now. Life with the Chunta had thickened his skin. Pushing past pain and injuries were part of life, and his body had already begun to adapt to it. He thought of Feesa for a moment, wondering what would become of the beast and if she was still alive. Part of him would miss her companionship. In the most basic sense, they were two of a kind, hunters both. But they would have clashed eventually, and Kenyon had no illusions about who would have won that fight. Parting ways with the Chunta was a good thing. And if they were all dead, even better.

Hutchins's hand went to his ear. He wasn't wearing the earphones that were customary in helicopters, blocking out the ambient noise, but he must have been wearing an earbud. "Copy that, weapons free. Engage." When he took his hand away, he said, "We have incoming."

Kenyon started to sit up, but his body protested.

"Sir," Hutchins said. "You shouldn't—"

Kenyon lifted his good arm up. "I want to see."

Hutchins shook his head, but smiled. "Nothing can keep you down."

"Not for long. Not yet."

Hutchins pulled Kenyon up, helped him onto a bench, and quickly strapped him in. "Give us a view," Hutchins said into his comms.

The chopper banked and turned. Through the side window, they watched the Apache tear through the sky on a collision course with what looked like an inflated squid, pulsing and flapping through the sky. Kenyon had no idea if the thing had started out as a denizen of the sea or not, but he didn't care. All that really mattered was that it be killed.

While he had allied himself with the Chunta, their days had always been numbered. That was the point of RC-714 and the Change it kicked off. Why bother culling life on Earth through a virus, a nuclear war or some other equally messy means, when you could let the planet eat itself into extinction? There was no radioactivity to deal with and no corpses to clean up. The Change had whittled life down to a few million Apex predators, and they would slowly but surely come into contact with each other. In the end, there might be a few hundred creatures separated by vast distances. When that happened, ExoGen would take care of the rest. The planet would be pristine once more, Eden reborn and awaiting its inheritors. Killing the ExoGenetic creatures they came across only hastened that eventuality, so he watched the event with a smile on his face.

When the flying creature turned to face the pair of helicopters, its tendrils open, ready to grasp, a series of bright flashes flared on either side of the Apache. Smoke trails snaked through the sky, chasing a swarm of rockets. Fire and flesh ruptured into the blue sky.

Beautiful, Kenyon thought, as the liquefied creature rained down toward the land below. When they flew through the pink mist lingering in the sky, Kenyon sat back, feeling hopeful.

"Where to?" Hutchins asked. "We need to stop for supplies and fuel, but we can map out a route once we have a destination."

Kenyon looked out the window, watching the blur of trees and empty homes passing by below them. The world was nearly empty, but not quite empty enough, and it wouldn't be until Peter Crane and his son, were dead. Lost and feral among the Chunta, he had desired Ella and Anne's lives too, but that was when he thought his dreams of the future were dead. But now...now everything could be his.

Everything.

"Beantown," he said, smiling at his blood-caked reflection. He turned to Hutchins, who looked as confused as Kenyon expected him to. "Boston. Take me to Boston."

THIRTY-EIGHT

When it came to war, people generally focused on the fighting. It's dramatic, and violent, painful and exciting. Adrenaline pumps. Bullets fly. Hoorahs fill the air as the enemy falls. Fewer people think about what follows a war, which for a soldier, is sometimes physically agonizing, sometimes emotionally taxing and always—always—long winded.

Everyday noises become explosions.

Kids playing sound like kids burning.

Life transforms into a confusing world of chaotic illusion, and soldiers lie awake at night with the realization that the enemy they killed were human beings.

And no one liked to talk about that. Better to pretend it's not a problem. They're soldiers, after all. They can deal, right?

Peter had dealt, but not on his own. PTSD had left him shaken and exhausted, but he had pushed through it with the help of family, friends and three good therapists. It was a longer, harder battle than the war itself, and now, in the wake of the fight for Hellhole Bay, he felt the familiar emotional and physical twitches creeping up on him.

The war's not over, he told himself, trying to stuff the emotions back down. *Deal with this shit when we're done.*

Done with what? he wondered, and then answered, *Saving the human race.* But it was simpler than that. He never really focused on the big picture, just on what was in front of him. His family. His son. They were reason enough to fight a war. As determination took root, the PTSD symptoms retreated, biding their time.

But Peter was not alone in his struggles. All around Hellhole Bay were the faces of men and women who had fought for their lives. And their battle began long before Peter or Kenyon set foot in the compound. Mason had seen to that.

And he had received his just reward, but that didn't change what he had done. Nor did it help those who dutifully obeyed him.

Boone was alive, but in the new status quo, he was the lowest of the low. The man looked relieved when he saw Mason's dead body, but it would be a long time before the people of Hellhole Bay trusted him.

Although they didn't have much of a choice. With all of Boone's men killed, and most of the still living residents of Hellhole lacking any kind of fighting ability, he was their best chance of survival. In the days following the attack, people had rallied against Boone, demanding his weapons, but Peter had stood beside the man. Technically, he'd sat beside the man. Three days passed before he could stand without much pain. A week before he could walk.

It had now been two weeks.

Boone wasn't their leader. Hellhole Bay was now a democracy of sorts, split into mini-sections of government that covered food, energy, sanitation and defense. Given their knowledge of most of the camp's functionality, the three former maids, Shawna, Charlotte and Sabine wound up in charge of the first three. They had begrudgingly allowed Boone to oversee the camp's defense, along with some unlikely allies.

The Chunta were staying. Five females, including Feesa, along with two Woolies, had survived the battle. There had been some tension at first. The citizens of Hellhole had killed a few of the Chunta, but Feesa explained Kenyon's deception and that Peter and his kin were family, a title never bestowed on Eddie. The creatures, who were already predisposed to symbiotic living, now resided in the swamps surrounding the compound, watching over the people within. And Boone was busy training those who were willing and able to carry weapons. Willie was his second-in-command and would be more than willing to put a bullet in his boss, if Boone ever got out of control. Said as much, right to his face, which Boone accepted with a grateful nod. He knew it was more than he deserved.

The girl who had helped Anne and Jakob's insurrection, Carrie, survived the knife in her chest. Barely. She was laid up in one of the beds, and would likely stay there for another few weeks. The wound had been deep, but missed her heart, lungs and major arteries. Shawna and Charlotte had experience patching up Boone's men in the past, and Sabine had been a nurse. Without them, Carrie would have died. The three women had been busy since the two choppers flew away, patching up the wounded and getting food and water to everyone.

They had tended to Peter and his family, and had even sewn up Alia's cheek, inside and out. The girl would have scars, emotional and physical, for the rest of her life, but she had survived. It didn't change the haunted look in her eyes, though. Kenyon had broken her.

Kenyon...

As far as they knew, he was alive. And Peter now knew better than to assume the opposite. Peter wouldn't believe the man was dead until he saw him bleeding out at his feet. Until he saw the life leave Kenyon's eyes. War was generally not a personal affair. But Kenyon had made it one. At the same time, Peter would do his best to avoid the man. Better to win the war without fighting. A soldier who could do that was the very best.

At the same time, Kenyon knew they were headed to Boston. He didn't know where, which was good for the people already on George's Island, but he'd be there, waiting for them.

Hope for the best, Peter thought, *prepare for the worst.*

He dropped *Beastmaster*'s hood and pronounced the vehicle fit for duty. It had a lot of cosmetic damage, but it had survived the battle in one piece.

"Good to go?" Jakob asked. He stood in the bed, cleaning the machine gun. During the day, he seemed like his old self. At night...not so much.

Nightmares were common, especially when they walked the Earth, but Jakob's fears got the best of him. He was plagued by doubt, and by guilt over what had happened to Alia. Blamed himself for letting her be part of that fight. For not reaching her sooner. According to Ella, it was chivalrous bullshit, but Peter understood. He blamed himself for everything that happened after running into Boone on the road. He could have backtracked. Could have run and found another way around. Could'a, would'a, should'a. It *was* all bullshit. Hindsight and all that. What happened wasn't Jakob's fault any more than it was Peter's. They'd done their best, and their family was alive and present because of it.

"Good as it's going to get," Peter said, patting his hand against the armored siding. "Are you ready?"

Anne leaned out of the truck's open side window. "To live without big walls, and beds, and electricity and running water? Ooh, can't wait."

Peter grinned at the girl's sarcasm, which had slowly returned with each passing day. She had taken her lumps along with the rest of them, but she seemed to recover more resiliently. Then again, she, like Ella, had fought her way through the wild for far longer than Peter and Jakob. For her, living out there might feel more normal. And what was normal for Anne? Before trekking through the ExoGenetic landscape, she'd lived in a protected facility. Until she and Ella fled with a group of scientists, the girl hadn't set foot outside. Weird was her normal.

"I'm good," Jakob said, but he didn't sound very convincing. Then his face lit up a little. Alia was headed toward them.

Jakob hopped down from the side of the truck and wiped his greasy hands off on his pants. "Where's your stuff?"

As reward for aiding in the liberation of Hellhole Bay, the residents had made sure they were leaving fully stocked. They had fresh clothes and plenty of food and water. Of course, they would cover the clothing and their clean bodies with mud after leaving the compound, but they didn't tell *them* that.

Alia's eyes flicked from Jakob to Peter and back again. Peter knew what was coming before the girl spoke. Had suspected it for more than a week now. "I-I'm not coming."

Jakob deflated, but he didn't seem surprised.

"It's for the best," Anne said. "She'd just get you killed."

"Screw off, Anne," Jakob said.

Anne was about to launch a verbal counterstrike when Peter gave her a look that mirrored Jakob's message and defused the girl's bravado. She rolled her eyes and sat back in the truck.

"She's right," Alia said. "You're distracted when I'm around. Everyone is. I can't track, or forage, or fight, or even stay out of the way. I can't even get canned food from an empty grocery store without freaking out. What you're doing... I can't do it."

"I know," Jakob said.

Alia's eyebrows raised. "You *know?* And you still wanted me to come?"

"You got kitchen duty, right?" Jakob asked.

"Charlotte asked me today...just twenty minutes ago. How—"

"I told her you were a good cook," Jakob said with a grin and a shrug.

"I'm a *horrible* cook."

"Then you'll learn fast."

"She's a slow learner, too," Anne said from the backseat, and when everyone present glared at her, the window slid up, shielding her from rebuke.

"That doesn't mean I didn't want you to come," Jakob said, "But I understand why you'd stay. And we'll come back for you." He looked to Peter. "Right?"

"Without a doubt," Peter said, trying to hide his doubt. If they survived, he had every intention of returning to Hellhole. If humanity had a chance of rebuilding, it was here. Not necessarily inside these walls, but with these people. He'd also warned Boone that if he returned to find Hellhole devolved into another monarchy, there would be actual hell to pay.

Peter gave Alia a gentle touch on her head. "I'll take care of him." Then he left the pair to say their goodbyes, make their promises and share a farewell kiss. Ella was walking toward him, accompanied by the newest member of their small crew: Lyn Askew. She'd slowly returned to health over the past few weeks, and despite her treatment at the hands of Mason and the death of her husband, she was eager to help set things right. Her work at Hellhole, modifying the ExoGenetic crops so they could be eaten, was a good step, but it was the human genome that needed a tweak, and she could help get that done in Boston. If she survived the trip. She wasn't a fighter, and she was still quite skinny and frail looking, but she had the right kind of determination— the kind that pushes a person to see things through to the end, even if the end is death.

Boone was with them, carrying bags.

"Meet you in the truck," Peter said to the ladies, who continued on past.

Boone stopped and held the bags out to Peter. "More food. Root veggies. Should keep for some time. We got more than enough."

Peter nodded his thanks and took the bags. One of them was a lot heavier than vegetables should be.

Boone pointed at it. "That one there is something special for you. Made a run last night."

"That wasn't smart," Peter said. With Hellhole Bay being self-sufficient, there wasn't any reason Boone or anyone else had to leave. Doing so could attract the wrong kind of attention.

"Them hairy Chunta ladies were with me," Boone said. "Can't say I like the way they been looking at me, all horny an shit, but they're playing nice." When Peter put the bag on the ground, Boone flinched and said, "Be gentle with it."

Peter buzzed the zipper open to reveal a collection of grenades.

"Fragmentation, flashbangs, smokers and offensive, if you need something with a little more kick. You're heading into a shit storm, right? Ain't nothing better in a shit storm than a bunch of grenades."

"A tank would be nice," Peter said. "But thanks."

Peter shook Boone's hand, parting with the words, "Keep them safe and the world might just have a future."

"I'll do what needs doing," Boone said. "S' long as you do the same."

Peter gave him a nod, recovered the bags and headed for the truck. "So long, Redneck." Boone had adapted the Redneck Raiders term for his own personal use as a callsign.

"See you soon, Ricochet," Boone replied, using Peter's old callsign, which he had learned from Jakob, while regaling the boy with the story of how he and his father had faced off against the ExoGator.

Back at the truck, everyone was inside and waiting. Ella sat in front. Lyn sat in the back seat, between the kids, both of whom looked to be dealing with their own personal miseries. Alia was nowhere to be seen. Peter climbed into the truck, slid behind the wheel and let out a sigh.

"You okay?" Ella asked.

"Will be, when this is over."

She gave his arm a rub and said, "We should go."

It was just seven in the morning, but they wanted to reach their first destination long before the sun set, giving them time to search for the kinds of weapons that would allow them to stand up to an Apache attack helicopter, not to mention the ever-evolving ExoGenetic creatures between Hellhole and Boston.

"We're waiting on one more," Peter said, and when the back of the truck sank down a bit, he knew she had arrived.

"Am here, family," Feesa said through the open back window.

Stunned eyes looked from the Chunta warrior to Peter.

"She insisted," Peter said.

"Protect family," Feesa said. "Kill Eddie."

"Good enough for me," Ella said.

"Her breath smells like a Woolie fart," Anne said, which got a hoot of laughter from their Rider compatriot and kept the girl from joking again.

"Family," Jakob said, and he held his fist out to Feesa. She pushed her larger fist against it, gave an approving nod. Then she leaned back out of the window, sitting in the truck bed, arm up on the side as though ready for a nice drive in the sun, which was probably as far from the truth as you could get.

Peter started the engine, shifted into drive and left the safety and comfort of hell behind. "Next stop, Fort Bragg."

EPILOGUE

Anne leaned her head against the window, watching the endless streaks of crops pass by. Bored by the monotony, she started naming the vegetation, whispering to herself. "Asparagus. Beets. Corn. Peas."

And then at some point during the brain game, she didn't know when, she switched to the crops' formal identifications. "Chenopodium quinoa. Spinacia oleracea. Lycopersicon esculentum. Triticum aestivum."

The words were an audiobook narrator's worst nightmare come true, but she could rattle them off as quickly as the crops shifted from one to the next. She'd become fluent in her mother's botanical geek speak. She'd also decided to keep her growing knowledge, and the memories that came with it, from her family.

Because as the amount of information stored on the USB drive leached into her head increased, so did more recent memories. And with every new memory came the growing fear that she couldn't fully trust the woman who had grown her, dragged her across the country and introduced her to her biological father.

Ella, she was beginning to realize, was a first class manipulator. Anne knew it was a useful skill to have in the current state of the world. Anything to stay alive. But she didn't think that applied to her father. Sure, she'd only met him just over a month ago. And yeah, he hadn't willingly donated his DNA. But they *were* family. By blood, and now more.

Anne knew her feelings for Peter and Jakob were genuine. But her mother's feelings? She wasn't sure.

Memories peppered her like nearly forgotten dreams.

She remembered them the way that steam wisped above a boiling pot, clear for a moment and then dispersed into the air. She could feel its lingering humidity, but could no longer see it or experience it directly.

And one of those memories left her worried.

She couldn't recall the events around it.

Couldn't tell you where she—where Ella—was, or what she was wearing, or what the room smelled like. But she could remember the emotion, raw and angry, close to how she imagined an ExoGen felt every time it saw another living thing.

But it wasn't hunger Ella felt, it was *hate*.

For Peter.

She looked away from the blur of crops and watched her parents. Peter was behind the wheel, keeping them at a steady forty miles per hour, eyes on the highway headed north. Ella sat beside him, scanning back and forth, always vigilant despite the relative quiet they'd experienced since leaving the swamps of South Carolina behind. Their shaved heads, now covered in a thin layer of scent-concealing dirt, matched. As far as the post-apocalypse went, they looked like a couple. More than Jakob and Alia ever had.

And they acted... Well, they acted married. Happy in an intense way. Trustworthy. A team. Everything she wanted them to be. But those were the best deceptions. The ones that were too good to be true. Eddie learned that the hard way.

Would Peter?

The question conflicted Anne, because as much as she loved Peter and Jakob, she felt the same for her mother. But on top of that love was the unshakable belief that her mother's every action since leaving ExoGen was solely for Anne's benefit. And ultimately the world's. So she still trusted her mother.

For now.

Maybe Ella really did hate Peter. Maybe he wasn't even Anne's biological father. Maybe she had no father at all, and no brother. The questions put a deep ache in her chest and nearly brought tears to her eyes.

Grow up, she told herself. *Life is about surviving. There's no place in the world for tears.*

Ella had spoken those words to her a week after they first fled into the wild. They had resonated and become part of Anne's core belief system.

But no matter how hard she tried to ignore the questions, and the emotions they unraveled, she couldn't help but wonder about it all. If she was going to help save humanity, she wanted to know that it was worth saving. That they were on the right side. And that her mother wasn't also lying to her.

So Anne rested her head against the window glass and tried to remember more.

Tried to remember everything.

ABOUT THE AUTHOR

JEREMIAH KNIGHT is the secret (not really) identity for an international bestselling author of more than fifty horror, thriller and sci-fi novels, and comic books. *Hunger*, the #1 post-apocalyptic bestseller, was the first novel under the Knight name, which Suspense Magazine called, "A riveting post-apocalyptic epic of man's rush to save the world and the harsh consequences that follow."

For more on Knight and his alter-egos, visit bewareofmonsters.com.

BOOK 1 OF THE BERSERKER SAGA

VIKING
TOMORROW
JEREMIAH KNIGHT
BESTSELLING AUTHOR OF *HUNGER*

Coming in 2016

"JEREMY ROBINSON SPINS MONSTER YARNS SO WELL THAT YOU CANNOT STOP TURNING PAGES."
--FAMOUS MONSTERS OF FILMLAND

UNITY

JEREMY ROBINSON

INTERNATIONAL BESTSELLING AUTHOR OF *PROJECT NEMESIS* AND *APOCALYPSE MACHINE*

Coming in 2016

"JEREMY ROBINSON SPINS MONSTER YARNS SO WELL THAT YOU CANNOT STOP TURNING PAGES."
–FAMOUS MONSTERS OF FILMLAND

APOCALYPSE MACHINE

A KAIJU THRILLER

JEREMY ROBINSON

INTERNATIONAL BESTSELLING AUTHOR OF *PROJECT NEMESIS* AND *ISLAND 731*

Available Now

62301932R00154

Made in the USA
Lexington, KY
03 April 2017